ZigZag

ZigZag

Landon J. Napoleon

A NOVEL

Henry Holt and Company

New York

Henry Holt and Company, Inc.
Publishers since 1866
115 West 18th Street
New York, New York 10011

Henry Holt® is a registered
trademark of Henry Holt and Company, Inc.

Library of Congress Cataloging-in-Publication Data
Napoleon, Landon J.
ZigZag / Landon J. Napoleon.
p.   cm.
ISBN 0-8050-6048-0 (alk. paper)
1. Afro-Americans—Fiction.   I. Title.
PS3564.A56Z35   1999
813'.54—dc21   98-42408

Henry Holt books are available for special
promotions and premiums. For details contact:
Director, Special Markets.

First Edition 1999

Designed by Paula Russell Szafranski

3   5   7   9   10   8   6   4

For Carol, always

But now they drift on the still water,
Mysterious, beautiful;
Among what rushes will they build,
By what lake's edge or pool
Delight men's eyes when I awake some day
To find they have flown away?

—William Butler Yeats,
   The Wild Swans at Coole

zig·zag (zîg′zâg) *n.* **1.a.** a line or course that proceeds by sharp turns in alternating directions **b.** one of a series of such sharp turns

Acknowledgments

Many grateful bows to agent Simon Trewin and editor Tracy Brown; special thanks to Philip Hobsbaum and Willy Maley, whose voices echoed in my head throughout the writing of this book; and most of all thanks to my little bro, Johnny Cleveland, for everything.

Even when you got supertuned cells in your head, it don't stop the sting of the punches. At least since my new big brother give me the special powers, my dad ain't beating on me as much as he used to. I learned how to move like the light, so fast or slow people eyes don't know which. Half of me around a stack of plates, while the other half loads the machine with pink soap, all night surrounded by food stink but never notice because my nose can ZigZag the smells. Just like that, two big Z's and two little g's.

This is the worst part, when you don't know if the beating's done or if he just taking a little break, sizing you up like a football needs kicking. Now's when you got to use all your special powers to keep the noise blocked out, keep it out your head in case there's more punches or a boot on the way. A hard punch low in my back throws the noise into my head so loud it knocks all the air out my body. My hands crawl around on the ground like they going on their own to find some air, but all they find is pavement and little

3

pebbles. Just when everything's getting all dark, the air finally comes back and the coughing starts, which hurts just as bad. My forehead's on the ground now, which don't feel too good, but my body won't listen to what my brain's telling it. The air starts coming a little easier . . . better . . . better . . . but it's still too early. Give in now, and the noise comes back twice as loud with the next punch.

"He ain't movin at all. . . ."

". . . pop your cherry and you disrespect me? Had enough you want a little more?"

My dad ain't too smart, always asking mixed-up questions that only mean more noise no matter what answer you give. Best thing is act like he just gave you the worst beating you ever had so he lose interest. Singer taught me that long time before he give me my new name.

"Listenin to me, you little fuck?"

"I do think you got the boy's attention."

They laughing now, Eddie and my dad thinking they so funny. The air's back in my head so the smell of the booze is real strong even way down here on the ground. I don't need to smell no booze to know they been drinking. When my dad leans down, I see all the red in his eyes.

"Now you listen to me, boy. You ain't paid your rent. Same deal as before. Two hundred bucks. By Friday or I'll beat you like you never seen . . . and your sorry ass can find somewhere else to live. Ain't no free ride around here. Understand what I'm sayin?"

I feel my head nodding *yes,* but inside my body's saying *no, no, no.* I can think whatever I want around my dad without having to worry about him picking it up. Even if he had radar like the Toad, the booze would mess it up. He'll never see what I think on the inside.

"Answer me, motherfucker!"

He grabs me and pulls his fist back. My body goes automatic all on its own, tensing up full tight, eyes closed, air held down inside

ZigZag

waiting for the blast . . . waiting . . . waiting . . . then when the blast don't come, one eye opens to see if it's safe for everyone to come out. The fist is gone away, but my body keeps tense. You can't never give in to the noise.

"Yeah, OK."

"Yeah, OK what?" he yells.

"Yeah, OK I'll give you two zero zero."

"By?"

"By Friday."

"Or else what?"

"Or else my black ass on the street."

"Ain't as dumb as you say," Eddie says. "Catches on fast."

"We'll see. Now get the fuck out my face."

I don't so much get the fuck out his face as he gets out mine because they go up the stairs and back into the apartment. It seems like a long time before I can get up, the pain mostly deep inside my back, music and voices coming loud out the apartment again. I try to push myself up, but my shoulder has a real bad hurt inside. Instead I roll the other way, real slow, and use the arm don't hurt to push myself up. Feels like punches still in my stomach and back, hurts every time I breathe. Only way to keep the hurt away is to take little baby breaths.

Once the noise drifts away just a little, the head can start doing some thinking. He ain't getting my paycheck again, no way, not ever again. I got to think me up a plan and quick because today's . . . Monday. That means Friday's got to be pretty soon, I think, but the best thing is tomorrow be Singer Day. He's good at thinking up plans. Couldn't tell you how many plans Singer came up with all these years like giving me a new name. My dad the only one still calls me Louis. That right there shows you how stupid he is. Louis was before I learned to ZigZag.

I get back on my bike, slow, slow, the one they knocked me off after I walked in and my dad was sticking his thing inside some girl from behind. Eddie had his thing in her mouth. They stopped soon as they saw me and started yelling. That's the first time I ever seen a real naked woman, and dad and Eddie both had things ten times bigger and shinier than the one I got. My dad threw a black Nike at my head, but I was out the door and on my bike, and somehow they still got their pants on and caught me.

ZigZag will think on that one later, though, because it's time to go see the Toad.

At work I watch the Toad open the office safe and remember the numbers in my head for later. The Toad's short and round, and he's got shiny skin looks wet, or is wet, no matter what time you see him. If he got a real name, ain't no one ever said it since I worked here. He's bent over turning that dial so I have to force my eyes away from his greasy crack. It's hard not to look at something you know you don't want to see, but damn if those little white numbers don't look six feet tall. Maybe this will be one plan Singer won't have to think up. That's what happens when you got special powers like me; you always seeing stuff you ain't even supposed to know about.

The Toad stands up and turns real quick like he detects my mind on him. All frogs got this same radar helps them catch flies they eyes can't even see. Then I think maybe I'm repeating the numbers in my head too loud. I look at the floor, trying to push the numbers out my head but somehow remember them at the same time because I'm sure his radar's picking them up. I can hear him chewing on the white tip of that little cigar he never lights. I look up. Even without smoke something about the Toad makes your eyes water and your head roll back.

"Louis, why do I always get the feeling you're up to something?" I forgot, the Toad's the other one calls me that. And like my dad, he's always asking questions he really don't want no one to answer.

"I ain't did nothin."

"Precisely."

I just flash him a ZigZag. This is pretty much how it goes with the Toad. He's always acting like he onto something, while I'm still trying to understand what he's asking. I shake my head, feeling better now. I got my own radar, better than his, telling me the Toad ain't picked up nothin; he's just out fishing for some juicy flies. I grab my check so fast I can see the surprise in his eye white.

"Only thing I'm up to is gettin started on them dishes." Really I'm the one should be handing him a check for the numbers he just give me, which are coming back into my head but not too loud just in case.

"Remember, shit stain, I got a hundred people could replace you yesterday. So the only way you keep this job is to keep not fucking up. Little spick in here yesterday asking . . ."

The Toad's got a lot of different names for people work here. We got redskins, spicks, niggers, coons, faggots, butt munchers, chollos, kikes, gooks, wops, cunts, whores, sows, and white trailer trash. With owning the restaurant and all the people he's got to yell at, I don't know when he's got time to think up all them names. I block out what he's saying so I can pull back them numbers. The more he keeps talking, the more my mind swims farther away, like when my dad and Eddie were hitting me. Finally, I get down to a place where I can see the Toad's frog mouth moving but I don't hear him. That's the place where I can think. That's what so great about washing dishes; you ain't got to talk to nobody except in your own head. I do most of my talking on the inside, so people think they always got to talk extra when they around me to fill up space. Funny thing is you don't need to hear people's words to know what they saying. I don't say nothin, just stay down inside, safe, until the Toad finally shakes his head and waves me away like a fly he'll eat later.

Back in the kitchen the cooks are talking, laughing, and chopping lettuce. I got it blocked out, just catching bits here and there. I punch my time card and float over to my dish station.

". . . you one crazy African, ZigZag. Why don't you ever talk to us? You are dumber than this fuckin soup spoon."

I see the flash of silver leave his hand, and pull my head back. The spoon hits the mirrored window and cracks the glass. On the other side of that one-way mirror is the Toad's office.

". . . you fucked up good now. Your ass is . . ."

My mind lets go of whatever they saying because it don't really matter when you're repeating numbers in your head and you got dishes piled up from the lunch shift. Lunch bastards always skating out early because they know ZigZag can punch in and clean up they shit before the tumblers in the time clock move a notch. Sometimes my own mind don't even tell me what will happen next, like whether these numbers will stay in my head or take a ride down to my fingers. The Toad comes into the kitchen and yells at everyone, but mostly he looks at me. "Which one of you birth defects broke my goddamn window?"

The cooks keep cutting lettuce, steady sound of them heavy knives hitting the cutting boards, but they ain't laughing no more. I keep washing, concentrating on the numbers because I never write anything down unless Ms. Tate makes me. Better to just think things in your head. Not too loud, though, with the Toad so close. The Toad walks toward me and leans across the dish station so he can run his finger along the crack in the glass. Nothing real around here until the Toad feels it. He don't say nothin to the cooks, just looks at them and back at me through the steam coming up. Everything quiet now except them knives: *foop, foop, foop, foop* . . .

"You break my window, fuckhead?"

I shake my head.

"Louis . . . what did I just tell you not more than three minutes ago?"

"Numbers to the safe" jumps out my mouth so quick I ain't got time to grab it back.

"Uh-huh. You got numbers on the brain. Now tell me who broke the window, or it comes out of your next check."

"I didn't break no damn window, less movin my head out the way flying spoon counts."

"All right then. Who?"

The Toad's really working that little cigar, around and around in the corner of his mouth. His forehead gets extra shiny whenever someone breaks something, even by accident. The little craters on his neck filled up with wet now and makes me want to ZigZag extra small and hide in one of them, underwater, where they ain't no noise. I look at the cooks and can mostly remember how two of them locked me in the walk-in for so long took me three days warm back up. The big Indian never did nothin to me, like a tree got a ponytail, about the same size and never makes a sound. Can't decide yes or no whether he likes them other cooks.

"Didn't break no damn window."

"One more time, Louis. Tell me who did it, or it comes out of your next check."

I got to think—because the check he just give me only one five nine two one, and my dad wants two zero zero, and now the Toad wants money—but I can't with everyone staring, and the noise starts up slow, slow, then faster . . . like a far-off rumble you know only going to get worse, louder, louder . . . then right in the side my head where I can't get it out, the pain so bad, everywhere pain, and the Toad keeps yelling but now I really can't hear him, the brain just goes soft, no more, make it stop . . . big Indian looking at me with some kind of chicken skin hanging off that black-handled knife, sting of the punches rising in my back except ain't no one hitting on me . . . running out the door? no, dad grabbing me, holding me tight . . . making me watch Eddie play with his big shiny thing, dad pushing me to the ground, his knee across my throat with his big shiny thing in my face, I can't breathe . . . someone trying to take off my pants . . . the naked lady, music and laughing, the naked lady still trying to get my jeans down . . . don't matter, need air . . . need air . . . can't breathe, hands looking for air, looking, my hand on something cold and heavy, swing it up at dad's head, and the air comes back. . . .

"Jesus Christ, Louis. Take it easy. Forget about the fuckin window. Take it easy . . . just don't throw anything else."

When my head comes back, I'm underneath my dish station, which is where I go to make the noise stop. All the pieces of slippery food and greasy buckets and bleach bottles don't bother me none because I know it safe down here. Sometimes I can't remember how I got here; I always know why. A whole crowd's staring down at me, the Toad, big Indian, the other cooks, waiters and waitresses, like they paid money and waiting for the show to start. That's when I sense the tumblers in the time clock about to make they move, my supertuned cells buzzing cus all the lunch dishes still piled high. I ZigZag into position so fast everyone make a noise together like *oooohhh . . .* , and then I'm flying through the stack, feeding full racks into the machine so fast its gears and wheels be smokin—

"Louis! C'mon. Stop it." The Toad's got a hold of me by both shoulders like he afraid of what he seen, too much speed for his brain to soak up. "Take it easy. Fuckin chill!"

He's just afraid I almost ZigZag right out his universe and then he ain't got no one to wash the dishes Monday, Wednesday, Thursday, Friday. Sometimes when you got the special powers you got to slow things down, always slow, slow, slow, so no one get scared.

"I'm all right. Don't worry none about me."

"Jesus, don't flip out on me like this. Bawlin your head off throwin my dishes one minute, then acting like a goddamn maniac. I'm not running a day-care, so get your shit together. Just used up your last chance. Got it?"

I nod, but I can't hardly concentrate because my fingers itching to load dishes. When the dishes piled up high like this, they give a sound, like little bells only I can hear ringing that don't stop until the dishes clean. I dig into the stack, slower, slower, just half speed so I don't scare the Toad again.

"Christ," he says, walking toward the door. "What a fuckin night, and it hasn't even started."

ZigZag

Soon as the door swings shut behind him, I ZigZag back up to full speed, faster, faster, my left hand working the sprayer while my right feeds the dishes onto the racks and into the machine, the noise gone, pushed way far away, until all I hear is the machine spitting hot water and chewing on dishes and the numbers to the Toad's safe, over and over again in my head.

I got my radar turned up extra sensitive in case the Toad's got secret agents work at night. Little frog helpers with red eyes hiding in the dark to tell the Toad later what happened. I got the numbers real loud in my head over and over, ZigZag my way to the safe. I got a little place in the attic where I sleep sometimes that no one knows about except Singer. I just hang there until all the bar crew gone, then drop down into the Toad's office through the ceiling. Kitchen lights stay on because breakfast crew be here soon, so I got enough light coming through the little cracked window. My heart's going all crazy, but how else I'm going to get the two zero zero for my dad and who knows how much for the Toad's damn window?

I crouch down low like I seen the Toad do and start spinning the little black dial around and around like a clock. I watched the Toad open the safe lots of times, except just out the corner my eye so he never noticed. After plenty of spins to get it warmed up, I

12

stop on the first number, then spin it back around and stop on the second, just like that, back and forth until I empty all the numbers out my head. My heart really starts going crazy when I reach for the long silver handle, which is cold but moves down easy and makes a big *CLICK* sound. The little door swings open easy, too, but I can't see nothin so I just got to feel around with my hands. I empty everything in there into my pillowcase and then climb back onto the Toad's desk and into the ceiling, careful to move the white panel back exactly the way it was, my heart going so crazy feels like it might explode out my chest. The attic is hot and dusty in my eyes and throat. I climb up the little ladder and through the door onto the roof so I can breathe easier, even though it's pretty damn cold outside.

Mostly seems like the Toad keeps nothin but stupid papers in his safe, except for one little box I seen him carrying back and forth to the bar. When I open the box, there's more money inside than I ever seen: five two four one. ZigZag rich! I put the metal money in my pocket and everything else in the pillowcase. I go back inside to the attic to get out the cold and hide the pillowcase behind some boxes. It ain't bad here with the brand-new sleeping bag Singer bought me, a flashlight, some of my clothes in a box, and a little radio Singer give me so I can listen to music at night. I turn on the radio but don't really listen because all I can think is what I'll be buying with all this money. Maybe me and Singer will move away somewhere now since we rich, some place where he don't have to work all the time and my dad can't punch me. Long as we find a place for me to ZigZag some dishes cus that's what keep the noise out my head for good.

Seems like it took forever to fall asleep, but next thing I know I'm waking up to the smell of coffee and eggs. I double-check to make sure the five two four one is still in my pocket cus you never know about those little secret frog agents the Toad's got. I ain't ever seen one, but you don't got to see some things to know they there. The Toad's money is still there, but I take it out and count it just to make sure. Then I get a plan so good I think Singer whispered it right into my head. I'll ride my bike back to my dad's apartment, get the rest my clothes and my black jacket cus it's getting colder, and then stay in the Toad's attic permanent. I ain't got time for the Fellowes School today with all the stuff I got to do, and besides today's Singer Day.

I get dressed fast and climb up the ladder and then down another ladder by the trash dumpsters where I keep my bike. I move in so fast the big Indian jumps back until his eyes have time to adjust. He drops the trash bag into the dumpster and then looks up towards the roof like he's expecting more people to be coming down the ladder.

"Just me," I say, shaking my head. I dial the combination to my bike lock, careful not to mix the two three three five six with the Toad's numbers. The Indian don't say nothin. He does his talking on the inside like me. I walk past him with my bike and forget where I'm going, so I stop at the gas station and buy some candy bars with some of my new money. Three two six for the food, so now I got five two three seven seven four left. I use two of the metal money to call Singer at six four four eight nine eight eight, see how he's doing, so now I got five two three seven three nine left.

"Singer?" Why some lady answering his phone?

"Hold on. See if he's around."

I'm starting my second candy bar when I hear his voice. "Hey ZigZag."

"How'd you know?"

"Lucky guess. You at school?"

"School?"

"Yeah. School."

"I got too much business today."

"Where are you calling from? You at a pay phone?"

ZigZag

Damn if Singer don't have the best radar I ever seen. He knows everything before I even tell him, so I might as well tell him about the Toad's money since he'll probably ask about that next.

"I got five two four one from the Toad, except after the candy bars and this phone call it's five two three seven three nine."

"Slow down. What?"

No one knows where I might ZigZag next, not even Singer, and he's the smartest man I ever seen. Slow down, slow down, ZigZag, everyone always asking me to slow down.

"ZigZag?"

Now I remember: I got to get my clothes from my dad's and especially my jacket because it's cold out here. I hang up and jump on my bike and ride with one hand and keep the other one under my arm to keep it warm and then switch so the other one stays warm too. I'm happy I get to see my big brother today. Singer ain't my real brother, and you'd know if you ever saw him cus he don't look like me at all. I'm skinny; he's a lot shorter. Last few months he been coming around he ain't got no hair! He wears a hat, but he still looks pretty funny. He says he's sick, but he looks the same to me except no hair. He says once he's done taking some kind of special medicine, all his hair will come back.

I don't really care if his hair grows back or not. Singer been more real than any other family I got. I ain't never met my mom, she already dead. I ain't got no brothers or sisters, so really it's just my dad and me and Singer. But Singer ain't never hit me, not even when I broke something or did some other stupid things. He's been coming to see me once a week for a long time, and we done so many things I can't even remember everything. Thing I like most about Singer is that he's smarter than me, helps me think up good plans for what to do. Singer give me a new name and got me into the Fellowes School where I should be right now. He's the one got me the job washing dishes Monday, Wednesday, Thursday, Friday so my dad wouldn't have as much time to beat on me. Lot of times I sleep on Singer's couch at his apartment, which I

15

really like because it's a lot more quiet and softer than the Toad's attic, and he got a big color TV we watch movies on, and I cook me my own bowl of popcorn with lots of butter.

The noise ain't never got into my head when Singer and me together.

The noise explodes inside my head when I walk into the dark apartment. Right across the back my neck real hard and makes me fall down to the floor. The supertuned cells in my head just stay focused on the five two three seven three nine and how the noise going away for good once I get out this place.

"Goddamn, nigger. Scare the shit out of me. Why the fuck you ain't at school?"

Eddie and that naked woman are on the bed, both they mouths wide open and Eddie snoring real loud. My dad's still naked, except his thing is a lot smaller now, less shiny. My radar's telling me he ain't in a beating mood, but my body stays tensed up just in case.

"Nigger, don't get silent on me," he yells, throwing a little pillow at my head. I ZigZag out the way so fast the pillow misses and hits Eddie right in the head. He just keeps snoring. When I look back at my dad, some red rises up in his eyes, like maybe they do got some beating in them.

"I got business."

"Business, shit," he says, laughing a little. "What the fuck you know about business?"

"Five two three seven three nine. That's what ZigZag knows."

"Don't start with those goddamn numbers. Too fuckin early for that shit." He unscrews the lid off a bottle looks like the ones the Toad keeps lined up behind the bar. Then he takes a sip and makes a face like he don't like the taste.

"Goddamn," he says, wiping his mouth with his thumb. "See that bitch there?"

This one of those questions I suppose to answer or no?

"See the bitch?"

I nod.

"I tell you about motherfuckin business. Bitch wanted two hundred to fuck and suck me and Eddie nine ways to Sunday. No problem, we said. But we ain't payin her shit. Not a fuckin dime. Only thing this fuckin crack whore's gettin is more of my black dick up her ass."

I don't know what my dad's talking about, so I go to the closet and take out my black jacket and my box of clothes. Good thing about not having too many clothes is they all fit in two boxes.

"The fuck you doin?"

"I got you two zero zero."

"What I just say about that number bullshit?"

"The two zero zero you wanted. From yesterday."

"Talk fuckin English, Negro. Didn't see your sorry ass yesterday."

Sometimes the noise makes it hard to know what's inside my head and what's outside, like the beating and the knee on my throat and that naked lady. Maybe that was all in my head last night in the Toad's attic. I flip on my radar extra sensitive see what I can find out.

"Goddamn, you fucked up." He drinks again from the bottle and scratches his stomach. "What you talkin about 'two zero zero'?"

"For rent. You said by Friday I got to give you two zero zero."

He looks at me like maybe I'm trying to trick him somehow. Then he tips his head to one side a little. "I said that?"

"Uh-huh. Right out front before I went to wash the Toad's dishes."

He takes another drink from the bottle he don't like. "All right. Yeah . . . fuck yeah, now I remember. I told you by Friday. So you got it now?"

I nod.

"Then what you waitin for? Can't you see I got a bitch needs fuckin? Hand it over."

I pull out the money and hand him two zero zero, but when he screams I jump and drop the money. It goes all over the floor.

"God . . . damn boy! Where the fuck you get all this?"

He's down on his knees touching the money and holding it up close to his face. I ain't never seen dad this happy like I really done something good.

"Got five two four one last night out the Toad's safe."

"What you talkin about 'safe'?"

I run the numbers through my head just like when they went down into my fingers. "One in the Toad's office."

Now he's laughing, holding his stomach. "You stole this shit from that fat fuck cracker you workin for?"

I nod again. He's counting the money, except I already know it's five zero three seven not counting the coins minus the two zero zero.

"You bullshittin me, boy? How the fuck you get all this? Five thousand dollars here!"

"Easy. Just watch the Toad open the safe and remember the numbers in my head for later."

"Goddamn, Ne—gro. We fuckin stylin now!"

I smile and try to grab the Toad's money back. My radar don't see the fist coming, the noise blasting into my head on the left side. I fall down, and his fists follow me to the floor, low and hard into my stomach until he knocks the air out again, the noise so loud now I can't see anything except him laughing. . . .

". . . goddamn hands off my shit . . . clear my ass with Cadillac Tom . . . where you got five grand, you can get me some more. . . ."

When the noise stops, I'm on the floor where I can see my dad's butt going up and down real fast on top the naked lady. She making all kinds of noise, but Eddie still snoring on the bed like he dead or something. I hurt bad so it takes me a while to get up. I put on the black leather jacket Singer gave me and grab the box of clothes, but I don't know what my dad done with the Toad's money. I ZigZag around for a few minutes seeing if I can find it, extra silent so my dad don't see me. He's too busy bouncing on top the naked lady.

Finally, when I can't find the money nowhere, I just leave. Dad might got the Toad's money, but ZigZag still got the Toad's numbers in my head. The noise pretty loud still, so I just try to concentrate on one thing at a time, back on my bike, hold the box of clothes with one hand and steer with the other, just ride back to the restaurant and then later Singer can help me come up with a new plan like he always does. Singer the only one in this noisy world always be there for me.

When I get back to the Toad's restaurant, there's a police car in the parking lot. I lock my bike where it always goes behind the dumpster and ZigZag up the ladder to the roof so fast I go invisible, back through the little door and down another ladder, then over real quiet until I'm right above the Toad's office. The voices are all messed up, except when I press my ear down on the panel that moves, I can hear the Toad and another voice I ain't never heard.

". . . the safe?"

"About five grand and change. All cash. When I find the prick that did this, I'm going to scoop his fucking eyeballs out with a teaspoon and shove them up his ass."

"So . . . you normally keep about five thousand in the safe?"

"No. Depends. Sometimes less, sometimes more. I've had as much as twenty grand in there on holiday weekends. Fuckin meeting I had yesterday, bank closed before I could get there."

"Could someone else have seen you open the safe? An employee maybe?"

Whoever this man is he sure asks a lot of questions. Usually, the Toad's the one asking all the questions. The Toad don't say nothin, and I wonder if maybe he's looking up at the ceiling right now, his radar remembering back to when he gave me my check. "I don't know. I doubt it."

"Why?"

"It's a six-number combination. Plus when I open it, I crouch down like this . . . so even if someone was standing where you are . . . you know, it's so simple, I'm telling you it's either that fuckin chink slag Williams or that stink-gash Cindy. They knew right when to do it."

"Your assistant managers."

"Fuckin-a they are. I'll assist their sorry asses right to jail."

"Uh, why don't you leave that to us. They're number one on our list."

"Yeah, I never trusted either of them. You get any prints?"

"Couple of good ones off the lever. But that alone doesn't do us much good—"

"Because every one of those bastards' greasy hands has been all over my safe."

"Exactly. Including yours. But you never know. Sometimes fingerprints surprise us."

"Yeah, sure. Fuckin Prince Charles did it, right?"

"Better yet, someone who works here, the last person you'd ever expect. Some box of marbles who can't wipe his own ass."

The Toad laughs. "That's easy. But no way, not in a thousand years. This fuck-brain puts the Rain Man to shame."

"That's your man. Seen it before."

"Yeah, right."

"You watch."

The Toad don't say nothin else, but I can hear him thinking real hard.

Singer drives up to the dumpster at five three zero like he always does on Tuesday. He started picking me up here at the restaurant instead of the apartment cus of how many times my dad tried to get in fights with Singer. I got so many things jammed up in my head to ask him about, like the police car and all the Toad's questions. I don't even know where to start, so he does most the talking while I get my mind slowed down.

". . . school today? ZigZag?"

"Didn't have time."

"Why's that?"

"Stuff to do. Like gettin this jacket you give me and my clothes so I can move out."

"Is that why you brought all your stuff? Your sleeping bag and pillow. You're moving out?"

"Yeah, except I ain't got no money no more."

"You got your check yesterday. Right?"

"One five nine two one. I mean the Toad's money my dad stole."

"What?"

"Five two four one I got out the Toad's safe, then gave my dad two zero zero, but he took the five zero three seven supposed to be for us to move so you ain't got to work no more. Long as I can ZigZag me some dishes."

"Hold on," he says, pulling into some video store parking lot. He turns down the heater, but I wish he'd leave it on because I'm still cold. I hope he don't mind now the inside of his car smells like the Toad's restaurant because of all my stuff in the backseat. Once you work at a restaurant, that smell stays with you no matter where you go. Singer's job is to drive a forklift, so I lean a little closer to see what kind of work smell he got.

"Say what you just said," Singer says. "Except slower."

"Just seeing if you got a work smell."

Singer gives me the same look most people give me when I talk outside.

"I won't ask. I meant before that. What you said about the Toad's money."

"Five two four one I got out the Toad's safe, then gave dad two zero zero—"

"You're saying you took $5,241 from the restaurant safe?"

"Then gave my dad—"

"You didn't really, ZigZag."

"Five two four one."

"Think for a minute. Was this inside or outside your head?"

Now he got me confuse, what's inside my head and what's outside all mixed up. . . . The soup spoon hitting the window, and the big Indian, and watching the Toad open the safe with one eye, and my dad's knee on my throat . . . Singer don't say nothin, just rubs his face and breathes a lot, loud, and shakes his bald head a few times. He's wearing a black hat.

"I think it was just a dream. Inside your head. Were you mad at your boss? Did he do something at work to make you mad?"

"Said I broke his damn window."

"But you didn't?"

I shake my head.

"So if you could, you'd open his safe and steal his money; that would be a good way to get back at him. Right?"

I nod. "I'll be damn those numbers don't look six feet tall."

"What numbers?"

"Little white numbers on the Toad's dial."

"OK . . . so maybe you saw him open the safe for real, outside your head, but inside you thought you saw the numbers."

"The Toad is goin to make me pay for the cracked window. Skinny cook did it, not me."

"Hold on. I'll help you get the money for the window, OK? Don't worry about that."

"I didn't break no damn window!"

"That doesn't matter. I'm just saying whether you did or didn't I'll help you sort it out. We'll talk to your boss together."

Singer sure got a way of making everything slow down, like I can feel the noise draining out my head. I just nod, and he nods too. That look on his face means we got us a new plan just like always when we're together.

"Now, why were you going to give your dad two hundred dollars?"

"He said I don't give him two zero zero before Friday, he beat me good and my black ass be out on the street."

"When did he say that?"

"Last night."

"Was he drinking?"

I nod. "He always hit harder when he been drinking."

Singer slams the steering wheel so hard it makes me jump. My body tenses up automatic.

"He hit you again?"

"Lot of times. Eddie, too."

"Fuck. I don't care what the agency says . . . legal guardian, that's bullshit. We're getting you out of there for good. You still want to leave, right?"

"Yeah, with you, move away from the noise where you ain't got to work no more, ZigZag me some dishes. We get in trouble with Ms. Tate when we say that."

"What?"

"*Fuck*."

This makes the smile sneak onto Singer's face. "Yeah, well, sometimes when you get really mad, like when you told me your dad hurt you again, then it's OK to say that."

"Really?" I ask. Grown-ups got some mixed-up rules, sometimes it's OK to say this, other times it's not, sometimes you do one thing it's OK, another time you do the same thing and you get punched in the head.

"Fuck yeah, it's OK, but only when you're really fuckin pissed off." He tickles me, but it stirs up the noise from all them punches. When he stops, I'm glad because the noise goes away again.

"So do you understand now? The window was real, but the safe wasn't. And you don't have to give your dad any money or feel bad about leaving because he's abused you long enough."

"Abude?"

"Hit you. Punched you. Hurt you."

"He done all those things plenty."

"Let's call Diane at the agency right away and see if she can help us."

"Singer, you wanna see my paycheck?"

"Yeah."

I reach in the backseat and grab the pillowcase. There's a lot of papers and other stuff I got to look through before I find the paycheck for one five nine two one. When I pull it out, some other papers fall out and Singer gets a look on his face I ain't never seen, like that noise coming back inside him or maybe I done something wrong again.

He's holding up some papers, looking at them and then at me, but he don't say nothin. It looks like he wants to talk, his mouth open but it ain't working. Finally the words come back from wherever they been: "Where did you get these?"

I'm about to say they look like the papers I got out the Toad's safe, but he just told me that was only inside my head so I don't know where they come from.

"Did you steal these from the safe at the restaurant?"

"You said that was only in my head."

"I know what I said, but where did these come from?"

Now I'm scared because Singer don't look too happy. Singer ain't wrong about too many things, but maybe he's wrong about what's inside my head and what's outside.

"Did you steal these from the safe?" he says even louder.

Singer's face either scared or mad, but I can't tell which so I just nod. Stuff outside my head got a different feel, like that little black dial between my fingers and the way the sprayer fits in my hand.

"These dinner checks are from your restaurant. All dated yesterday."

I don't know what he's talking about dinner checks, but it looks to me like they making Singer sick, and I still don't know if what I done is good or bad. You can't tell right away with Singer because he don't hit. He takes a lot of deep breaths and shakes his head a lot when he's thinking hard. It seems like a long time before Singer can talk again.

"ZigZag, listen. If you did steal the five thousand, you're in big trouble. Very big trouble. Do you understand?"

Not really, but I nod anyway because it sounds like Singer knows what he talking about. He just told me it was all inside my head.

"Now, we'll figure this out together, but first I need you to promise me you won't talk to anyone about this."

I nod.

"No one except me. Only talk inside your head. This is very important so promise me."

"ZigZag don't talk to no one except Singer about the Toad's money." Only inside my head.

"If anyone finds out about this, they'll send you away to a juvenile facility. We won't be able to see each other anymore."

"What's *juv-nile*?"

"Jail. They'll lock you up like they locked up your dad that time. Far away from me."

"I don't talk to no one except you." Except inside my head.

Singer wants me to tell him everything I remember about last night starting with when my dad asked me for the two zero zero, which is easy cus everything's so close in my head. Ask me about stuff that's far away like last week, and maybe my mind can't pull it back as clear. He backs out the parking lot, and then we start driving again. Singer's the best driver I ever seen. I talk for a long time until I pulled back the whole thing. Singer asks a lot of questions, especially about how I got the numbers to the safe and then went in there at night and opened it. A lot of times he says how he can't believe I actually got the safe open. I told him about everything I seen, like the police car, and even stuff I didn't see but knew was there, like secret frog agents hiding in the restaurant. Singer didn't say much when I finished, so I still can't tell if he's mad or not.

"Where we goin now, Singer?"

"To see if we can fix this mess."

"How we gonna do that?"

"First we need to get that money back from your dad."

It's half-dark outside when we pull up to where my dad lives. The apartment looks pretty quiet, except I wonder if my dad's butt still going up and down on that naked lady and Eddie still snoring. Or maybe they all drinking out that bottle gives you funny faces.

"Flip on your radar, ZigZag."

I nod. Singer's the one told me we all got special powers inside we don't even know about, like radar to detect what you can't even see with your eyes. Then he give me my new name cus he said nothing can catch you when you ZigZag. He's right, too, the noise ain't never got me for good.

"When were you last here?"

I dunno.

"Was it right after you called me? This morning? About eight, nine hours ago?"

Yeah, that sounds right, eight, nine, because it was full bright then. I nod.

"Was anyone else here?"

"Eddie here and the first naked lady I ever seen."

Singer shakes his head, laughs a little bit.

"You saw a naked lady?"

"Yeah."

"And?"

"And what?"

"Did you like seeing her?"

"No." I didn't like what she done, trying to pull down my jeans. "You ever seen a naked lady, Singer?"

"One or two."

"Why they got no thing between they legs?"

Singer laughs again. "Well, they do. It's just a different kind of thing. It's . . . more on the inside."

"You crazy." I don't know what he's talking about on the inside because I didn't see no thing. Singer gets out the car that's a lot of different colors. Singer says he ain't got enough money to paint it, so I think when we get back the Toad's money I'll give some to Singer so he can get his car painted all one color. I follow him up the stairs, my heart starting to go a little crazy now cus I can feel the noise coming on. My body gets tense whenever I get near the apartment. Punches on top of old punches about the worst hurt you ever had.

We stop outside the door. Singer puts his bald head flat against the door see if he can hear anything. Since Singer just picks me up at the restaurant now he ain't seen my dad for a long time. When Singer knocks on the door, it makes my heart go a little more crazy. Then when my dad don't open the door, my heart slows down a little. He's probably out spending the Toad's money.

"Not here," Singer says. He looks at his watch. "Any idea where he might be? Six fifteen on a Tuesday?"

I ain't got no idea where my dad goes when he's not in the apartment, so I just shake my head. The apartment's a lot more quiet when my dad and Eddie and the naked lady ain't around. I like things when they stay quiet.

"How about a job? Is he working now?"

"I dunno, Singer."

"You have a key?" Singer points at the door.

I nod and pull the key out my pocket and give it to him, which makes my heart start going crazy again.

"Why we gotta go in there, Singer? He ain't here."

"I know. It's OK. Let's just look around a little. Maybe we can find some of the money. Or something that will tell us where he is. We've got to find him before he spends it all because I sure as hell don't have that kind of money."

My dad's about the last thing I want to find, but Singer pushes open the door anyway. All we can see inside is black. There's no sounds coming out the apartment but a smell so bad, like the trash dumpster at the restaurant, that it hurts your head. There's a lot of kids running around near the street screaming now, but I block it out, slow, until I can just concentrate on whether there's a beating coming out of that black. I don't think so, not with Singer here, but I got my cells supertuned just in case.

"Hello?" Singer yells. "Anyone here? David?"

We step inside the apartment and it smells even worse, but at least it's still quiet. "Can we go, Singer? I don't like being here."

"Don't worry. I won't let him hurt you." I feel Singer's hand on my arm. I nod, but I'm still scared. It's good Singer's here, but my dad's bigger than me and Singer put together. I sure don't want no naked lady trying to pull off my jeans again. I want to ask Singer why the naked lady did that, but he's pretty busy now, looking through all the papers and bottles and cans and all kinds of junk piled on the counter.

"Jesus Christ!"

I jump back when Singer yells and put up my hands, my body tensed up waiting for the noise. . . .

"Sorry. Roach ran across my hand. Didn't mean to scare you."

It don't take long to look around the apartment because it's only one room with the couch that turns into a bed in the middle and the kitchen on one wall. If I'm sleeping in the bed when my dad ain't here and he comes home, he throws me on the floor, so whether he's here or not I pretty much sleep on the floor. That's why Singer got me the sleeping bag and I started staying in the Toad's attic, which is still a floor but different because I get a longer sleep where the noise stays away and the only thing comes into my head is good kitchen smells. I hope this is the last time I'm ever here again. Now Singer's looking through all the kitchen cupboards so I help him, but we don't find nothin except some more roaches. Singer yells each time one runs out, but they don't scare me since they been here from the first day me and my dad moved to this apartment. Singer looks under the mattress and in the drawers and in the little closet. We both look in the bathroom together, but we can't find the Toad's money nowhere. Really all we find is the smell under the couch, which is wrapped up in paper and covered with these tiny white worms.

"I don't want to know what that is," he says.

Then Singer drops down on the floor holding his stomach, like the noise is getting him except on the inside. I try to pick him up, get the noise out, but it's got him good and he can't get up. He's breathing hard and still holding his stomach and his forehead looks all shiny like the Toad's. I don't say nothin and then real slow he gets up on one knee and takes some deep breaths. That's when I see the noise float out his body like green smoke, and I wave my hand through the air to cut it in half.

"It's all right, Singer. That special medicine you're taking will keep the noise out your body."

Singer's face has to think about this one for a little while. "C'mere."

I go over, and we sit down in the only two chairs my dad got, one with a leg that bends out so the chair wiggles around when you sit in it. Singer's still got that shiny forehead and a different kind of look on his face, like a little bit of that noise floated back inside when I wasn't looking. Then he says, "There's something I need to tell you."

My big brother got the noise in his balls so bad they took one off. That's what he had to tell me. He said it didn't hurt none because they put him asleep. That's good because my dad's kicked me down there a lot of times, which makes you walk and talk crooked for a while. Singer says that noise is growing inside him the same way the special powers been growing in ZigZag. I want to ask Singer why some things growing inside kills you and other keeps you alive, so I walk down the hall to look for him even though he told me to wait in that chair. He went into this office to talk to some lady about my dad. We supposed to do fun stuff on Singer Day, not spend all our time looking for my dad and hanging around some lady's office. I can't see them in there, but the office door's open enough to hear.

"But he can't stay there. He can't go back to that apartment. Ever."

"I appreciate your concern, Dean, but unfortunately Positive Mentors—"

"I know, I know. It's not the agency, it's state law that keeps a fifteen-year-old kid with a father who beats him. There's got to be something we can do."

"Again, in cases like this about all we can do is call in family social services."

"And then what?"

"Well . . . they'll investigate and take corrective action if the situation merits."

"If the situation merits? Jesus Christ, he's beating him. How much fucking merit do they want?"

"Please watch your language, Dean; I don't make up the rules."

"Yeah, but you know your way around them."

They're both quiet for a minute.

"Well," she says, "the first step would probably be to get some help for Louis's father."

"That's it? What happens to Louis?"

"Again, Dean, this is out of our realm. Positive Mentors is about you helping Louis with his homework, taking him to the movies, being a good role model. Serious family issues like this are beyond our charter and, quite frankly, outside our legal means."

"In the last twenty-four hours Louis was blamed for breaking a window at work that he didn't break, he was beaten two separate times and robbed by his inebriated father, skipped school, saw his father and another man having sex with a prostitute, and spent the night in the restaurant attic. Talk about merit . . . where you think he'll be by the time he's eighteen?"

"How long have you guys been together now?"

"Five years next month. We've outlasted five of your caseworkers. Diane was number five. You're number six."

"I'm touched by how much you care about Louis, especially in light of your . . . illness. He really is lucky."

"It's OK to say it: testicular cancer. Or, to put it bluntly, they cut off one of my balls. But that has nothing to do with my commitment to Louis. The issue here is his well-being. Will you help or not?"

"Of course I will, but you need to be patient. We need to work within the system we have. Fair enough?"

Singer don't say nothin, but I can hear him nodding.

"OK, since I'm new, I'd like to go over his file with you. Get all the background."

"Sure. Fletcher, Louis, although he likes the nickname I gave him better."

"And what's that?"

"ZigZag."

"ZigZag. I like it. Now, he was ten when you were paired?"

"I had just gone through a pretty rough year: split up with my wife, fired from my job. I was depressed, getting fat. My doctor said something like this would give me some perspective. Shit, I planned on dropping the volunteer thing the minute I felt better. I had no idea I'd still be doing this five years later."

"He's lucky. Most of our pairs stay together one or two years. Now, this is the original report when you were first paired. It's not normal policy, but I'd like to read it aloud and make sure there are no discrepancies. If left unchecked, these things can follow a kid forever."

"Yeah, great."

It sounds funny, her voice reading a story about me I ain't never heard told start-to-finish, but all of it true:

Little Brother Profile: Louis Fletcher has had a rough start in life, and whether he is having a childhood at all is debatable. His mother died when he was an infant, although the details of her death are unclear. Louis's dad apparently seems to think that the transmission of sperm was his last official fatherly duty. There was, and continues to be, physical abuse, but the main form has been simple neglect. Louis has no brothers or sisters, and his father is rarely around except to administer beatings and eradicate any lingering strand of self-esteem. Louis and his father shuffle between one-room apartments rented by the week and girlfriends' places. His father, David, has no stable employment or prospects. When he is working, it's usually as a construction laborer.

Against that backdrop, Louis struggles to get to school on a regular basis. When he is in school, it's not surprising that he's inattentive and has a penchant for stealing. Currently age ten, Louis can't read and can't write his own name. About the only bright spot is that he shows skill at memorizing and recalling numbers. Nothing remotely approaching the abilities of an idiot savant, but at least Louis can remember and recite long lists of numbers such as his perpetually changing phone number.

Anytime Louis is in a stressful situation he retreats within himself. He won't talk to anyone, which can last days. Not even repeated beatings from his dad bring a word to his lips. He often wets himself during these long silences and throws nearby objects.

His father did not have the wherewithal to get his son help. Louis stumbled into the Positive Mentors program purely by serendipity when one of his more vigilant teachers arranged an after-school meeting in her classroom. Louis's father was invited but never showed.

Big Brother Profile: Dean Singer has volunteered for the minimum commitment of six months. From his application: "Don't be misled; I'm not a saint or a bleeding heart or someone out to save the world. I'm here for purely selfish reasons. I've been going through some difficult times, a divorce, mainly. My doctor suggested volunteer work as part of my therapy."

Although his commitment to Positive Mentors is borderline, I think Dean shows great potential as a role model to Louis. Dean has no college degree, and his work has been all blue-collar. He recently started a job driving a forklift at a warehouse. His new employer gives him high marks for punctuality, performance, and attitude. It is this last trait, his diligent approach, that could most benefit Louis.

I am recommending that we pair Louis and Dean immediately for the standard six-month trial period.

"How's that sound?"

After a few seconds Singer answers, "Like I was a selfish bastard. But it's accurate, I guess. I'm still working at the same company."

"Now I've got yearly updates here, as well, but you're saying his home situation hasn't improved?"

"It's worse. His dad's drinking more, and when he drinks he hits."

I can hear paper sounds. "Outside of the home situation, it looks like Louis has made some dramatic improvements."

"Oh yeah. He's in the Fellowes School now, learning to read, and he can write a little now. If he sticks with it, he could be ready for a G.E.D. class, maybe by the time he's nineteen or twenty. But he'll never make it unless we get him out of that apartment. I also helped get him a job washing dishes four nights a week, which he really likes. He's learning a lot from the experience, and he loves it when he gets his paycheck."

"And has he stayed out of trouble?"

"Well . . . yeah . . . pretty much. Couple little things here and there . . . but overall, yeah, he's stayed out of trouble. He's never had a run-in with the law."

"Good. I'm going to need to present a recommendation to my supervisor as to what we should do. Now because you're the closest one to the situation, what course of action would you recommend?"

"Recommend? Shit, I don't know. You're the caseworker. All I know is we need to get him away from his dad, but I don't want to see him get put into some state-run home."

"That's the unfortunate thing in these situations: there's no perfect solution."

"Well, there may be . . . I mean it may not be perfect, but what about . . . it's something I've thought about for quite a while now, it's just I don't know how. Or if it's even possible."

"I think I know what you're thinking."

"Yeah, I mean, is that even possible? I mean it is, I have a hide-a-bed in the living room and my apartment is close enough to his school that he could ride his bike, but I mean, legally? Could I somehow adopt him?"

"What you're saying is very commendable, especially in light of your original attitude toward this program. The chance, however, of a nonblood party getting legal custody from the biological parent is depressingly remote. And without meaning any disrespect, a terminal illness will negate any chance you might have. I know it's frustrating, but if you really want to help Louis, a boys' home is probably the best option."

Tonight all the lights in the city look like they too cold to stay lit and won't be full bright until summer. I'm glad when we finally left that place cus I was bored just listening to Singer and that lady talk. Now Singer got the heat turned up, but the heater makes a loud noise so we don't talk except in our heads. After we left that lady's office, Singer got us some food, the car filled up now with the smell of hamburgers and french fries. Singer said he's pretty tired from work and that noise in his one ball and trying to figure out how he's going to get the Toad's money back, so we're just going over to his apartment, which is great with me. I got my sleeping bag, and Singer's got a color TV with different movies all his own; you just pick which one you want and watch it as many times as you want. My favorite is one I can't remember the name, but it's got these kids who find this space monster and hide him in the closet and dress him like a girl. They give him the name ET, like Singer give me a new name.

"What were you and that lady talking about?"

He turns the heater down so we can hear each other. "About finding you a place to live. Where no one will hurt you."

"I'll live with you. You told that lady about where I sleep and I can ride my bike to school."

"You heard all that?"

I nod my head. "I got bored just sitting in that chair."

"It's complicated, but she said you can stay with me until we figure out a plan."

That right there shows how many plans Singer got in his head. That must be why he got such a good job driving that forklift; you gotta be smart to drive good. Whenever they need a plan at his work, all they got to do is just go ask Singer and he'll give them one.

"Singer, you told that lady I wasn't in no trouble. That mean we don't have to worry no more about the Toad's money?"

"No, we are still in trouble for that, and yes, we still need to get it back. I just don't know what to do yet."

"Singer, how come you only wanted to be with me for six months? I in trouble again?"

"What do you mean?"

"You told that lady you only wanted to volunteer for six months. You mad at me?"

Singer shakes his head and smiles. "You heard our entire conversation, didn't you?"

"I guess."

"You guess. Well what you heard was from a long time ago. A lot has changed in five years."

"We been together five years? Damn, I only been alive one five."

"Thanks a lot. Now I feel really old."

"Nah, you ain't old, Singer. I seen people coming in the restaurant at least six five or seven zero. Now they some old people. You know when you really old, Singer, cus your hair will be all white. You won't be that old for a long time, Singer."

Singer don't say nothin, but I can see him talking on the inside about what I said. Or maybe he's working on another new plan. I reach over and turn the heater up full power so he don't feel like he got to talk on the outside. We got to get Singer a new heater when we find the Toad's money. He looks at me and smiles, but it ain't the same smile he usually give me. It's more like a pretend smile.

No wonder Singer gets tired after driving that forklift all day and looking for the Toad's money and having meetings with that caseworker lady cus then he still got to think up plans to keep me out of trouble. I wonder maybe Singer got that noise in his balls cus I'm always giving him problems and making him tired like right now. He don't look so good, one hand on his stomach like maybe that noise is down deep inside where I can't see it. I flip on my radar and listen hard, see if any noise jumped in the car when I wasn't looking. When I go extra sensitive, I know some of that noise is underneath his face even though I can't see it. Supertuned cells in my head see the noise even when there ain't nothin to see on the outside. Singer's face don't look the same since he got that cancer in his balls, like all day he just got out his bed. He don't talk as much, either, like me when you got to use all your extra thinking just to keep the noise out your head. He'll be all right, though, especially with me nearby because nothing can catch you when you ZigZag. He just needs some rest and more of that special medicine makes his hair fall out. Then me and Singer will always be together keep the noise out each other's heads.

When we get to Singer's apartment, first thing I do is put that movie about the space monster into the machine and put a big bag of popcorn into the microwave. Someday maybe Singer will teach me to drive a forklift so I can make as much money as he got. He got his own bedroom with furniture and then a whole other room with the couch that folds into my bed and the TV and all the videos. Whatever you want to drink, he got it in the refrigerator. He keeps a lot of Dr Pepper for me. But the best thing about here is two things: one is the smell because there ain't one. Everywhere else I stayed got a smell you can't get out your head, like the kitchen smell in the Toad's attic or that stink under my dad's couch. This the only place I ever stayed my nose don't have to ZigZag the stink while I sleep. Second thing is that it don't matter whether it's winter or summer outside cus Singer's apartment always just right, not too cold or too hot.

"You want popcorn, Singer?"

"No thanks."

Singer must be working hard on our new plan cus he always has popcorn in the blue bowl. I always use the green bowl.

"Dr Pepper?"

"Nothing."

Singer always sits in his chair when we watch videos, and I sit on the couch. I can see two more of us in the sliding door, so it looks like two short bald people and two tall skinny people watching the TV. Right now that kid's putting the candy on the ground for the space monster. Then Singer gets up and goes over to my stuff that we brought in from his car. My radar picks up a little bit of that restaurant smell sneaking out my stuff into the room. Singer don't notice; he's back in his chair now and looking at the Toad's receipts. His head looks funny with no hair when he takes off his hat.

"What?"

Singer got the best radar I ever seen. He picks up my thoughts all the time. "Nothin," I say, careful now to keep my thoughts quiet while he's thinking.

"How are we going to get this money returned?"

Sometimes his questions just mean he's thinking outside his head. I know cus of the way his eyes look at me without really looking.

"I just don't have that kind of money. I've got maybe three hundred in my checking account, and they cut off my last credit card. . . ." Singer thinks outside his head for a long time and points at the candy for the space monster. "Too bad we can't do that."

He wants to give my dad candy? "He don't like candy too much."

"Not candy. But what if there was a way to make your dad come to us?"

"How about a naked lady and a bottle of that booze?"

Singer laughs, shakes his head. Then he comes and sits by me on the couch. "The naked lady idea is good. I like that. But no, even if we got your dad to come to us, we'd still be in the same spot. How do we get back the money he already took? And does he still have it?"

Singer usually asks a lot of questions on the outside when he's coming up with a plan, but it's always so complicated I don't know what he's talking about, plus I'm mostly trying to watch the space monster. Anyway, Singer's plans always work whether I talk on the outside or not.

"We've only got one choice: we go back over there and confront him. . . . ZigZag, listen. This is important."

I turn my head, but Singer don't know I'm only listening out one corner my ear. I can still see the backwards TV in the sliding door.

". . . talk to your dad in the morning before I take you to school and go to work. First we'll have to find out if he still has the money. Then I'll have to convince him to give it back to us. Good luck, right?"

I nod.

"And if all that works, we take the cash back to the restaurant. We could do it late tomorrow after you get off work. You think you can open that safe again?"

I say the six numbers so fast I got to say them again, slow, slow, slow, so Singer can hear.

I float through air so cold you can see it coming out people's heads and the car pipes. There's no snow, but the ground makes noises you never hear when the grass is green. I got my black leather jacket and gloves and a hat, but the cold touches my face and fills up my whole body all the way to my toes. It's so cold even the hole for Singer's car key don't want to turn. I get inside, and somehow it feels colder in here than outside. The cold's like the noise cus you can see it floating in the air and feel it inside your body, and you know there ain't nowhere it can't get. It takes a few tries to shake the cold out the engine.

Singer didn't used to let me start the car but I asked him so many times, probably one zero zero, until he finally taught me. I like floating out here first, make sure the lever is in the right position, then turn the key and blast the heater so loud you almost think it'd be better to stay cold. Then I jump back out and scrape all the cold stuck on the windows and watch them little flakes of cold float down to the ground, wondering where they gonna go when it's summer again. I go back in for Singer, who's still pulling on the same sock as when I left. That's what happens when you ZigZag in and out so fast, everyone around you always stuck in slow motion. When he's finally ready, we leave, Singer following in the warm path I cut through the air. His heater don't work so good but somehow throws enough cold off the seats to soften up the cracks. Singer's got his white cup that puffs out little clouds of hot coffee air. Sometimes I shrink down to coffee-cup size and sneak in there when Singer ain't looking to fill up my whole body with warm and be back in my seat normal size before he can take a single sip. Then he smiles to let me know he don't mind if I go extra small. You can't think nothin around Singer without him knowing about it.

My heart and stomach been a little crazy ever since last night when Singer said we were going to find my dad after seeing those kids leave the candy for the space monster. Probably would have been better to watch a different video, and then maybe we wouldn't be driving there right now. My radar's telling me we're driving closer and closer to some real bad noise. If there's one thing my dad don't like, it's being tricked out of his money. One time Eddie took two zero from my dad's wallet and left a note saying he'd pay him back later. Next time Eddie showed up at the door, I seen my dad hit him across the back of the head with a bat that ain't never hit a baseball in its life.

Dad called the bat Black Beauty since it was shiny and black, said she was the mom I never had. Whenever I did something wrong, he'd tell me it was time to ask Black Beauty what she thought, and he'd pull her out from behind the couch real slow and swing her through the air a few times to warm her up. One time dad used the Black Beauty to knock the noise into my head so loud, when I woke up it was a different day. When I got me a new big brother, one of the first things Singer helped me do was get rid of Black Beauty. We sneaked the Black Beauty out the apartment when my dad was asleep and drove a long time until we were outside the city. I never seen so many trees as that day, real green all along the river. Singer told me to throw her in the river, and it filled me up with good on the inside to watch her float away. Singer said it ain't right to kill no one, except he said it was OK what we done to Black Beauty.

"Singer, I don't think it's such a good idea we go to find my dad."

"Don't worry. If it gets out of hand, we'll just leave. I won't let him hurt you."

"What if he got him another Black Beauty?"

"What? No . . . that was when I first met you. Long time ago."

I dunno, sure don't seem like a long time ago, and maybe my dad found Black Beauty floating in the river, got her out with a long stick, dried her off, and hid her somewhere in the apartment.

"Hey, don't worry. We'll be all right."

Singer puts his hand on my leg, which helps, but my heart's still going crazy when he pulls up slow along the curb and we see my dad's car, which is the only car I ever seen looks worse than Singer's. The back bumper on my dad's car hangs down low on one side, crooked, so close no one can sit in the backseat or the bumper scrapes the ground. Whenever we go somewhere with Eddie, we all got to crowd up front to keep that damn bumper quiet.

Singer shuts off the car, and we just stare up at the apartment to give our radar a chance to get tuned in to the air around here.

"Well . . . he's up there," Singer says, pointing at my dad's car.

I concentrate my mind like Singer taught me to keep the noise out, think about something good, like how the sprayer feels heavy and slippery in my left hand while hot grease balls jump off the big black pots and stick my arm like little pins. That's my favorite time, right at the beginning of my shift when I'm flying through a huge pile of plates and cups and cold silverware the lunch bastards left, and the sun comes in the high kitchen window and bounces off the white wall so bright I got to work by feel. Then everything goes on the inside, automatic, too much light the same as dark. I just look at Singer, his words ain't sinking in full yet. Singer touches my leg and gives me a serious kind of look.

"Remember our plan?"

"No."

"You stay here. I'll go up and talk to him, see if I can get the money back."

"Singer, how come you think he'll give it back?"

"I guess I don't. But I don't know what else to do. Either we get that money back soon, or you're going to get sent away. God knows I'm probably an accomplice by now." He scratches his bald head through the black baseball hat. "One thing at a time. You wait here, and I'll be right back."

Singer slips out the car real fast before I can say watch out for the noise, but I say it anyway cus he got his radar on. He goes up the stairs, slow, wearing the black leather jacket just like the one he gave me except his is smaller. When he gets to the door, my heart really goes crazy, like it's me standing up there not knowing whether the noise is about to explode. He turns his head sideways and presses it up against the door to see if my dad is making that naked lady scream or if Eddie is in there snoring. Only thing worse than waking up my dad is waking up Eddie when he's snoring. One time the TV woke up Eddie, and he threw a bottle that flew past my head and smashed the TV. Then when my dad came home, he wouldn't believe me that Eddie done it. My dad said the only way to find out the truth was to ask my mother. Black Beauty, he said, never lies.

Singer looks down at me and nods his head a little like it's all quiet and then knocks three times loud. I hope he knows around my dad it's always real quiet right before it gets real loud. Even though the sun's shining on Singer, I can see the little puffs of cold coming out his head. He knocks again, *one, two, three,* and waits, and then three again. When he turns and walks away, my body lets up cus I think it's better we never see my dad again. Singer can be my new dad, even though he ain't really old like most dads I seen.

Then just out the corner my eye a black crack opens up along the edge of the door, gets bigger, bigger, now big enough my dad comes out the door behind Singer. My voice tries to scream, but it's like my heart is double crazy and jammed up in my throat. Singer don't hear my dad moving up behind him dressed only in a towel, got a brown baseball bat above his head. Since my voice ain't working, I throw my fists against the window try to make some sound, but my gloves are real quiet on the glass. Just before Singer gets to the top of the stairs, his radar must kick in cus he turns and *WHOOOO*, my dad swings hard, Singer's bald head just low enough that all the bat knocks off is the hat. The bat slams into the side of the building, and little white chips tear off the wall. My dad almost falls down, and the metal railing catches the towel and pulls it off. Singer falls, too, then starts kind of crawling down the stairs backwards and talking, but all I can see is puffs of cold and no words with the window up. Then my dad starts towards him, full naked, his thing shrunk up from the cold, swinging the bat with both hands and yelling at Singer. The bat makes noises loud enough to wake up the whole city, *DING, DING, DING*, each time it hits the metal railing. Then my dad stops swinging the bat, picks up his towel, and wraps up again before his thing freezes.

Singer's down at the bottom of the stairs now, my dad standing at the top with nothin on but that towel. My heart's really going crazy the way my dad stands there surrounded by puffs of frozen air, but he don't shake or shiver, like he's made out of some kind of metal don't feel the cold. I roll the window down just a little so I can hear.

". . . fuck should I do that?"

"He's your son. He needs your help."

"What the fuck you know about my son?"

"More than you apparently."

"Fuck you, bitch. You crackers don't know shit about what goes on around here."

"I know he's gonna get sent away."

"Sent away . . . shit. You talking like they going to send him upstate. He'll do a year max, juvenile." My dad picks up Singer's hat and throws it down at him. Singer leans down and puts it back on his bald head.

"So you don't care if he goes into the system?"

"Fuck you know about the system? System supposed to keep the niggers locked up. Ain't that right?"

"That's bullshit."

"Easy for a white boy to say."

"This isn't about black and white. This is about doing what's right for your son."

"I *been* doing what's right. Beat his ass keep him tough. I knew one day he'd get sent away. Now he's ready."

"That's touching. If only all parents could be so loving."

"Fuck you, you little punk motherfucker." My dad comes down a few stairs and then stops. "Best get your bald white ass out here fore I come down there and fuck up your shit."

"That money you took is stolen."

"What you talkin about 'money'?"

"You know what I'm talking about. From yesterday."

"Yeah? So the same money been stole twice. You think I give a fuck?"

"You should. He goes down, you go down. Either we put the money back . . ."

"Or what, motherfucker? What the fuck you goin to do about it? You gonna come up here and do something about it?"

"You still have it?"

"Fuck you. Ain't none of your business."

"Just tell me. It's gone, right?"

"Damn, you a determined little bitch."

"I care what happens to Louis."

"Shit, nigger ain't got but half a brain. And the half he's got is all fucked up. Always be talkin about numbers and shit and—"

"So what about the money?"

"You want that money so bad, you go ax Cadillac Tom. Down the Monkey Club. Ax him the five grand I give him yesterday. Tell him you want it, and see what he say." My dad's laughing now.

"You gave him all of it?"

"Don't be surprised he tells you to suck his nine."

"The Monkey Club?"

"And I ain't talkin about the one in his pants."

My dad laughs even harder after he says that, covering his mouth with the hand still got the bat and holding the towel with the other. Singer's walking back to the car now, and just before he gets in my dad yells again and pulls off the towel so he standing there full naked with little clouds of cold air around his head.

"Come on up here, boy, and bring your little nigger girlfriend there. I'll let you earn back fifty bucks." My dad waves his thing at us with his hand, the bat in the other, and laughs again. Singer gets in the car without saying anything, but his face ain't too happy. He starts the car. As we drive away, I can see my dad still out there full naked, stretching his arms like he thinks it's summer and he about to jump in the pool, those little clouds of cold air still swirling around his head.

"What my dad mean about that five zero?"

"Nothing. He was just joking."

"So how we gonna get the Toad's money back now?"

"Only one thing we can do."

"What's that?"

"I'm gonna get off work early and pick you up at school."

"Then what?"

"Then we're going to find Cadillac Tom."

At the Fellowes School we watch a video about a man got some stuff called botulism injected into his face make the wrinkles go away. Another lady got fat sucked out her leg and shot in her thing suppose to make it prettier. When the video ends, Ms. Tate says we're starting a new unit about the self-esteem, which she says means how you feel on the inside. Ms. Tate says you got to have the self-esteem before you can do good stuff on the outside. I don't know what the self-esteem has to do with some lady getting fat sucked out her leg, but what I think Ms. Tate is really talking about is the special powers you got to have to keep the noise from getting you.

Ms. Tate has been my teacher ever since I come to the Fellowes School, which she says is a place for kids got special needs, kids like me too stupid or too messed up to go to the regular school. Singer says I ain't stupid or messed up, that I just learn different from the other kids. Singer told me about some guy named

Albert who's real good with numbers like me. Albert's so smart he flunked out the regular school, too, and then he wrote the theory of relatives. I ain't wrote no theories, but my body can ZigZag ways make people rub they eyes see if they dreaming.

I always like coming to the Fellowes School to see Ms. Tate. She always smells like flowers no matter what the air's like outside. Singer says it's been five years since we met, but five years, five weeks, five minutes, five months; all feels the same to me. Ms. Tate's a lot prettier than that naked lady at my dad's apartment. Since Singer and Ms. Tate about the two nicest people I know, they should get married, then I'll have me a regular family who don't knock the noise into your head and try to pull your jeans off for no good reason.

". . . Louis? Louis?"

I nod; I guess she the other one calls me Louis.

"Can you tell us what you think?"

This the part I hate about school, when all they eyes on me at once with no sounds, and Ms. Tate smiling nice but I don't know what to say or what she wants to know, and then I feel it again, that noise in the back my neck, somehow slips in my body when ain't no one close enough to even touch me, all them eyes just waiting, waiting, waiting. Then the room gets darker like the noise blocking everything out again, and I can see Ms. Tate trying to reach out and save me, her face different, her mouth moving and the kids laughing but no sound comes out nowhere, everything silent, big holes in they heads with green noise slipping out towards me until I just got to slap them jaws shut, close them ugly holes keep the noise locked up where it can't get inside me, but there's at least one five holes all opened up now, with the green smoke pouring into the room until I can't breathe . . .

"You all right?"

Ms. Tate got about the best damn voice you ever want to see and real smooth skin, and when she this close, that flower smell fills up my head. Maybe if Singer don't marry Ms. Tate, I'll marry her for myself. Ms. Tate won't mind none if Singer comes to live with us. I nod, and she smiles and then leans down to help me off the floor. Then she moves away from my desk to talk about the self-esteem. Inside my head's real quiet now because I got the smell inside, and now I know Ms. Tate won't ask me any questions for a while.

She's reading us a true story out the newspaper about some kids that raped and beat on a ten-year-old girl, stuck her panties in her mouth, and drew pictures all over her body with markers. A janitor found the girl barely alive not too far from here. No one knows what rape is, so Ms. Tate has to explain, like she always does when we don't understand words she uses. Then she talks about how if those kids had better self-esteem, they would never be able to do something like that to another human being. One kid, Alice, asks Ms. Tate what a human being is, and everyone laughs, even me, but then I listen to Ms. Tate's answer just to make sure.

Ms. Tate says we get the self-esteem from the time we little babies to now depending a lot on whether people make us feel good about ourselves. She tells us to close our eyes and think about the people that have had the most positive influence in our lives. She says it can be anybody, mom, dad, uncle, aunt, cousin, teacher, friend, grandma, but I don't even got to think to know who give me the most self-esteem, and it sure ain't my dad or my mom since she died when I was a baby.

Then Ms. Tate tells us to take out a paper and pen and write about who's given us the self-esteem. Some kids saying they don't have no one makes them feel good about themselves except Ms. Tate, but she says that's fine, they can write about anybody they want. Then some kids yell about how that's cheating to write about Ms. Tate giving us the self-esteem. Then more and more questions, everyone except me asking so many questions, like they always do when Ms. Tate gives us some work to do. I keep all my questions on the inside and then just listen close to all of Ms.

Tate's answers. If no one asks the question I'm thinking of, then I just push it out my head and forget about it for good. Ms. Tate must get tired of so many questions all the time:

"What if we ain't never had self-esteem?"

"What about Bugs Bunny? Watching him gives me the self-esteem."

"How do we know if someone gives us the self-esteem?"

"You got any paper, Ms. Tate?"

"If I already got the self-esteem, I still gotta do this?"

"Why didn't you show us the part in that video when that lady got the fat injected up her thing?"

"You ever got fat shot up your thing, Ms. Tate?"

When all the questions are over, Ms. Tate says the assignment is to write down why the person we chose makes us feel good. That way, she says, we can concentrate on getting more of the self-esteem. Then she writes *self-esteem* on the board because she knows none of us is smart enough to spell big words right. I hate this part, where we got to write. If Ms. Tate had the special powers, I could just think on the inside and she could understand without having to spend so long always writing, writing, writing. It takes a long time to write down what you can think in your head a lot quicker. I look around, and everyone else is finally quiet, and, since we ain't going to see Cadillac Tom for a while, I get out a paper and pen.

self-esteem
By ZigZag

siner my new bigg bruther five years makes me fel good.
we go eat togethur & latter watch the video et.

Siner got me a jod washhing the dishis for the tod munday winsday, thirsday, fryday.

Today he shod me not too be afrad my dad.

ZigZag

1 time siner help me kill the black buty ded ded ded. gone for good! i got more self-estem cus siner is my frend. I'll never do the rape to no one.

siner and me be togethur four ever.

allways.

ZigZag

At least three of Singer's car could fit inside the long black car Cadillac Tom drives. Me and Singer are sitting across the street, not talking, just looking at that car for a long time while the heater blows loud. The sun's been out all day, but it ain't done much because everyone walking down the sidewalk still got the cold air coming out their heads. Singer picked me up at the Fellowes School, and I showed him the story I wrote about him giving me the self-esteem. He hugged me after he read it and said I done an excellent job. Then we got on the freeway and drove down here to a place Singer said is called the Monkey Club. It's a long pink building, but instead of monkeys it has naked ladies painted on the outside.

"This is a long shot if I've ever seen one," he says, taking off his hat and scratching his head. One time he let me rub it just cus I kept bugging him about how it feels with no hair. It feels like the bottom of the glass bowls I wash at the Toad's restaurant.

"Even if we find him . . . there's no way he's going to give us back the money."

"But it ain't his, it's ours."

"Actually, no, it's not his, and it's not ours either. The money belongs to your boss."

"Really?"

"Uh-huh. Really."

"So we gonna tell him the money belongs to the Toad?"

"I don't know . . . and what do I call him? Cadillac? Mr. Tom? This is right out of Elmore Leonard."

"What do you mean?"

"Nothing. He writes books. Maybe this isn't such a good idea."

Singer didn't take no college, but he still got more books than I ever seen except at the library, two whole shelves got nothin but books, probably two zero or three zero books. Singer's still got his eye on that long black car or the pink building, I can't tell which. Then he reaches down and turns off the engine, and the car gets real quiet without the heater. I wonder how long we're going to sit here like this, the cold waiting for us right on the other side of the window.

"OK, we'll go in and tell him the situation. Either he says yes, or he says no. Right?"

"Or maybe he's the one found the Black Beauty."

"ZigZag, there is no more Black Beauty. Let's just hope your dad wasn't right."

"About what?"

"Never mind. All right, flip on your radar, and stay close to me. We'll be in and out in five minutes. Ready?"

I nod, and we get out and wait for the cars to clear before we run across the street toward the pink building. Singer slows down and looks at the long black car so shiny it shows what we look like walking together, Singer on one side, short, little wider, me on the other side, taller. When we get to the door, Singer pulls it open, and we step into a place so dark my eyes don't work, loud music rolling up in my head. Then real slow my eyes come back, and I can see Singer talking to a girl behind a little window with a hole in the middle. The girl's smoking a cigarette.

"There a guy named . . . Tom works here?"

"Tom?" She blows out some smoke and shakes her head. "No one calls him that."

"What's he go by?"

"Cadillac."

"Is he in?"

"Who's the kid?" She points at me with her cigarette the way the Toad does with his little cigar.

"My little brother."

She looks at Singer like he's crazy. "Ten-dollar cover. Kid can't go in."

"No, I just need to talk to . . . Cadillac. Out here's fine."

She blows some smoke out her mouth, sideways. "Ten-dollar cover. And the kid waits outside."

"Ten dollars just to talk to him? Out here?"

"He ain't out here, he's in there."

"Would he come out if you asked him?"

"I don't know. Ten dollars, and you can ask him that yourself."

Singer looks around and then back at the girl. "But I need him to meet Zig—Louis. Could you maybe page him or something. Have him come out?"

"I look like a secretary?"

"I'd really appreciate it."

"This is good," she says, nodding her head and puffing on the cigarette. "The silent kid act is good."

"What?" Singer asks, looking real confuse.

"We've had you guys down here before, but this silent kid act is a new one."

"You've had what guys down here before?"

"Liquor board."

"Liquor board? We're not with the liquor board."

"One time," she says, leaning back and folding her arms, tapping the cigarette in a glass ashtray like the ones we got at the restaurant, "they sent in a girl saying she got locked out of her house and could she go in and find her dad? She even had ponytails and braces. You know what I told her?"

Singer just looks at the lady.

"Told her to fuck off."

"That's really great, but we're not with any liquor board. I just need to talk to him for a minute, about some money that was stolen."

"Ten-dollar cover—"

"I know. The kid waits outside." Singer looks at me and shakes his head, then back to the girl. "If you see him, could you at least ask him . . . or tell him Dean Singer and Louis Fletcher," Singer pointing at me, "he's David Fletcher's son, and I'm—"

"For ten bucks you can tell him all this yourself."

"Never mind. Forget it. Don't say anything."

Me and Singer go back outside, and the light blasts us full bright. I got to squint to see, my eyes coming back slow in the bright. We wait for the cars again and walk back across the street. We just sit here in Singer's car without talking on the outside and watch that big black car like it's about to do something all on its own.

"This is boring. How long we gonna sit here, Singer?"

"Until this Cadillac Tom comes out. We have to get that money back, or we're fu . . . in big trouble."

"When you going to stop taking that special medicine makes your hair fall out?"

Singer looks at me without talking. Finally he says, "Soon, I hope."

"Why it makes your hair fall out again?"

"It's a special treatment. Eats up the bad cells."

We watch the cars pass back and forth between us and the big black car. Some men come in and out the pink building, two with black cowboy hats and black leather jackets. For some reason with Singer I talk more on the outside than with anyone else I ever been around.

"Singer, I was thinking, when we get that money we could get your car painted one color. Maybe black like that car."

"That would be nice. But when we get that money it's going right back in the safe."

"Then how will we paint your car—"

"There he is."

Singer leans forward and points across the street.

"How you know there he is?"

"Look at him."

Singer's damn smart cus I don't see nothing looks like a name tag says Cadillac Tom. He's short like Singer and got a girl taller than he is on each side. Then he stops at the long black car, over on the curb, and both girls get inside. That big car with a good bumper in back, and they all jammed in the front seat?

"Come on. Come with me."

My heart starts going a little crazy when we ZigZag across the street so fast Cadillac Tom blinks twice make sure we real.

"Cadillac?"

He don't say nothin. He walks past like we're both invisible and opens the driver door.

"My name's Dean Singer. This is Louis, David Fletcher's son."

Cadillac Tom's got skin in between white and black with real short black hair. He leans on his car and looks across at us standing on the sidewalk. "Some reason I should be listening to you, or do you just want to take a picture?"

"David Fletcher gave you five thousand dollars yesterday."

Cadillac Tom looks like he don't care or can't remember, I can't tell which. He's looking at his fingernails.

"The money he gave you was stolen by Louis, his son." Singer touches me on the shoulder.

Cadillac Tom must like to look at his fingernails cus that's where he looks when he talks. "I like stories that have a point. So far I don't like your story."

Singer starts talking faster. "Louis stole the money from the restaurant where he works, and his dad stole it from him and then gave it to you. We think. If you don't, or if we don't, get that money back, Louis could get sent away. To a juvenile home. I was just hoping you could help us."

Cadillac Tom got a toothpick in his mouth like the Toad got that unlit cigar. He rolls it around, around, working it with his tongue, now looking up at us for the first time. Then he takes the toothpick out and flicks it across the car. It bounces off Singer's face and lands on the sidewalk.

"Sad story."

Cadillac Tom gets in the long black car and starts the engine. Singer looks at me, then walks around the front of the car and taps on the window. I float behind to keep my eye on Cadillac Tom just in case he's got the Black Beauty hidden down under the seat.

"Please. Wait. He's only fifteen. He shouldn't have to go down because his dad owed you money."

Now the black window comes down, slow and even, until it stops halfway. Cadillac Tom's already working a clean toothpick, just staring at Singer through sunglasses so black you can't see his eyes. Singer's still talking. "C'mon. I don't know what it was for, but David Fletcher, he gave you five grand yesterday?"

Cadillac Tom just looks at Singer. "You after money, you should go to a bank. You girls have a nice day."

Singer got all kinds of mad on his face. He just stares at Cadillac Tom for a few seconds before he lets go the car and steps back. Cadillac Tom smiles and slips the lever down, and the car is gone. Me and Singer just stand there in the road while the cars fly by us both directions. Then Singer nods toward his car, and we run back across the street. When I ask Singer what are we gonna do now, he gives me a look I ain't never seen before, like maybe he don't have a new plan for us.

● ● ●

The sprayer fits into my left hand like it's been there since I was born and my skin grew around it. The silver metal gets hotter each time I squeeze the handle and blast the scraps off the plates. I'm only working at half speed, one eye on the dishes while the other looks around for the Toad. Singer just dropped me off here a few minutes ago since we couldn't get the money from Cadillac Tom. Usually I look forward to coming here on Wednesday, but today I'd rather go on home with Singer and cook some popcorn and watch the videos. I told Singer maybe I should stop washing dishes for the Toad in case he knows I was in the safe. Singer said that's why I got to use all the special powers right now and act like nothin happened. Singer said we just need a little more time to get the money back, and everything will be all right. But the more I act like nothin happened, feels like everyone's eyes looking inside me, where they see the numbers to the safe and that five two three seven my dad took.

So now instead of half speed I go full speed, so no one thinks anything's different, act like nothin happened, and I know it's all right because they eyes get big when they walk past and see me stacking hot plates off the racks so fast my fingers ain't got time to feel the burn. Before the stamp dries on my time card, I got the lunch bastards' mess cleaned up and my dish station ready for the night. I always make sure the two pink soap bottles on my machine full up and the disposal is all cleaned out and ready to chew up all the food scraps I'll be feeding it later. After I run the squeegee back and forth and get the station dry, I take the tall stacks of clean plates out to the cooks. I got to use the supertuned cells in my head when I deliver the clean dishes cus the cooks always try to make me drop the stack. One time I did drop a full stack and the Toad hit me on the side my head, which made me slip and cut open the corner my eye on the door. Toad said if I broke that many plates again, I'd be out on my ass for good.

ZigZag

Then he walked away without helping me up. I ain't broke none since.

Once I get the plates delivered, I take the racks of clean glasses to slide them into the slots in the waiter stations, three different ones in the restaurant. A busboy and a busgirl are talking in the first one.

"Hey, Louis. Hear what happened to the Toad?" the busboy asks.

I don't say nothin in case he works for the Toad. I just act like Singer said, except busboy's in my way so I can't slide the rack in its slot.

"You'd tell us if it was you? Right?"

He's laughing, me leaning down and trying to push the rack in, but his legs are still in the way.

"Leave him alone. Louis wouldn't steal anything," the busgirl says. "Would you, Louis?"

I just shake my head, flash them both a quick ZigZag, and try to slide the glasses in the rack again. Why they got to ask so many questions?

"Why don't you ever talk?"

Do my talking on the inside, just like nothin happened, got to block out the numbers and the five two three seven my dad knocked out my hand, his knee across my throat . . .

". . . Toad's offering a thousand bucks to anyone who helps catch the guy."

"And how do you know it wasn't a woman?" she says.

"Woman? Women don't steal stuff. Crooks are always guys."

"Are not."

"OK, name me one famous woman criminal."

"Lizzie Borden," she says real quick.

"Never heard of her."

"That's cus you're an idiot. She's famous."

"For what? Shoplifting?"

"Chopped up her parents with an ax."

He makes a funny face. "Shut up, you lie."

"Do not. It's totally true."

"Yeah, so what if it is? What's that have to do with this retard cracking a safe?"

"Shut up," she says. "He's not a retard."

"How do you know?"

"Leave him alone."

"He your boyfriend?"

"Please . . ."

"Ask him. You retarded, Louis?"

I don't care about retard or not retard, I just got to get these glasses in that slot and go back to the kitchen like nothin happened, nothin happened. . . .

Then she says, "He couldn't work here if he was retarded."

"Yeah, right. A monkey could do his job."

"Shut up."

"He'll still be washing dishes here when he's like forty years old. The Toad will be like eighty, still chewing his ass. Right, monkey boy?"

"You're a jerk. Move your leg, he's trying to work."

I smile at her cus finally I can slide the rack in and be back in the kitchen before he's got time to start asking more questions. Then the cook big as a tree comes around the ice machine and makes my heart go extra crazy. He got a pan full of chicken all cut up, and he looks down at me with these brown eyes that see everything. We just stare at each other and fill up our brains with information without saying a word. He got black hair goes halfway down his back in a ponytail and skin in between white and black like Cadillac Tom. It seems like a long time we stand like that, him letting me know what he knows, and me checking to see if he's said something to the Toad. Then when we done talking on the inside, he turns and carries his pan of cut-up chicken out to the grill. So I go back to my dish station, where the cooks already piled up some pots. I sprinkle the scrub powder inside a pot and watch the water turn it blue. I think maybe when we get the

Toad's money back from Cadillac Tom, we'll give some to that big cook. Then before I got time to empty out my head, I hear the Toad's voice coming from the other side of the ice machine.

". . . take it out and make ten gallons of the green goddess. Check the blue cheese, too, but I think we have enough until the weekend . . ."

I focus on the scrubber in my hand, back and forth so fast the black on the pot ain't got time to know what hit it, the scratched silver rising up fast under my fingers. The smell of the scrub powder floats up and tickles deep inside my nose. I see the Toad on the other side of the ice machine now with a clipboard in his hand talking to the little cook that threw the spoon at my head and broke the window. Even though I don't look or think for too long, I can feel the Toad moving over this way. When I look up from the pot, he's standing right in front of the dish station.

I watch the little cigar with the white plastic tip, unlit, back and forth from one corner his mouth to the other, and the tiny spit strings that break when he pulls the cigar away. His face is shiny like always, looking at me like the big cook to see what he can find out. Just to test him I flash him five two four one and pull it back before it hits his radar. Then he pulls the little cigar out and looks at it like he's wondering why he never lights it.

"Hear what happened Monday night?"

"Didn't hear nothin."

"Yeah? Well some jisbag took five grand out of my safe. You hear that?"

I don't say nothin, just try to keep the numbers out my head in case the Toad got his equipment tuned extra sensitive. Damn, it's hard to keep what you thinking about the most out your head. Then the Toad comes around to my side of the dish station, something I never seen him do, and stands so close I can smell the little cigar and see the greasy circle on top his head where he ain't got no hair. He's so close the supertuned cells in my head can feel the heat coming off his radar equipment.

"Sure you don't know anything?"

I shake my head, but my insides are all twisted up now cus of what Singer said about getting sent to the juvenile if they find out. Toad takes a step back, still on this side of the dish station, the black mat making wet sounds under his feet.

"You were in my office on Monday. You remember that?"

"I dunno. Been in there a lot of times."

"Yeah, well I only been robbed once, and that was Monday. I gave you your check."

"I always come in there when you give me my check."

"Well, Monday was different. I gave you your check, and then two minutes later one of you fuckin yahoos broke my window. You with me, Einstein?"

"Just because I go to the Fellowes School don't mean I can't remember nothin."

"Good, then you'll remember one other thing happened that day." The Toad pauses. It's getting a little hard to see like he's stirring up some noise deep down in my head. I just keep thinking about what Singer said about act like nothin happened, act like nothin happened, over and over again in my head. ". . . said something about the numbers to the safe. Remember?"

I shake my head. Now I'm really getting scared cus I wasn't even thinking about the numbers, but maybe when he's this close his radar can pick up things ain't even in my head, things I'm about to think about.

"We know it was someone who had the combination. Cops got fingerprints. Even a pea-brain like yourself should know it won't take long to figure out who did this."

"I ain't did nothin."

"That's what you said about the window."

"I didn't break the window. And I don't know nothin about your safe." Except how that long silver handle felt cold and made the big *CLICK* sound when I finished spinning those numbers.

"I know you don't. Chances that you opened my safe are about as good as my odds of . . . what?" Then to a cocktail waitress walking past he says, "Getting a blow job from Queen Elizabeth." She shakes her head and speeds up her walk. "Nothing goes on around here I don't know about. You fart on my property, and I'll smell it before your sphincter does. Think about it."

He stays up close for a few seconds and then steps back and points the plastic white tip of that little cigar at me. It's shiny with spit. "You hear anything, you come tell me. There's a little reward for anyone who helps catch this stool sample."

"Reward?"

"Yeah, a little extra cash."

"Cash?"

"Cash reward: you help me catch the bad guy, I give you money. How fucking hard is that?"

"How much?"

"How much . . . now all of a sudden he's fucking Dick Tracy. For you, Louis . . . five hundred bucks. Could you use an extra five hundred?"

I nod. Me and Singer could use the five zero zero to maybe go away from all the noise.

"Better move fast, Sherlock, because I've told every greasy hump working for me about the reward. Never seen so much motivation around this place. Like a bunch of goddamn weasels in heat."

I don't know what the Toad's talking about Sherlock and weasels with the heat. Mostly I just watch him close, see if he got his radar turned off yet.

". . . anyway. You hear anything, I'll make it worth your while."

Then he picks up his clipboard and walks out the kitchen, fast, like he's going to get a new white-tipped cigar ain't all covered in spit before he moves in close to check someone else with his radar.

All through my shift I stay behind my dish station, *like nothin happened* over and over so many times in my head, now I believe it myself. ZigZag ain't did nothin wrong. The dishes are coming back fast for a Wednesday, busboy and busgirl dropping them off in black tubs slippery from all the food, busboy calling me a new name, monkey boy, every time he comes back. I don't listen, just tear into the dishes superfast, spray and rack the plates and grab the good food pieces all at once. Sometimes I eat the good stuff right away, like a big hunk of lobster or steak doesn't want to spend the rest of its life getting spun around in my disposal. Or sometimes I pile up the good scraps in a little white bucket I got hidden with a napkin on top cus the Toad don't want no one works for him to eat during their shift even though it's a restaurant. The Toad says he owns everything here, all the plates and dishes and ice cubes in the ice machine, even the food people don't want is his. He told me my first day everything here is his, right down to the turds once they hit his toilet water. That means, he said, even the garbage is his until the truck hauls it off his property. I ain't never seen him laugh so hard as when I said, *So we can't eat the garbage?* He laughed so much he had tears. When he finally stopped, he said, *Yeah, it's OK to eat the garbage if your ass is waving to me from inside the back of the garbage truck.* Then he laughed again until the tears came back. I still don't know what he means except sometimes it's OK to eat his garbage and other times it ain't, so I always hide the food scraps in the bucket underneath the dish station.

"Louis. Phone call. It's Dean. Toad will be pissed he finds you on the phone. Hustle up."

I ZigZag into the kitchen office and grab the phone from the head cook so fast he looks at me like I spun out of control.

"Singer?"

"Hey, ZigZag. When do you think you'll be off?"

One thing about working in restaurants is everyone is always asking, *When will you be off? When will you be off?* Except you never know until all the dishes are done and you're already off. That's when you'll be off. Even smart people like Singer, though, just keep asking. "I dunno. Probably one one zero zero."

"All right. I'll be in the parking lot waiting for you at eleven. Oh, I talked to Jasmine at the agency, and she said it's OK for you to stay with me while child services investigates your home situation. That sound good?"

"That sounds great, Singer! I'll cook us up some popcorn, and we'll watch the videos tonight. Right?"

"Well, first we're gonna go for a little drive."

"Where?"

"To see Cadillac Tom again."

My sneakers are puffing out little clouds like they do sometimes when they wet. I like to see how long before the cold eats up the little clouds. I got my dishes done early and ZigZag out here instead of waiting around in the kitchen, where the Toad might sneak up on me with his radar. Singer will be here soon, at one one zero zero, he said, so we can go get the money back from Cadillac Tom. I like standing here by the side of the building cus it's quiet except for the cars going back and forth, and the cold air feels good after washing the Toad's dishes. The cells in my head work better at night cus there's less you got to see. The daytime lights up every-thing so bright your head fills up before you got time to think.

The kitchen door opens, and the big cook steps out carrying a garbage can. I press my back into the cold wall and watch him walk this way. He's carrying the garbage can like it don't weigh any more than that pan of cut-up chicken. I got to drag the garbage cans on the ground with both hands, so heavy with wet food scraps you can barely move them. Then I got to get someone to help me empty them into the dumpster. He walks regular speed, his eyes looking inside me for a few seconds as he goes past. I hear the plastic garbage can hit the side of the dumpster like he tossed it up there with one hand, and he's already coming back towards me carrying the empty can same way he carries it full. Then his eyes got mine again, and he stops. My dad and this cook the only ones I ever had to tip my head back to look in they eyes. Instead of just his sneakers, the air's pouring off his whole body, like he's on fire and he knows just how long he's got to stand here before the fire will go out. Then he lets go of the garbage can, and a hand big as a bus tub rises real slow, like his machinery is rusted or been stuck on low speed all his life.

"Dale."

I reach up and shake his hand like he's some kind of bear learned to talk at the circus and he's hiding here until they catch him. "ZigZag."

We don't say nothin for a while, me wondering how long it takes someone this big to cool off. "You a Indian?"

"Part."

I don't know what that means: part makes him so big or the part gives him the in-between skin. Could be the part gives him that long black ponytail cus that's what most of the Indians I seen on the videos have.

"Dale don't sound like no Indian name."

"Neither does ZigZag."

Dale either smarter or dumber than me, I don't know which, cus I don't know what he's saying. Now I know it's Singer's car turning into the parking lot. The little orange light hangs out by a wire like some kind of eyeball that's swinging around outside your head but can still see. Dale don't squint when the headlights flash across his face. He's got to step towards me so Singer can pull right up alongside us. Singer waves. I open the door and turn to say good-bye, but Dale's already walking back towards the square of light coming out the kitchen, still carrying the garbage can like that pan of cut-up chicken. Singer turns the heater down when I get in, and drives away.

"Who was that?"

"Dale."

"Big boy. How was work? What did your boss say?"

"Said he give us five zero zero we catch whoever took his money. Almost told him I did so we'd get that money reward."

"No, no. Don't do that. Don't say anything."

"Don't tell him for the reward?"

"No, just keep acting like I told you, like nothing happened." Just like Singer, always got a good plan. "Did he act like he knows anything?"

"Always acts like he knows."

"Does he think it's you?"

"He got in real close with his radar."

"What did he say?"

"Something about the queen giving him a blow job."

"What else?"

"He said he remembers I was in the office on Monday and seen him open the safe."

"He did? Shit . . . what else?"

"Said the cops got fingerprints and even a pea-brain like me knows it won't take long to figure out who did it. Then he explained *reward.*"

"Fingerprints? Oh, shit . . . but we don't know whose. They could be anybody's."

We're driving down the road that runs alongside the restaurant. Soon as we past the doughnut store on the corner, I look down the street I ride on to get to my dad's apartment. My bike's been locked up by the Toad's dumpster ever since I been living with Singer. I like driving in the car better cus my hands don't get so cold, always switching one hand in my pocket, one steering. Singer's loud heater keeps both hands equal warm.

"Singer, how long I lived with you?"

"*Lived* with me?"

"Yeah. How long it's been?"

Singer look a little confuse like he can't remember so far back. "Well, officially, starting last night."

"So how long is that?"

"One night."

One night? Sure seems a lot longer, like one year. "What about the five you said?"

"Five years since we met."

"That's what I mean. Since we met."

Singer turns on a street that's lit up full bright and got cars everywhere. Most cars ain't like Singer's cus they only got one color. I like this street. It's long and straight and got every kind of store and places to eat and buildings so tall they got little red lights on top to remind you where they end.

"Do you remember that first day?" Singer asks.

"First day?"

"When we met?"

"Not really."

Singer's a damn good driver cus he can drive and do a lot of talking on the outside without getting messed up. I'm going to need to practice real hard and probably never talk on the outside when I learn to drive. That's what I got to do when I ZigZag the dishes, keep focus on the smell of the soap and how the same plate feels so many different ways, cold and slippery going in, and then so hot it smokes coming out, the supertuned cells telling me when I got to slow down, slow down, slow down, so the gears and wheels in the machine don't melt they spinning so fast, watch for flying soup spoons and rack the dishes just by feel, like my hands are tiny people who know what to do without my eyes always having to tell them. Makes the noise sneak into my head to think how you do all that and talk on the outside at the same time like Singer's doing right now.

". . . with Global Express. I had just turned twenty-four. I can't believe I'm still working there. Remember, we met at your school with that first caseworker."

"We met at the Fellowes School?"

"Right before then. You were at that other school . . . I can't remember the name."

I don't remember no school except the Fellowes School and Ms. Tate smelling good like flowers.

". . . skinny ten-year-old . . ." Singer's smile looks nice, so I give him a smile back. ". . . didn't say a word to me the first month I knew you. I didn't know what to do. I was ready to call it quits. I even called the caseworker and told her it wasn't working. She told me to give it another month. So another month went by. I came to pick you up every week at that apartment on Essex Place. Anyway, you'd get in the car, and I'd ask you questions until I ran out of things to ask. That took about ten minutes. And then for four hours we wouldn't talk." He laughs. "You never said a word."

Singer grabs my leg and smiles again. Now we're turning onto the street that's got the Monkey Club. This street is darker than where we just were, more paper and stuff blowing around when the cars drive by. Up ahead I can see the pink building. Now the little naked ladies on the side are lit up with purple lights. We park on the same side as before, across from the same long black car, except a little farther back. That car looks really shiny at night, almost like it's wet. Singer shuts off the car, and we just sit here looking across the street. The black-and-pink door to the Monkey Club never stops swinging open and closed, open and closed, open and closed. . . .

"Well," Singer says, taking a deep breath and letting it out real long and slow. "Here we go again." Tonight he's wearing black everything: T-shirt, jeans, baseball hat with a little white skull on it, leather jacket. "Do we go in and try to deal with that girl at the door again, or wait for him to come out? What do you think?"

What I think is Singer's the one should make up the plans cus he always got the good ones. The wind is blowing now, loud outside the car, making all them papers move up high in the air and then come down real fast before they blow back up again. Little white cups, too, up, around, and then back down.

". . . eleven twenty. We could be out here a couple hours if we wait for him. Let's give it another shot."

Singer gets out, and I follow him, right behind him as we cross the street, pass Cadillac Tom's long car, and right inside the Monkey Club. When it's night out, my eyes work better inside here. There's a different girl behind the little window, but the same loud music is coming from behind the thick black curtains.

"Need to see Cadillac. Right away."

"Ten dollars each. Need to see some ID for him." She points at me with a handful of cash.

Singer takes out his wallet and hands her a bill says two zero. "That's yours if you could do me a favor."

"Favor?"

"Just tell Cadillac someone's here needs to see him. Urgent business. We'll wait right out front."

She blows a big pink bubble and looks at Singer. "What if he don't come out?"

"You keep the twenty."

She scans the money, checking maybe to see it's real. "All right. No promises, though."

Me and Singer stand outside the door of the Monkey Club watching the wind blow that trash up into the air. Even with the wind the cold don't feel as bad it did today. When the door opens, it's the lady with the gum instead of Cadillac Tom.

"He said go around back, and he'll talk to you in the office. Back around that way."

We have to go past a bunch of stores before there's a place we can get around to the back of the buildings and then walk up the alley the way we just come.

"You think he got a bat?"

"At least."

I don't know what that means, *at least*, standing now at a black door ain't got no handle, just looks like part of the wall. Singer pounds his fist on it three times. The door opens, and a man looks like that skinny little cook moves his head for us to come in, my heart going a little crazy now every time we walk inside this Monkey Club. The man slams the door, loud, and we follow him down a skinny hallway to another door.

"Wait here."

The man leaves, and two women, one black, one white, walk by with nothin on but little underwear and shoes and no shirts. One blinks an eye at me. Singer looks at me and smiles.

"Three naked women in three days."

"Those two ain't naked, Singer."

"Close enough."

"First one I seen was full naked, saw the hair between her legs but no thing."

"Don't tell Jasmine I brought you here. Or Ms. Tate."

"Like I done with the Toad? Act like nothin happened?"

"Perfect. Just like that."

The little man comes back, and we follow him again down another hallway. We walk past a room full of women. Singer and the man keep walking, but I stop, then ZigZag back real slow, silent, and slide my head around. It's a big room with little tables and mirrors all along one wall, hooks on the other side with clothes on them. There's maybe one five, half-naked, full naked, full dressed, so many now I lost track how many I seen total. The ones sitting at the little tables lean their faces real close into the mirrors and rub little black brushes on they eyes and spray big clouds from cans, like in the video to give them the self-esteem. Some of the women are getting dressed or undressed, I can't tell which cus none of them wear many clothes here.

My nose got to ZigZag all the different flower smells to keep it from itching. I watch the way they bodies are all different shapes and colors and sizes, soft rounds like Ms. Tate got under her clothes. The one closest to me is standing at a mirror, nothing on but some sparkling blue shoes, trying to decide whether she should wear the black underwear or the green. The hair between her legs grows straight up in a skinny strip.

"Uh, hello? Who the fuck is this guy?"

She's looking at me without turning around, in the mirror, her chest swelled up three different levels. Then a couple of the other ones look at me in the mirrors, waving me away like the Toad. One of them yells, "Close the door!" and I pull back my face just before her leg swings around and the door slams. I start walking the direction I seen Singer and the little man go. Except my thing feels different in my pants, and when I squeeze it feels hard. I tap it a few times. It don't hurt but just feels weird, like some kind of big rock in my pants.

I see Singer sitting in a small office, him on one side of a desk, Cadillac Tom on the other, the little man standing by the wall. Cadillac Tom's working a toothpick again, around and around his mouth. I ZigZag in and sit next to Singer so fast no one notices I wasn't there the whole time instead of watching the women.

"Ziggy, these boys came by earlier and told me a real boring story. You ready in case they start telling me a story I already heard?"

The little man just smiles, got one tooth made of shiny yellow metal. "Sure."

"Sixty seconds, egghead. Clock him, Ziggy."

Singer looks at the little man, who's got a watch out now, then at me real quick and back at Cadillac Tom. Singer looks good in all black. All I gotta do is act like nothin happened.

"OK . . ." Singer leans forward on the little metal chair. I can still hear the music coming loud but not as loud as in front by the woman who blows pink bubbles. ". . . different story this time." Then the door swings open, and a girl's head pops in.

"Cadillac, Trudy's got her period so she won't . . . oh, sorry."

"Anybody fuckin knock around here?" Cadillac Tom asks the ceiling. She's standing there in red shoes and a red robe.

"Anyway, so she won't be in until Friday."

"Thank you for that late-breaking news flash. Is that all, Barbara Walters?"

"Sorry. Fuck you too." She slams the door.

Cadillac Tom breathes out and shakes his head. "Sixty-five dancers I got. You know what that's like? Need a goddamn computer to schedule around all those menstrual cycles." Then he looks at Singer. "You through yet?"

"I was just going to say—"

"Time," the little man says.

"Sorry, girls. Time's up."

"Wait," Singer says. "She used up all our time. Start the clock over."

"Boss?"

Everyone looks at Cadillac Tom working that toothpick, who looks at Ziggy, then me and Singer. "Thirty seconds, Ziggy. Clock em."

"Not our fault she came in."

"Twenty-five," the little man says.

"OK, I've got an idea," Singer says.

"Twenty."

"Is that really necessary?"

"Fifteen."

The door swings open again, this time a different girl with lots of black hair and no top, her soft rounds right out in the open. "What the hell you just say to Ricki?"

"What'd I tell you?"

"She's all pissed off and says she's leaving," the girl says. "Better apologize, or she's fuckin out of here."

She slams the door even louder than the first, the music still going, Cadillac Tom rubbing his hands real fast on his hair ain't much longer than Singer's.

"Time."

"Get the fuck out of here," Cadillac Tom says, standing up. "I don't have time for this bullshit."

ZigZag

Now Singer's standing up, me the only one sitting, so I stand up by the door, my heart starting to speed up. Cadillac Tom has that look in his eyes like he's wondering where did he leave the Black Beauty.

"We didn't come here to give you a sob story," Singer says, now getting pushed backwards by the little man.

"Get them out of here," Cadillac Tom says, waving us away like the Toad. Little man pulls open the door, pushes me through where the music is louder, everything black in this Monkey Club: walls, ceiling, doors. Now Singer's out in the hallway by me, except he pushes the little man away and looks back into the office.

"I came here with a business proposition," Singer says.

"Get home. It's past your bedtime. Ziggy!?"

"Come on, punk. Time to go bye-bye."

The little man grabs Singer's jacket, but Singer pushes him away so hard the little man falls on the floor and almost makes a half-naked woman trip. She kicks him with her shoe that's got long skinny heels.

"Watch it, asshole."

Now Singer's back in the office talking to Cadillac Tom—I can't hear what they saying—little man pushing himself off the ground with that look in his eye, sliding his hand under his jacket, except instead of a bat his hand comes out with a little knife with a black handle, the noise starting up low, filling my head so quick I can't . . .

Breathe.

Breathe.

Breathe.

I'm trying to yell, but my heart's stuck back up in my throat. Singer still standing there talking with his back this way, that little man up now and giving me a look makes me sink back up against the wall and go invisible, the pain everywhere, everything so loud and bright there ain't no sound or color, no more music or black or nothing, just one thing blurred together at the edges by the noise until I can't separate what's inside from what's outside. Flowers.

● ● ●

Some lady's got me, smells good like the flowers but different from Ms. Tate, holding me, both of us down on the floor, people eyes all around looking at me.

"Check out Jordan's new lap dance technique."

"Fuck off. Can you please shut up and help me? Get him off my tit."

"You OK, buddy?" Next to Ms. Tate's flower smell, that is about the best damn sound I ever seen. "Come on. Let's get you up."

"Thank you." The half-naked lady gets up now, looking down at her soft round.

"Thanks for helping him," Singer says. Who did she help?

"Kid's dusted," she says, taking a paper towel from one of the other girls and rubbing it on her soft round. "Disgusting."

"All right, show's over," Cadillac Tom says, waving away all the women circled around. "Go on. Back out there."

Singer's got me up now, lights brighter, music loud again, women walking away, but all different flower smells stay in my head. Like nothin happened, just act like nothin happened. . . .

"You all right?"

I nod at Singer.

Cadillac Tom look confuse. "She right? I don't need some dusted-out kid going toe tag in my club."

"Fuckin elephant seizure," the little man says.

"Wasn't a seizure," Singer says. "And he doesn't take drugs."

Cadillac Tom looks at me. "You sure, cowboy? I seen some juiced-up wackos in my time, and looks to me like this kid is tripping."

Then the little man says, "Scared the shit out of me when he yelled. Sounded like a goddamn cat passing a kidney stone."

"He just has these spells sometimes."

Cadillac Tom got his toothpick going again, flipping it around on his tongue. "You like a social worker or what?"

"Just a friend."

"He always been that fucked up?" the little man says.

Singer just gives the little man a look. Cadillac Tom points his toothpick at Singer. "So how you two get hooked up?"

"Positive Mentors."

"So what, you take him to ball games and help him with his homework and shit?"

"That's the basic idea."

"Ain't he a little young for topless bars?"

Cadillac Tom and the little man laugh real hard.

"So how often you two get together? Like once a month?"

"Every week," Singer says.

"Every week? For how long?"

"Been five years now."

"Five years?" the little man says. "Shit, they saw you coming."

"How much they pay you?" Cadillac Tom asks.

Singer shakes his head, smiles a little. "It's volunteer."

Everyone starts laughing, except I stop when I see Singer ain't even smiling.

"There's nine hundred kids on the waiting list at Positive Mentors," Singer says. "And that's just in this city."

"You sure got a hard-on to bail out other people's kids," Cadillac Tom says.

"Look, can we just talk about this money thing?"

"Two of you are out there. Fuckin Pluto. C'mon."

We walk back into the office, Cadillac Tom on the other side of the desk, me and Singer over here, that little man standing behind us in the doorway. Now it's back in my head clear, the knife with the black handle. I turn up my radar extra sensitive make sure he doesn't pull that out again. Still makes me scared he's back there where my regular eyes can't see him. Cadillac Tom pulls a brown paper bag out the desk drawer all wrinkled up.

"Five years? You get a coffee mug or something?"

Singer looks at me, then at Cadillac Tom. "No, but since we're on the subject of community, maybe you'd like to make a small donation on behalf of Positive Mentors."

"Community . . . yeah, I like that. I'm a businessman. I'll tell you what. Normal vig's twenty-five percent a week. Until you pay back the entire principal. For the kid here, I'll go twenty."

"That's your donation?"

"Yeah, I like this community shit."

"How about ten?"

"You trying to insult me? I'd charge the fuckin pope fifteen."

"So give us his rate."

"You got some big balls, egghead, asking for the pope's rate."

"Well?"

"Well nothing. You're getting greedy."

"Mr. Twenty-five Percent, and you're calling me greedy?"

"Get cocky on me, it goes to thirty."

Singer breathes deep, chews his lip. "One question."

"Shoot."

"If I got to borrow from you in the first place, where am I going to get money for the . . . vig every week?"

"You don't like the terms and conditions, go to Citibank."

"Should we write this down or something?"

"I don't write nothing down. It's bad luck. We got a deal?"

Singer looks at Cadillac Tom, then at me again, breathing deep a few times like he's working us up a new plan. "So when would the first . . . vig be due?"

"You said one question."

"Last one. Promise."

"What, you want a fuckin payment book? Every seven days. Thursday at midnight. Come on, I'm a busy man here."

Singer takes another deep breath, looking around.

"Last chance," Cadillac Tom says, standing up now. "Yes or no?"

"OK . . . deal."

Then Singer reaches across the desk, shakes Cadillac Tom's hand, and takes the wrinkled-up brown sack.

That noise in Singer's ball hit him so hard he stopped talking, grabbing his chest now try to squeeze out the hurt. I ain't never seen Singer like this since I known him, rolled up in a little ball using all the special powers he's got. Like I just done on the sleep side, *ZigZag out the way before the knee goes across my throat, laughing at my dad he moves so slow, smack him on the head to get his clothes on. When he and Eddie opened the door, a light full bright blasted my dad's apartment, he and Eddie gone, and all them naked and half-naked ladies walking in, some chests swelled up big, some swelled up little, but all look nice and soft. We was in the Toad's restaurant, so I had to keep the radar on him like nothin happened but still watch the half-naked ladies. The one by the door takes my hand and puts it on one of them soft rounds. You like it, honey? Feels real good, right there in my dish station with Ms. Tate like little electricity down in my toes. You like it, honey?*

Then all the half-naked women gone, and only Singer was

here. I close my eyes and try to go back to my dish station with Ms. Tate, but she's gone from my head. I ZigZag up and dress so fast Singer was still sitting on the couch rubbing his eyes. Then when I came back from starting the car and scraping all the cold off the windows, I find Singer here, half-dressed but don't look like he's goin nowhere.

"You all right, Singer?"

"Yeah. I'll be OK."

"You using the special powers like you taught me? Get that noise out?"

"Trying."

"I ain't got to go to the Fellowes School today."

"Yes you do. You might be a little late, but I'll take you."

"Why I always got to go to school? School boring."

"You just do. To learn."

"What do I got to learn? I don't need to learn nothin. I already got me the job, live here with you."

"How about reading and writing?"

"Writing's stupid, takes too long. I ain't got to read and write at the restaurant."

"Gets easier with practice."

"You could teach me to practice."

"I have to go to work."

"I could just stay here while you work. . . . What day it is?"

"Thursday."

"Monday, Wednesday, Thursday, so later I'll go wash me some dishes."

Singer gets up slow until he's on his knees with his hands on the bed, breathing, still holding his chest. That special medicine he's taking don't seem to work too good except for making his hair fall out. It's real good at doing that. Now he's sitting on the bed, his body smooth like his head.

"What shirt you want, Singer?"

"Brown work shirt."

Singer's closet is supersmall, and everything's so tight it's hard to pull what you want out. All kinds of papers and old magazines and everything jammed up in here. I give him a brown work shirt got a white patch says DEAN.

"Bit of a role reversal," he says, pulling on the shirt.

"What's *reversal*?"

"I've been looking after you for five years."

When Singer grabs his chest again, I can see the noise on his face. He leans down on the bed again and then goes flat on his back. "Dammit . . ."

"You need more of that special medicine, Singer?"

He shakes his head, breathes deep a few times, in . . . out . . . in . . . out, real slow like that over and over. I just sit here on the bed watching him with one eye, the other eye scanning the room for the green noise. Then my fingertips get the little electricity tingle thinking about the dishes they be washing later, the Toad all greasy from being around kitchens too long, his equipment choked up with the sweat pools in them little holes all over his face and neck, running around the kitchen in the summer with a dish towel wrapped around his head to keep the frog sweat from dripping in the food.

"Singer, how long I got to keep acting like nothin happened?"

"What?"

"When the Toad comes around with his extra sensitive equipment, see if I was the one in his safe."

"We talked about this last night. On the way home?"

My mind tries to pull it back, last night, today, all them good flower smells, the man getting the botulism injected into his face. Last night? "Dale carries the full garbage can same as he does a pan of cut-up chicken."

"Who's Dale?"

"He's the guy part Indian at the Toad's restaurant. He got a long ponytail."

"Not right now . . ."

"Last night I remember Dale carried that pan first, then the big garbage can the same."

"After that. After we went to see Cadillac Tom at the Monkey Club? He gave me the brown sack with the money in it?"

"Money in that sack?"

"ZigZag . . . just try to remember."

"I remember the good flower smells in my head. Explain it again."

"Later. Time for school."

"Singer?"

"What?"

"What you call those soft rounds?"

"Soft rounds?"

"Them women last night had them on they chests. That first naked lady I seen, too."

Singer breathes out, that noise still on his face.

"Breasts."

"Brett-s?"

"Breasts," he says louder, a little bit of the beating sound sneaking in his voice.

"How come I ain't got them? You neither."

"Just women have them."

"What for?"

"They ever tell you about this at the Fellowes School? . . . birds and the bees?"

"We learned about the spiders one time, black window, got a red dot on them. They birds?"

"*Widow*. I'll explain it to you later."

"Why not now, Singer? You the one said I got to learn everything—"

"I said later, goddammit! Do you fucking understand English? Later!"

My body goes automatic on itself, tensed up tight now, Singer's eyes full of that same look my dad got right before he brought out the Black Beauty, everything closed up and held deep down inside waiting for the blast. . . .

Wait.

Wait.

Wait.

Supertuned cells keep it locked up tight cus the noise comes twice as hard when you let up, everything black and loud like a roar in my head but no pain coming in anywhere.

Not yet.

Maybe Singer's the one got the Black Beauty out the river.

Yeah.

Going to pull her from under the bed to show how he tricked me. Pulled her out that river with his special powers and got her all shined up . . . still waiting. Singer's voice now talking about my mama the Black Beauty, let's see what she's got to say about all this. . . .

Breathe.

Breathe.

Breathe.

Then a loud sound, and something touches me. . . .

Here it comes. . . .

Here it comes. . . .

Confuse.

It's a soft touch.

No noise.

No hurt.

No hurt anywhere. Then Singer's voice, except he ain't talking about the Black Beauty. "C'mon. Let's go. Time for school."

Singer and me do all our talking on the inside on the way to the Fellowes School. My heart's all crazy cus I done something wrong to make Singer mad, so I got my eyes slammed down tight, just listen to the sounds and colors, sun warm on my face, but the air cold cus Singer ain't got the heater on, the air clean like it's been put through my machine and came out this morning with the pink soap smell. When I open my eyes, Singer got one hand on his stomach like that noise still got him good. We're stopped in the middle of the road cus there's so many cars and trucks, surrounding us now on all sides. So many things I want to ask on the outside but don't in case Singer's got that Black Beauty hidden under his seat.

"Sorry I yelled at you. I'm really feeling like shit today."

I just look at Singer, all those things I wanted to say on the outside somehow slipping out my head.

"Apology accepted?"

I close my eyes back down and swim down deep, away from the noise and all the questions until I'm safe. . . .

"Fine, you know . . . sometimes this silent treatment gets real old. Fucking fighting for my life here, trying to keep your ass out of jail and hold down my job because if I lose my health insurance then you can just kiss my bald ass good-bye right now. And I'm getting no support here, not from your dad, not from the agency, not from that scumbag fuck Cadillac Tom. You'd think that piece of shit would cut me a break, right? No way, fuckin dickstick. So now I got to come up with a grand I don't have by next Thursday on top of the five I already borrowed. Can my life possibly get any more fucked up? Huh? What do you think? Can it?"

My stomach confuse, Singer starting to ask questions that don't have a good answer same as my dad. I ain't never seen Singer like this, his eyes red, but his whole head looks white and cold like a plate before it goes in the machine.

"No? I don't think so either. We're basically fucked. And for what? Maybe you should get sent away. Teach you a lesson. Just give Cadillac Tom his five grand back and tell the Toad what happened and, like your dad said, you'll probably only do a year, tops. Juvenile. I don't think I can keep this all together. You know? Where am I going to get a thousand dollars? And then another five on top of that?"

ZigZag

I learned quick with my dad that anything I say when he's mad just means more beating on top of the beating he already had planned. Even if Singer does have the Black Beauty hidden, he ain't never used it on me. Besides, I got a plan so good I'll risk the Black Beauty. "You said Cadillac Tom give you five zero zero zero. Give one zero zero zero to Cadillac Tom."

"ZigZag, no . . . that's not how it works."

"How it works then?"

"Please. Just let me think. . . ."

Please, please, please, and then slow down, slow down, slow down. ZigZag moves too fast.

Ms. Tate's teaching us about the sentence today, how you build it out of two blocks, one the subject and one the predicate. Ms. Tate got to explain for a long time before we understand the subject and the predicate, and even then I don't get it too good. Then she shows us how we suppose to make up one zero of our own sentences. One zero! Instead of writing the sentences, mostly I notice now how Ms. Tate got them soft rounds, about middle size, and think about how they look under her white shirt. Why those women at the Monkey Club don't wear shirts and Ms. Tate always do? I raise my hand, and she gets up from her desk and walks over. Before she even gets here, I can smell the flowers. Everyone else is writing the sentences.

"Yes, Louis?"

"Can I see your bretts, Ms. Tate?"

"Excuse me?"

"Your bretts."

"Barrettes? I don't understand what you're saying."

"Bretts!"

"Is it in this room?"

I nod. They right there.

"Point to it."

I push my finger in, and it sinks in pretty far until she grabs my wrist so fast I think maybe she got the special powers.

"Louis, no. That's not appropriate. We don't touch people there. That's private. Understand?"

"Women at the Monkey Club ain't private."

Ms. Tate kneels down by my desk, gets in so close that flower smell fills up my head. She talks real quiet. "Women at the where?"

"The Monkey Club."

"What do you know about the Monkey Club?"

"Singer took me . . . last night? Some night, where they got naked ladies."

"Dean Singer took you there?"

I nod.

"Your Positive Mentor took you to the Monkey Club?"

How many times she going to ask? "Yeah, to get the Toad's money back from Cadillac Tom."

"Who's Cadillac Tom?"

"Some guy got a long black car. Says he needs a computer to schedule all his minstrel cycles."

"Minstrel cycles?"

"Uh-huh. Then he gave Singer the five zero zero zero so we . . ." My radar goes automatic, Singer's voice in my head like he's standing right here: *just act like nothin happened.* Even around Ms. Tate? Yeah, act like nothin happened, act like nothin happened, keep it all pushed out my head just in case . . .

"Are you OK, Louis?"

I nod, but keeping it all inside cus maybe I said too much on the outside already, telling Ms. Tate about Cadillac Tom and the Monkey Club and all them naked women.

"What did you mean 'five zero zero zero'? Five thousand dollars?"

My throat gets tight to keep me from talking, which is good cus I don't know what to say or not say on the outside, wishing now Ms. Tate would go back up to her desk, even though the flower smell makes me feel safe.

"Louis?"

I take out my paper and pencil. Please stay and let me smell the flower smell, but no more questions about the Toad's money or what Singer and me done. Please . . . I start trying to write a sentence, but I only got one in my head:

Siner god

"That's a good start," she says, maybe now what we were talking about is floating out her head. "How about this?" She takes my pen and writes below my sentence:

Singer is good.

"Remember what we said. Subject, verb. Try one with just a subject and a verb."

So I write:

mis tat smel.

She takes my pen and writes below it:

Ms. Tate smells.

"Meaning you like my perfume, or I forgot to take a bath?"

I don't know. She smiles, so I just nod, even though who knows what she's talking about forgot to take a bath. Sentences confuse.

"Go ahead and write your ten," she says, standing up. "When Dean comes to pick you up, I'll talk to him about what you said."

That's good, talk to Singer cus he'll have the plan about what to say, and I'll just act like nothin happened. I watch Ms. Tate walk away, looking real nice, breathe in deep that flower smell. Maybe some day she will marry me or Singer. Just so she's always around with that good smell. Then I write me eight more sentences so fast my pen smokes:

Landon J. Napoleon

bresst is nice
munkey clubb pink
catilak tom got a black car
Siner bald.
siner short
siner mad at ZigZag
ZigZag ZigZag the dishis
sop pink

"He asked if he could see my breasts, right in the middle of class, right before he told me about your night at the . . . what did you call it, Louis?"

"The Monkey Club."

"Ah yes, the cultural apex of our city: the Monkey Club."

Singer gives me a look maybe to remind me that Black Beauty is still out in his car. Then he looks back to Ms. Tate. "I can explain."

"That would be very helpful," she says, holding up some papers stapled together. "Since I have here an evaluation form from family social services asking me to judge your capacity to act as legal guardian to Louis."

"Really?"

"Oh yeah. Really."

"I mean the form, so they're actually considering me?"

"At this stage I would put a strong emphasis on *considering*."

"OK, look, here's the deal. Friend of mine got into some trouble. Now without going into a lot of detail—"

"What kind of trouble? Better not be drugs."

"No. Nothing like that."

"What then?"

"I'd rather not say."

"I'd rather you did say."

"He had to borrow some money from a loan shark."

"Five thousand sound about right?"

Singer flashes me a look so fast his eyes are back on Ms. Tate before the chill hits my skin. "Ballpark, yeah."

"So . . . ?"

"So I said I'd go talk to this guy sort of as a go-between, see if I could work out an arrangement. That's all."

"And you just decided it would be educational to take Louis to a topless bar?"

"No, not like that. We didn't even go in . . . to the club. We were back by the office and . . . do we really need to go into the details?"

"Yes, we do."

Singer waits, scratches his neck before he starts talking again. "He saw some of the dancers in their dressing room. That's all. It's not like we were in the club getting table dances. He couldn't get in anyway."

"Dressing room? What you mean is he saw a room full of naked women."

"Naked? Not necessarily. Not all of them."

"Not all of them . . . you want to know what I think?"

"I know you're about to tell me."

"I think you're the one owes this loan shark five thousand dollars, and I don't think it's right mixing Louis up in this."

"Well, that might be how it appears, but I promise you that's not—"

"Look, I don't really care because I know how good you've been to Louis. But don't insult me by feeding me some stupid story and expecting me to buy it. Give me more respect than that."

Singer nods.

"Now, I plan to give you an excellent recommendation, but I don't want to pick up the newspaper and see your face on page one because Louis is the one who will suffer. He needs you now more than he ever has. Understand my point?"

"Totally. I totally agree."

"Whatever you're into or not into or used to be into, that's your business. And I don't mean any disrespect, with your illness and all. Believe me, what you're trying to do is great. But when you're talking about taking Louis in, then everything becomes my business. I just want that to be clear before I sign this form."

Singer looks at me and pulls me into his chest, my body tensing up at first and then going relax when he just gives me a good hug.

"You don't have anything to worry about, Ms. Tate. I've got everything under control."

At the Toad's restaurant the busboys tell me I got to squirt ketchup on busgirl's cunt, or they'll pour more pepper in my eyes. They trapped me in the dry storage when I was stacking the clean salt and pepper shakers on the shelf like I always do, except I wasn't fast enough. I always try to ZigZag out of here on superspeed because dry storage is at the back of the kitchen and full of table-cloths, napkins, and all kinds of stuff that grabs your voice right out your mouth.

When I tried to ZigZag past, somehow they caught me with some kind of invisible net. Then the shorter fat one pushed me back, hard, and the other one closed the big metal door. Ain't no one going to hear me back here now. They talked at me, but I blocked it out, like nothin happened, just like nothin happened, until one of them took the big can of pepper, pinched some out with his fingers, and flicked it at my head. Seemed like the pepper landed in my eye but felt like it was inside my head, the burn down deep. Don't seem right how the busboys could make such a loud noise in my head without touching me.

"You got it, monkey boy?"

I shake my head, my eye still on fire and that pepper taste in my whole head, cus I don't know what they talking about. Feels like someone's got little pins they sticking in my eye. They still got me held down.

"Listen: you take this packet of ketchup and squirt it on Tawny's cunt. If you don't, we'll pour this whole can of pepper in your eyes." He's holding up a can of pepper that, out one eye, looks big as a house.

"Understand?"

I shake my head. "What's *cunt*?"

They both laugh, shaking their heads, the shorter fat one pointing at me. "Between her legs, monkey boy."

"What do you call it? Goomba? Snatch? How about twat?"

"Her thing?" I ask.

"Yeah, her thing. Monkey boy knows what we're talking about."

My head's still on fire from the pepper, but now I really confuse. "Women ain't got no thing, except some hair."

"Oh, like you've ever seen a naked woman."

"I did. Saw one five last night at the Monkey Club. Lots of breasts."

"Yeah, right. You gotta be twenty-one to get in there."

"I seen lots. You ever seen a naked woman?" They give me a look like they don't know what to say. Then they look at each other like they still confuse.

"Don't try to change the subject. You do what we said, or you'll get all this in your eye. Got it?"

I nod just to make them let go, still confuse why they want me to squirt the ketchup on Tawny's thing even though she ain't got one. They open the door, and as soon as they gone I ZigZag out the dry storage so fast I crash into one of the cooks.

"Goddammit, you idiot," he yells, both of us on the floor with squished tomatoes and that pepper burn still in my head. I don't say nothin, like nothin happened, just ZigZag back up and over to the sprayer and give my eyes a full blast of the water until the burn goes away.

For a long time I just stay behind my dish station like nothin happened, full speed into the dishes, my head full of numbers from the safe and instructions from Singer and the busboys while my radar listens for the Toad see if he knows I was the one in his safe. Each time the busboys come back, they give me a look make sure I don't forget what they said, and then when Tawny comes back I ZigZag some looks down between her legs, but I can't see nothin except light brown pants. Then when I look up, her eyes are right on me. I give my sprayer a full squeeze and blast the hot water so the steam rolls up. I feel safer in the steam. Then she just shakes her head and smiles and walks out the kitchen with a clean bus tub.

I tear into the tub she left so fast it tries to slide away from me. A juicy piece of steak is in my mouth before it has time to know what hit it. The kitchen is empty right now except for ZigZag and my machine and the cooks over on the other side of the ice machine. This is the best time of the night, when there's lots of dishes coming back, and the cooks and waitresses and waiters and busboys and busgirl and the Toad all got so much other stuff to do they ain't got time to mess with ZigZag. The steam rolls off the clean racks and sticks hot to my face.

> now's when I go automatic
> my arms do what my brain don't see
> my brain do what my arms don't see
> scrape and rack
> rack and stack
> scrape and rack and rack and stack

> stack and rack and rack and rack and stack and rack
> faster
> faster
> noise gone away can't never come back
> rack and stack don't never bite back

My radar sees the Toad in the kitchen before my eyes do, and when I look up he's standing on the other side of the dish station with a man in a suit I never seen before. The man's taller than the Toad, but so is everyone. He got little round glasses and some kind of papers in his hand. The Toad's looking at a clipboard. I give the sprayer another full blast, maybe mess up his radar with the heat, but he's already looking right at me.

"Take a break, Louis. We need to talk to you."

"I don't need no break."

"It's not optional."

"Opshul?"

"Op—tion—al. It means get your bony ass over here right now."

I let go the sprayer and start toward them, *just like nothin happened, just like nothin happened,* over and over in my head, keeping the numbers outside.

"Louis, Detective Hawke. Detective Hawke, Louis."

"Hello, Louis." He puts out his hand. I don't say nothin or reach out to shake his hand, too busy concentrating on *nothin happened, nothin happened.*

"Our boy here's a little short on the Cheese whiz," the Toad says.

"I just need to ask you a few questions, Louis. Will that be all right?" Then to the Toad, "How old is he?"

"Why?"

"I can't interview a minor without at least one of his parents present."

"That won't be necessary. Our boy here just turned eighteen. Right, Louis?" The Toad slaps me on the back and smiles, two things he ain't never done to me since I asked about eating his garbage. "All right, let's go. We can use my office." The Toad pushes me low in the back.

"Could I see his driver's license?" the man in the suit asks the Toad.

"Fuck he needs a driver's license for? He's a dishwasher."

They talk like I gone invisible now, like a lot of people do when I'm standing right here.

"I'll need something to verify his age before we do the interview."

"I just told you he's eighteen. I'm his employer. There's your verification."

"Look, if I do this interview and we find out later he's a minor, you know whose ass is on the line?"

Then the Toad leans in and whispers, "It's not like he's our prime suspect. He's dumber than all the other dishwashers put together." The Toad works the little cigar around to the other corner of his mouth, then pulls it out and spits a little brown flake. He points the cigar at the man in the suit: "Louis has no one. Do you want to kiss ass down at social services for two weeks, or just ask him a few quick questions and get on with the real investigation?"

Over on the other side of the kitchen I hear the heat sound coming off the cook's pans, and my stomach makes a loud hungry noise. Waiters and waitresses are rushing past us on both sides with big trays and the food smells following close behind. I look over at my machine when it spits out the last rack and then goes silent like it got me beat, the electricity tingle rising up again in my fingers, thinking now about shoving the dirty racks in so fast the machine don't ever stop running.

"All right," the man in the suit says, folding up his papers. "Just a couple of quick questions. Officially, we're off the record. What do I call him?"

"Louis."

"ZigZag" comes out my mouth automatic.

ZigZag

"ZigZag?"

I nod.

"OK, ZigZag. Do you remember—"

"He's stupid, not deaf," the Toad says. "You don't have to scream at him."

"Singer says I ain't stupid. You're the one stupid."

"That's right, I forgot. I'm stupid. Louis here is the first dishwasher in history to win the Nobel Prize." The Toad laughs and looks at the man in the suit, who just gives him a look like he as confuse as me. Then the man in the suit looks back at me. "On Monday you were in the office with Mr. Walters—"

"Who Mr. Walters?"

"Mr. Walters, your boss." Except he's pointing at the Toad.

"The Toad?"

Then the Toad yells across the whole kitchen: "Next person I hear call me that is going home with grill marks on their gonads!"

The man in the suit looks at the Toad. "You ever had a visit from the folks at the employment commission?"

"No, but you know what I'd tell those government bung sores if I did?"

"God help us."

"Way I see it, employees are like dairy cows: keep em locked in the barn and milk em dry."

The man in the suit gives the Toad a long look.

"Anyway . . . on Monday Mr. Walters and you were in his office. You watched him open the safe, and then he gave you your check. Remember?"

Like nothin happened, just like nothin happened. My hands are all hot and sticky, but it ain't from the sprayer.

"Don't start this silent bullshit, Louis."

Just act like nothin happened.

Nothin.

Nothin.

"Louis?"

"Nothin happened."

"What do you mean, Louis?"

"Nothin happened. Singer said nothin happened, saw him open the safe outside my head, numbers inside. Never took a ride down my fingers. Never broke no damn window. Window real, safe wasn't no real."

"What's he saying?"

The Toad pulls out his little cigar and picks a little brown flake off his lip. Then he scratches his nose, which is shiny with the wet. "Kid's a nutcase, career dishwasher. Most of the time he's quiet as a rock. Then when he does talk, it's nonsense and numbers bullshit. Sometimes he wigs out like he's having some kind of attack. Happened Monday when he broke that window." He points across the kitchen at the window looks like a little mirror, cracked, except on the other side are the little red frog eyes, those secret frog agents watching us all the time from the office.

"Do you remember breaking the window, Louis?"

I look at the man in the suit, then back at the Toad. Just like nothin happened, Singer said, just like nothin happened.

"Louis?"

"You're wasting your time with him. I know it's Cindy Monroe."

"Yeah, maybe. But we've got zero physical evidence."

"Physical evidence? She had the combination. Her prints were on the safe. You said it was an inside job. Case closed; that slop cunt's guilty as fuck."

"And your prints were on the safe. And the two assistant managers' prints were on the safe."

"I tell you she's banging one of the bartenders? Thinks I don't know."

"Yes, and you also told me that in the end all women are whores because one way or another they fuck you out of your money."

"Yeah?"

"Yeah, well, to get a conviction we're probably going to need a little more evidence than 'Your honor, the suspect had the combination to the safe and, of course, the most damning revelation: she's a woman.'"

"Maybe. But you're still wasting your time with our genius Louis Pasteur here. Get it? Louis?" Except he says *Loo-ee*.

"Don't forget what I told you. Everyone's a suspect."

"Kid can barely tie his own shoes."

I sneak away while they're talking, ZigZag slow back over to the dish station, little bells ringing in my head from all the dishes piling up. Four bus tubs came back since we been standing here, machine still quiet, except it got a big smile like it done beat me for good.

> got to burn
> got to burn
> smell the cool gears inside
> got to heat them up
> smoke those monkey boys
> pour the pepper till it burns

"Where you going? We're not done yet. Back over here."

The Toad's looking at me again, waving that clipboard at me. I walk back around the dish station and stand closer to the man in the suit. Something about him reminds me of Singer, but I don't know what cus he ain't bald.

"I'll be back in a second," the Toad says.

My body goes a little relax when the Toad leaves and it's just me and the man in the suit standing by the reach-in cooler where we keep all the ice cream.

"Your boss must be an interesting man to work for."

Yeah, he's interesting all right. Singer told me the best way to talk to people is block out they words and climb down deep into they eyes. What they saying out their mouth don't matter. Get inside they eyes. You got the special powers, you see this man got the kind of eyes don't want to beat no one. My body goes even more relax.

"Just a couple of quick questions," he says, "then you can get back to your work."

I don't say nothin or nod, just stand there, like nothin happened, let him talk outside.

"Your boss tells me you're good at remembering numbers."

I push the numbers to the Toad's safe out my head, but not so far out I can't grab em back cus me and Singer got to put that five two four one back tonight.

"Is that true?"

"What true?"

"You good with numbers?"

"Dunno."

"Do you remember watching, uh," he looks both ways and then, "the Toad open the safe on Monday?" He smiles. I nod, just like nothin happened.

"Did you see the numbers?"

"Numbers?"

"To the safe."

"Course I seen those" jumps out, but I stop my mouth before it starts showing off how it knows those numbers.

"Well enough to open the safe?"

"What you mean 'well enough'?"

"If you knew the numbers, do you think you could open the safe?"

"Nothin happened."

"Nothin happened when?"

"Monday night, just ask the little frog agents, didn't see no nothin nowhere."

"Late Monday night?"

"Yeah, late."

"Late Monday night, no one else was here. That's when nothing happened?"

"Uh-huh. Just like Singer says, nothin happened."

"Who's Singer?"

"Bout the best damn driver you ever seen."

"Singer's a driver?"

"Drives a forklift."

"And how do you know him?"

"He give me the special powers."

"Special powers?"

"Give me my new name, ZigZag." Just like that, two big Z's and two little g's.

"I see. And is Singer in your family?"

"He's my big brother."

"Your brother."

"He ain't for real."

"He isn't for real?"

"For real my big brother."

"He's your stepbrother?"

"Step?"

"Do you and Singer have the same parents?"

"Don't think Singer got no parents."

"Everyone has parents."

"Maybe. I ain't never seen Singer's."

"So your parents adopted Singer?"

"Adopt?"

"*Adopted.* It means, uh . . . never mind. Let's go back to what you said. So your big brother, Singer, he told you to say nothing happened on Monday night?"

"Nothin happened."

Then the man takes out his little pad of paper and a pen. "Singer. Like it sounds?"

I confuse. Then he says some letters.

"That's his first name?"

"I just call him Singer."

"Do you know how old Singer is?"

"Easy. ZigZag one five, Singer two nine."

"Two nine . . . Singer's twenty-nine?"

I nod, slow, slow, slow, always slow down cus ain't that what I just said? Then I see the Toad's head through the little square window on the kitchen door. There's something green stuck on the window or stuck on his head, can't tell which. He's talking and waving his hands when he comes through the door, he's still got that clipboard in one hand, wet face, that little cigar stuck in his mouth.

"Pin the Kennedy assassination on him yet?"

Man in the suit just looks at the Toad, puts away his little notepad. He reaches out and shakes my hand. "Thanks for your time, Louis. Sorry . . . ZigZag."

ZigZag.

Time to ZigZag them dishes.

"Well?" the Toad says.

"You were right," he says. "Nothing there."

"That's everybody then."

"Still got a couple waiters and waitresses."

"When are you going to stop fucking around with these worker bees and go after the queen? Monroe's our prime suspect."

"Our?"

"Yeah, I'm telling you it's her."

"And I'm telling you I still need to question—"

"I want a new detective."

"What?"

"I'm a taxpayer. I want a new detective assigned to this case. Someone older. Knows what they're doing."

"Knows what they're doing . . ."

"How old are you?"

The man in the suit looks at me, smiling, then looks back at the Toad. "You think you can do better? Be my guest."

"All right. I will. The fuck you lookin at, Louis?"

Before he goes out the kitchen door, the man in the suit stops.

ZigZag

"Just remember one thing: no one cares about your pathetic little five thousand dollars. But at least I act like I do." Then to me, "Take it easy, ZigZag."

I ZigZag into the dishes full speed, hot spray and grease and little food scraps everywhere, faster, faster, numbers back in my head, block it all out.

I can feel the Toad by the door, still standing there.

ZigZag faster.

Faster.

Without looking up, I know the Toad's still there, watching me close with his radar and smoking his cigar he never lights, my skin on fire when he looks at me same as that pepper burn.

Monkey boys got pepper gonna burn you down. Biggest pepper can I ever seen. Moving through the steam, mean smiles, heat sound coming loud off the cook's pans. Voices and shouts, no one nearby to help me.

Monkey boys got pepper gonna burn you down.

Closer. Closer.

Where I'm supposed to squirt the ketchup? She ain't got no thing. I move my feet until my back presses up against the machine, hot and loud inside like it's chewing on a dog, gears and little rubber wheels smoking, little vibrations through my back.

Monkey boys got pepper gonna burn you down.

They on the black mat now, squishy sound from all the brown water under my feet, pepper burn already in my head even though they ain't touched me yet.

Monkey boys.

Monkey boys.

ZigZag

Words coming out those mean smiles but no sound, just words I can't see, now a long, empty noise in the bottom of my head. Bright lights get louder, now everything go quiet. Special powers to block out the pepper burn, squeeze the sprayer full speed and soak they faces, then on the floor so fast they eyes go big. ZigZag deeper and deeper down into the mat, down into the brown water now feels so good, so small now I gone invisible, no sound or noise or pepper burn. Legs kicking crazy, arms going wild all on they own.

They still got me.

A punch in my back knocks the noise into my head. Legs kick harder, hands on they own trying to get me out, reach through to the other side of the dish station. Underneath the dish station now, sideways, my eyes and mouth and head filled with the brown water and bleach smell, bottle tipped over. I pick up the food scrap bucket and throw it at they heads.

The air goes out my body when the soft part on the front of my leg hits the metal post, the noise shooting out like the worse white light you ever felt. My hands go down to help my leg, my face pressed into the squishy black mat and the water and food scraps and a little green scrubber pad. Now my body goes automatic, tensed full tight, everything closed down waiting for the next blast.

Eyes shut.

Brain shut.

Stomach shut.

Hands shut.

Teeth shut.

Butt shut tight keep out the noise.

Then . . . they hands go away.

Monkey boys gone?

Waiting . . .

Waiting . . .

Can't give in yet.

Monkey boys got pepper gonna burn you down.

Don't let the noise back in, my leg now sending the noise through my whole body that comes out my teeth in a little rhythm, *BUMPH BUMPH BUMPH*. I go relax just a little, let some air in, and the bleach smell jumps inside my head, chokes off the air again until I cough it out, back on my hands and knees, everything soaked brown.

Then I ZigZag straight up toward the ceiling, like I got special floating powers I ain't learned about, leg on fire and bleach burn in my head. When I go full straight, the crack in the Toad's mirrored window cuts Dale's face down the middle. He lets go, and I dip back towards the floor cus my leg gone relax. I balance on the leg don't hurt and turn around. Dale barely fits behind my dish station.

"You OK?"

I'm still trying to wipe the bleach smell out my head, but it's in there deep, mixing up with the pepper. My leg don't feel OK. I feel like I might throw up real soon. "They put pepper in your eyes, too?" I ask Dale.

Dale shakes his head, smiles a little. Then he holds up the giant pepper can. Somehow now it looks smaller and less scary in Dale's big hands. Then my radar goes off. My machine got the mean smile again. I put my hand flat on the side.

Cool and quiet.

No vibrations.

It done spit out the dog.

I ZigZag back into position, then remember I got to stand on one leg until the noise gets out the other one. The bleach smell is still full bright in my head. I empty two tubs and feed the racks into the machine as fast as I can.

> choke it
> choke it, choke it, choke it
> choke it and smoke it

ZigZag

smoke it and choke it and burn it down
choke that monkey boy till he don't come back

I jump when I feel something heavy on the back of my legs. I turn around and look down. Dale, down on his knees picking up the bus tubs, stacking them back under the dish station. When I ZigZag down, he screws the lid on the bleach bottle and hands it to me. I put it back in its regular spot. The stupid monkey boys knocked the little tube out that feeds the machine pink soap. I got to crawl back underneath the machine. The floor's cold and slippery. I twist the tube back into the bottle. When I get out of there, Dale hands me my food scraps bucket.

"What's this?"

"Nothin." I grab it from him, trying to hide it in case he's one of the Toad's secret agents.

Questions, questions, questions.

The Toad.

Man in the suit.

Singer.

Ms. Tate.

Now Dale.

Everyone with all the questions and always slow down, slow down, slow down, please don't ZigZag right out our universe. My food bucket's half full of brown water.

"You don't need that," he says.

I got my radar on, though, like nothin happened, still trying to see if Dale's working for the Toad. Then he stands up. From down here he looks like a building except no red light on top.

"You get hungry? Come see me."

Then he walks away carrying that can of pepper same as he carries a pan of cut-up chicken and the garbage can, full or empty.

The air moves in slow motion, frozen up by the cold. It comes out my head in white clouds that float away and then go invisible. My pants are still wet from being on the floor, the cold sneaking around and already found a way in. The black leather jacket Singer gave me keeps my top half warm, my hands down deep in the pockets. I look back at the white light around the edges of the kitchen door, think about going in there to wait. I kick at the black snow along the edge of the pavement. At least it's never cold in the Toad's kitchen. A little chunk of snow breaks off and slides across the Toad's parking lot. I run after it and kick it again before it stops sliding, and it breaks all apart.

Two zero zero.

My dad?

I look around like maybe my radar turned on automatic and seen him coming. Back there's the Toad's long skinny building, all dark except the square of white around the edges of the kitchen door. I turn the other way and see the gas station, still open, full bright, and all the cars going both ways on the street. Now the cold creeps in closer and makes my body shake all on its own. I got to get back in that kitchen, go sit by my machine, stick my face in that steam. My sneakers go silent on the parking lot, back towards the kitchen door, then that crunch sound when they hit patches of snow. Before I get to the door, I see headlights coming this way, then the orange eye hanging sideways off Singer's car. I run to his window.

"Singer!"

He rolls down the window, the heater sound sneaking out before I feel the warm air on my face.

"You crazy? You're gonna freeze out here. You should wait inside. Supposed to get down to single digits tonight."

"One, two, three, four—"

"Five, six, seven, eight, nine, yeah. Get in."

Singer rolls up his window, so I run to the other side. Damn, it feels good in here, that hot air blowing on my wet jeans already frozen by the cold. Singer turns the wheel and parks the car. I'm glad he keeps it running so we don't freeze up, the heater still going full speed.

"You ready to do this?"

"Ready?"

"Tonight. You think you can open that safe again?"

I fire the numbers through my head so fast I got to do it again, slower, just to make sure them numbers lined up proper.

"Can you do it?" he asks.

"I still got the numbers in my head."

"OK. Good. I've got the money."

Singer reaches under the front seat and pulls out a black plastic sack. He unwraps it and holds up the Toad's money, five two four one. "Five thousand two hundred and forty-one dollars. I had to go to the bank, after I dropped you off, to get the two hundred and forty-one. That leaves seventy-six bucks in my checking account, five hundred dollars' worth of bills at home."

"Five zero zero?"

"Yep. Five zero zero. Not to mention the six grand I owe Cadillac Tom."

"Six grand?"

Singer's got on his black baseball hat with the white skull and his leather jacket like mine. I'm glad Singer got two jackets the same for us. Now Singer's looking around the parking lot, then at his wrist.

"Eleven-thirty now. What time do the breakfast cooks come in?"

"They start early. When I slept in the Toad's attic, I'd smell the coffee before it was light outside."

Singer's got his hat off now, scratching his head. He puts it back on and plays with the Toad's money with his thumb. The money makes a sound like little drums. Now he's got a red pen out, the one he likes to chew on when he's thinking. I go silent on the outside, just listen to the heater and practice the numbers in my head so Singer can do his talking on the inside.

"All right. Here's the plan: we'll go home and sleep for a few hours. Then we'll come back at three-thirty, after the bar's closed and before the breakfast cooks show up."

I look at Singer and nod. That sounds like a damn good plan to me.

At three three zero in the night, there's no white around the edges of the kitchen door, no cars in the Toad's parking lot. The gas station on the corner is the only thing still lit up full bright. Everything else is black and silent. Even all the cars are asleep except one or two that drive by along the road next to the restaurant.

When the air goes single digits, it stings your nose and freezes the inside of your head every time you breathe. Singer said we had to leave the car a few blocks away, which we did, and then walk to the restaurant. Now we're almost to the gate by the trash dumpsters. We got black everything on: hats, coats, gloves, pants, and sneakers. Somehow the cold still gets me through all these clothes. We ain't talking on the outside, just moving invisible across the parking lot, Singer leading us around the snow so we don't make the crunch sound.

The gate's so cold it don't want to open. Singer pulls the latch again, harder, but it still don't open. He looks around and whispers,

"Climb over." I ZigZag over the fence so fast I'm on the other side before Singer knows what happened.

"Shhhhh," he says, but I ain't said nothin.

Then I see his gloves on top of the wood, then that little white skull on his hat kind of glows in the dark. He drops down on this side and points to the ladder.

"There?"

I nod.

"You first," he says, still whispering. "You know the way."

What he says warms me up inside. This is about the first time I ever known the way better than Singer. The metal ladder is skinny silver metal stuck right on the side of the Toad's building. Now I feel Singer's hand on my shoulder.

"Go up it as fast as you can and then hide on the roof. We can't let anyone see us."

I ZigZag up the ladder like Singer tells me, fast, then jump down low and close everything up tight. I don't open my eyes until I feel Singer's hand. Now he's down low, the little black pack on his back with the Toad's money inside. After a car drives past, he leans close to me.

"All right, we need to do this as quick as we can. You're the boss. Lead the way to the office."

Singer touches me nice on my back, gives me the good warm inside again, maybe what Ms. Tate calls the self-esteem. I point towards the metal door that takes us to where I used to sleep, before I moved in with Singer. The door opens easy but makes a loud noise.

"Shhhhh."

I go down the little ladder first, the restaurant smell warm on my face. Singer closes the door and everything goes full black. Then a little light turns on, and he comes down the ladder.

"Why the hell doesn't he lock that?"

I whisper back, "If he did, how would we get in?"

Singer's shining his little light around. He shakes his head, whispers again, "Never mind. Let's go."

But I'm already going, my heart a little crazy, my radar up extra sensitive to watch for them little frog agents I know are in here, little red eyes over there in the corners. Don't matter I can't see them; I know they out there. It makes my skin go cold to think about them, so I push it out and start repeating the numbers make sure I got them in order.

Now I get the numbers full loud in my head, over and over and over, block out everything else make sure I get them right. Now we're above the Toad's office, a little light coming up from the kitchen along the cracks. I point down, and Singer nods. Singer sure look quiet, but I wonder if his heart's going crazy like mine.

We lift out the ceiling square, and my nose has to ZigZag the Toad smell rising up. Singer gets low next to me and shines the little light all around the Toad's office. It looks just like the Toad, like it ain't been cleaned for a long time. Singer gives me a little push. I go in first. When I put my leg on the desk, the noise tingles inside where it hit the metal post. Next thing I know, me and Singer are both in front of the Toad's safe with the kitchen light shining on the dial same as last time.

"That the window?"

"I didn't break it, Singer."

"I didn't say you did. I just asked if that was the one."

Singer pulls the backpack off and then his gloves, so I do the same. Underneath we got another pair of tighter gloves, white rubber, *like real bank robbers*, Singer said when we pulled them on. Singer looks at his wrist again.

"We're doing good. You ready?"

My heart starts goin extra crazy, more crazy than the first time. What if I can't get them numbers out right?

"You OK?"

My head nods automatic, but nothin feels OK.

"Go for it."

The dial spins easy between my fingers, around and around, get it warmed up, around and around, then stop on the first number, back around to the second, back and forth until all the numbers are used up. I look at Singer.

"Is that it?"

I nod. He reaches forward. My heart gets stuck up in my throat when he puts his hand on the silver lever. I shut my eyes and wait for that loud *CLICK*.

But there ain't no sound.

"It's not moving."

I open my eyes and push the lever same as I did before. It don't move.

"Try it again. Go slow. Make sure you've got the numbers right. Just do everything the same."

Everything the same.

Spin the dial. Around and around. One, two, three—

A door slams, and the light comes in full bright from the kitchen. Singer grabs my arm. Now voices from the kitchen.

"Shit. Someone's here."

Singer's up, looking through the cracked window. He whispers, "It's a man. And a woman. If they're cooks, they wouldn't have a key to the office, would they? Come see if you recognize them."

I ZigZag up and stand behind Singer. All the air goes out my body when I see the Toad walking this way.

"That's him, Singer."

"That's him who?"

"The Toad."

"You're kidding. Your boss? Oh, fuck. Go. Now."

I ZigZag onto the desk and reach for the ceiling.

Singer whisper-yells, "Goddammit, be quiet!" Then a weird sound, like my machine choking on dishes. I get up in the ceiling and look down into the office. Singer's on the floor, sideways, that noise inside him again.

"Singer?"

He's waving his hand, the other hand on his stomach trying to pull that noise out, his hat gone and the light shiny on his head. That green smoke tries to get inside me, too, but I got it blocked down. Got to get Singer out of there.

I jump back down onto the desk and land on the leg that smashed into the pole. The leg don't work right when my body comes down, the leg going relax, and I keep falling until I land on top of Singer. He makes sounds I ain't never heard come out of him, like a short blast, *EEEEOOOWWWW*, then little air sounds, *FOO FOO FOO FOO FOO.*

"That noise got you, Singer?"

He got his eyes shut down, nods yes. "Go. Get out. I'll take the fall."

"You already on the ground, Singer. Come on."

"Not that kind of fall."

Now them voices louder, louder, louder, Singer pushing me away, whisper-yelling, "Go! Go!"

But my legs don't move, everything frozen up solid, single digits in here now, voices louder, a blast of white light at the bottom of the door.

Singer's already got the chair out, crawling under the desk.

The Toad and a woman's voice so loud now it's like they in here with us.

Singer disappears under the desk. "Move the ceiling panel back."

I go on the desk supersilent, cover the hole, and ZigZag back down, jammed up tight in here with Singer.

A key sound in the lock.

Singer squeezes my arm. "Shit. The pack."

The office lights up.

I lean out, grab the pack, and ZigZag back under the desk just as a lady leg steps in front of us.

"What a pigsty. You always this messy?"

"You always so nosy?"

My heart's goin so crazy, superfast, shaking my whole body each time it beats. I can't see Singer cus he's behind me, but I can feel his air on my neck. Wish I could see whether that noise gone out his face. The lady's legs are straight towards us, and the Toad's legs are walking back and forth. He's got a bottle in one hand same as the one makes my dad's face go crazy.

"So how long you owned this place?" she asks.

"Want another drink?"

"Sure."

The Toad sets two glasses on the desk, right above our heads, then pours from the bottle. I don't have to see that little white-tipped cigar to know it's right in the corner of his mouth, still not lit.

"You didn't answer my question . . . how long you owned this?"

"Ten years. Worked in restaurants since I was thirteen."

"Married?"

"Barely. How bout you?"

"Ha ha. I see what men are like. I'm gonna sit at home scrubbing skid marks out of Jockey shorts while he's out banging some bimbo? I don't think so."

"I meant how long. As in how long you been a hooker?"

"I'm a student. At the community college. I started with Angel Escorts, I don't know, maybe six months ago?"

"What, you look in the classifieds?"

"Friend of mine, Jordan, is a dancer at the Monkey Club. Used to do escort. She's the one got me juiced in."

"I know the place. What if I got you out? Of the business, I mean."

"Don't tell me you're one of these closet feminists. I know, you think what I'm doing exploits women, that I'm a victim, that women have been marginalized by a misogynistic Western civilization for two thousand years, which only keeps us in a subservient role. Right?"

"No . . . you've got great tits. I want you to come work here."

"Waitressing? Kiss ass all night for thirty dollars in change? Sorry."

"My servers can make a hundred on weekend nights. And . . . as part of our deal you could earn something on the side."

Now all the legs are touching, no voices, just little wet sounds. The Toad's hand drops down, and I see the little cigar, the plastic white tip shiny with spit.

"I don't think so. You think spending six hours on my feet and then sucking your dick at the end of every shift sounds even remotely appealing?"

"I'd pay you. Five hundred a week. And that's on top of your tips."

"Don't insult me. I made seven hundred bucks last night. Two hours. No sex. Just had to clean this guy's house."

"Guy paid you seven hundred bucks to clean his house?"

"Not regular cleaning. I wore a G-string and carried around a feather duster. Bent over a lot. Then, get this, he asked me to stick my head in his microwave while he jerked off into a test tube. After he blows his load, he puts a label on the test tube with the date and asks me to sign it. I'm like, 'Hello, and when did you escape?' Then he shows me his freezer. He's got hundreds of these test tubes filled with his own sperm? I was like, whatever . . . thanks for the seven bills."

"Was it on?"

"What?"

"The microwave?"

"How could it be on if my head was in it?"

"Right. The door was open."

"So anyway, your time's up. I need to get back. I've got a couple of chapters to read tonight. Whose hat?"

She bends down and picks up Singer's skull hat.

"Not mine. Probably that bitch ripped me off."

"Nice skull."

"It's yours. Anyway, Jenna. How much for a little more of that sugar?"

"Uh-uh. Candy store's closed. I've got a class in . . . exactly seven hours."

"C'mon, just a quickie."

They legs touching again, the Toad so close I could reach out and grab him, block out everything in case he's got his radar on. It's hard to breathe the hot air under here, Singer's knees jammed up in my back and my leg still hurting bad.

"Unless we leave now, it'll cost you another hour, plus two hundred."

"How much more then?"

"Four hundred."

"That's over a grand I spent tonight. I get a free house cleaning?"

"I only get half of that, except for the tips. The agency gets the other half. Yes or no?"

The Toad takes her hand and puts it on his thing. "This answer your question?"

Then the legs get close again, his hands under her little skirt now, then inside her black underwear in the front, maybe looking for her thing he ain't never gonna find. I look close just in case she got one hidden. Then she pushes him away.

"Money first."

"You'll get it."

No words, just her hand opened up.

"Jesus Christ. A real romantic."

"Money first, then romance."

"How ironic." The Toad pulls out some money and puts it in her hand, his legs moving in close again.

"Not here."

"Why not here?"

"Because it's disgusting. Stinks in here. Out in the bar again."

"Fine. Go."

Her legs leave, then the Toad's, then the office goes black and the door slams. We hear the lock click shut and crawl out from under the desk. The air cooler now, feels good inside my head.

"Shit, I don't believe it. Jordan's the one that helped you that night."

My eyes are starting to work better in the black now. Singer's wiping the wet off his head.

"Wonder how well those girls know each other," he says, then, still whispering, "because if they're tight and she sees you here, they might put this together."

"I don't understand, Singer."

"Never mind. We've got to get out of here. They might come back."

"What about putting the Toad's money in the safe?"

Singer gives me that thinking look. "OK. Try it once more. Quick."

I do everything the way I did it the first time, spinning the dial, around and around, but after the last number the lever don't move. Singer tells me to try it again, except we do it three more times. That lever don't want to click down soft like it done the first time.

"He must have changed the combination."

"Why can't we just leave the Toad's money on his desk?"

"I thought about that. But now he'd know someone was in here after they were. Won't look right."

"I don't understand."

"Just trust me. We have to make it look like it was one of the assistant managers that stole the money and then got a guilty conscience. I have no idea how we'll do that . . . let's go."

Singer grabs my arm and helps me onto the desk. I move the ceiling panel and ZigZag up through the ceiling, dumping those useless numbers out my head, then go invisible into the black hole.

We both got the special powers, float through the night like steam coming off a rack of hot plates, think you see us then we gone. We ZigZag past the gas station, the lights full bright and shining off Singer's head, a man inside the glass booth reading a magazine.

Lift up the skirt.

Black underwear.

The Toad's little fat fingers slip under, quiet, move around looking for that thing.

Now feel the ZigZag thing, different, like that rock again. Reach on out from under that desk and touch the Toad, watch him float away like smoke. ZigZag under the black, so fast or slow she don't know which, see if she got that thing hid down in there good.

The snow crunches loud now under our feet, so Singer moves to the street. I follow him. All the houses and cars lined up along the street, so dark and quiet the only sound is the talking in my head. We float past, everything asleep except a cat under a car with eyes that light up. When I look at him, he crouches down almost flat. His little head turns to watch us walk past.

It takes us a little time to wake up Singer's car, everything frozen up, cold stuck on the windows I got to scrape off while he lets the engine run, the heater so loud I can hear it out here. When the last little flakes of cold come off the window, my head starts to feel real heavy, the sleep coming fast. I get in the car, and Singer drives away slow, the wheels making that crunch sound on the patches of snow.

The Toad's little fat fingers, fast and quiet, moving around. My eyes so heavy now, the white stripes on the road flashing by superfast. I turn sideways on the seat. Singer turns his head and smiles, rubs his hand on my leg.

"Tired?"

Just watching his head now, my eyes coming down slow and then fast back up.

"One hell of week, huh? Jesus."

The car stops, things lit up bright again. . . .

Now moving again, Singer working that lever up and down. . .

My eyes don't want to stay open no more, so I let them go. They close down fast. My ears are still open a little. Singer's words and the heater sounding extra loud now right before the sleep comes. ". . . promise me you won't tell Ms. Tate or our caseworker about any of this. Some mentor I am, huh? I'm just glad they went out to the bar to finish their business. Thank God it's Friday. We . . ."

When the day comes back full bright, I don't know where I am. Then I see Singer sitting at the table behind the cereal box. The TV's so low I can't hear it. Singer's couch feels good. This is the best place I ever sleep cus no bad kitchen smells and no one knocks the noise into your head in the middle of the night. The sun's got the room lit up so bright my eyes don't work so good.

Little drops of water are coming off the roof and landing on the junk piled up on Singer's balcony. An old bike he never rides, big stacks of newspapers, stuff in boxes he said he was gonna throw away a long time ago.

"You up?"

Singer's looking at me now, but my head's still moving in slow motion on the inside.

"Had to practically carry you up the stairs last night. You zonked out in the car. Jesus, that was close at the restaurant."

I watch Singer disappear, my eyes shut down again. I guess my body ain't ready to do any talking on the outside. Sleep coming fast again, Singer's voice loud for a second and then it's gone. . . .

Ms. Tate soft rounds. Money first then romance. Now Jenna sitting at a little table leans her face real close into the mirrors and rubs a little black brush on her eyes.

Hi, ZigZag. Come here. I'm a student at the community college. I started with Angel Escorts, I don't know, maybe six months ago. Then slip my finger under the black feel that hair grows between her legs in a skinny strip. I just wore a G-string and carried around a feather duster, bent over a lot. Feeling around for that soft thing got the flower smell. You think spending six hours on my feet and then sucking your dick at the end of my shift sounds even remotely appealing?

You get hungry? Come see me.

Money first then romance. Five zero zero zero. Money first then romance.

Fingers in the black, thing feels good, feels good, feels good. Soft rounds and sweet flower smell fill up my head.

Feels good. Faster now.

Faster.

Faster.

Faster.

Good, good. Good!

When I wake up, Singer is on the phone telling Ms. Tate I won't be in school today because we've got a bunch of stuff to do. Singer somehow got the noise knocked out his body cus he's smiling again today. Then it hits my brain like delay . . . no Fellowes School. I ZigZag off the couch and fold up my blanket so fast it makes Singer laugh. While I put the blanket and pillow in the hall closet, my mind's trying to pull back what was on the inside before I woke up cus it made me feel good. Except the harder I try to pull it back, seems like it's going the other way, farther and farther where I can't reach it. That's what it's like when you're stupid: lots of things is close in your head but not close enough to grab them up. Wish I was either really smart or even more stupid, not stuck in the middle where you're smart enough to know you're stupid but too stupid to pull things back when you want.

Then Singer yells for me to hurry up, we got a lot to do today. I ZigZag into the bathroom, start the hot water, and pull off my shorts. A strange smell comes out my shorts. I stick them up close to my face, and it goes full strong into my head, like that bleach bottle under the dish station. Then I feel something on my nose, sticky, like some of what comes off the Toad's pans. I wipe it off and look closer. That sticky is all over the insides of my shorts. ZigZag ain't peed the bed for a long time. Singer probably be mad if he knows. I roll the shorts tight into a little ball and hide them down deep in the blue trash can. Then I step full naked into the steam rolling out the shower.

When me and Singer go driving, the sun's out full bright. Lot of the cold that's been frozen up all week is gone liquid now. I ask Singer how that happens, cold frozen up one minute, then liquid, then superhot steam burns your face. He doesn't really say much, something about the oxygen and hydrogen molecules and then how he never did too good in science. The air's way above single digits so the heater's quiet.

I roll down my window. The air comes in cold and clean. Singer looks at me like I'm crazy cus maybe it ain't that warm, but I like to listen to the tires on the road. The tires are loud today cus the streets are covered with the melted cold, little pools that explode when the wheels cut through them. Sometimes when we hit a big puddle, the spray flies up, sneaks in the window, and sticks cold to my face. The air's still pretty damn cold, too, but it feels good.

"So how the hell do we get that cash back into the safe?"

"Five two four one?"

"Could mail it back." Singer looks at me like I should know if this is a good plan. I don't say nothin.

"Sure . . . the old Toad gets an anonymous package, bingo, there's his five grand."

"Five two four one."

"No way . . . we're going to trust the U.S. Postal Service with that much cash? Somehow we need to make it look like whoever did it got a guilty conscience."

"What's *guilty conscience*?"

Now we're stopped at a red light. "It's when you do something you know you shouldn't, and then you feel bad on the inside. That's guilt."

Singer might as well be a mind reader cus that's what he does all the time I'm with him. His special powers seen I got it good. "I got the guilt, Singer."

We're moving now, full sunshine but the air still cold enough we need our leather jackets.

"What do you mean?"

"I got the guilt for what I done to your couch. I'm sorry if I messed it up."

"Messed what up? What are you talking about?"

"Last night."

"What about last night?"

"I peed it."

Singer's face smiles, but when he reaches out my body goes automatic like he's about to knock some noise into my head. My dad's voice comes alive, so real it's like he's standing right here:

What kind punk ass bitch pisses his own bed? Fifteen years old. Sleeping in your own piss like a damn dog. You are one sorry little bitch. But my body keeps forgetting Singer ain't never hit me. Not once in five years. Instead he squeezes my leg and makes my body go relax.

"Believe me, that couch has had far worse than a little urine."

"Urine?"

"Urine. Pee. Same thing. Don't worry about it."

"You ain't mad?"

"Mad? Of course not. You know me better than that."

Know him better than what? I don't know. I'm just glad Singer ain't mad.

"That was about the best damn pee I ever felt."

Singer looking at me now. "What do you mean?"

"I dunno. Can't really remember except it felt damn good."

Singer's scratching his head, now rubbing his eye. He turns into a little store got black bars on all the windows. A man or woman, can't tell which, is sleeping in front of the store under a big pile of different colored blankets. When Singer shuts off the engine, it makes the choking noises before finally going silent.

"ZigZag, I don't think you peed the couch."

"Yeah I did, Singer. My shorts was wet and everything."

"But the couch wasn't. I sat on it while you were getting ready. Wasn't wet. No smell at all."

"But my shorts. They had the smell."

"What did it smell like?"

"Like the bleach bottle at work."

Singer scratching his head again, now looking at me. "How do I say this . . ."

"You said you ain't mad, Singer. Are you?"

"No, no, no, not at all," he says. My dad used to say that right before he brought out the Black Beauty, *no, no, no,* and then right across the back of my legs so hard I couldn't see. But it's different with Singer; I can see on his face what he says and what he's about to do are the same thing.

"Do you remember having any dreams last night?"

I remember trying to pull that one back, but never quite got it. Something about . . .

"Maybe one with the women we saw at the Monkey Club?"

Singer's radar so good he picks up the thoughts that float around outside my head. "Yeah, I seen Ms. Tate and Jenna sitting at the table at the Monkey Club with that little black eye brush."

"Right. Anything else?"

Now everything coming back like Singer unplugged a drain in my head, the pictures rushing in fast. "Ms. Tate was wearing the black underwear, and I slipped my finger in there looking for her thing."

"Well, I told you the other day I'd explain this to you. Guess now's as good a time as any for this talk." Singer breathes deep a couple times and scratches his head. "What you had last night"— both of us leaning in close to each other, without saying anything, like he's got a special secret to tell me—"that was a wet dream."

"A wet dream?"

"That's what it's called. You remember when I asked you about the birds and bees? No . . . forget that. That'll just confuse you more."

"I already confuse more, Singer."

He breathes deep again. "OK, remember when you saw the first naked lady, with your dad? And then you said she didn't have . . . a thing?"

"She didn't, less she got it hidden."

"Well, see, that's sort of true, it is hidden. Women have a thing called a *vagina*, and your thing is called a *penis*. God, why is this so hard?"

"Thought my thing is called a *thing*. No one ain't ever said nothin about no penis."

"Well, that's true. No one really calls it that. Just doctors, I guess. That's just a technical name."

"Tech-nal?"

"Like Louis Fletcher is your technical name. But I call you ZigZag."

"Tech-nal. I understand."

"So, OK, where do I start?" Singer's rubbing his hands together to help himself think. "Let me just explain everything, and then you can ask me questions when we're done. OK?"

I nod.

"So a man has a penis, and a woman has a vagina. You've heard these called lots of other names. For penis, things like *cock, johnson, dick*—"

"I heard *dick* before."

"Right. Just a different name for it. And for vagina, you've heard *pussy, snatch. Cunt?*"

"Toad calls people *cunt* all the time." Then I hear the monkey boys in my head, *Take this packet of ketchup and squirt it on Tawny's cunt.*

"OK, what happens is that when a man gets excited, his dick, or penis, gets hard. It fills up with blood. And a woman, her pussy gets wet."

Singer got both his hands up, one with a finger sticking out and one made into a little circle. "So then the man's dick goes inside the woman's pussy, back and forth like this, and then after a few minutes the man cums. He ejaculates—"

I confuse.

"See, that's what happened during your wet dream last night. Something called sperm comes out the end of the penis and shoots inside the woman's pussy. . . . I know it sounds really strange, but that's what happens."

"I shot sperm up a woman's pussy?"

Singer's laughing now, smiling big and shaking his head. "Not exactly. You see, if your dick gets hard, erect, then you can shoot your sperm anywhere. It doesn't have to be inside a woman."

"Like a test tube?"

"What?"

"Last night she said a guy paid her seven zero zero. Then he shot his sperm in a test tube."

"Yeah, that's the idea, but let's not use that as our example. Just try and forget you ever heard that. See, here's the main thing to remember: the man puts his dick inside the woman's pussy and shoots his sperm. It's called, well, it's called a lot of things. *Making love* is the nicest way to say it. Or *sex*. You've heard the other words: *fuck, screw*."

"I heard those a lot. Never knew what they mean, though."

"Right . . . so when a man and a woman are making love, now this is the really weird part, the little sperm swim up inside the pussy where they find a little egg. And when one of those sperm gets inside that egg, a baby starts to grow."

This sounds like some really weird stuff. "Women got eggs inside?"

"Uh-huh. That's how babies are born."

"Chicken babies?"

"No. Human babies. Like you and me."

"So I made me a baby last night?"

"No, it takes nine months. But first the sperm has to go inside a woman."

"Any woman?"

"Well, yeah. Roughly any woman between the ages of fifteen and forty."

"Like Ms. Tate."

"Yes . . . she falls within those parameters."

"You think she'd mind if I shoot my sperm inside her?"

Singer's laughing again, except I don't see what's so funny. This about the most confusing thing Singer ever tried to explain. When he finally stops laughing, he says, "I don't think that would be a good idea."

"Why not? I like that flower smell she got."

"Well, she's . . . your teacher."

"Teachers ain't got a pussy?"

"No, they have them, I mean *she* has one. Every woman has one."

"Then why can't I shoot my sperm in her?"

"It's more complicated than that. And for another thing, she's too old for you."

"You said any woman between one five and four zero."

"I know, but first you have to have a relationship. No, that's not true. OK, here: what you need to make a baby are two consenting people who want to make love together. That's the right way, at least. I don't think Ms. Tate would consent." Singer breathes out again, scratches his head. "I'm not doing too well, am I?"

"What?"

"You're probably more confused than before I started blabbering."

Singer's right again, so I nod.

"I've got it."

Singer starts the car and backs out the space. Then he has to wait a few minutes cus of all the cars and trucks before he pulls onto the street and cranks the car up to full speed.

"Where we going now?"

"What we need are visual aids."

It don't take my radar long to pick up Singer's work smell, paper, rolling off all the stacks of boxes and packages and envelopes, same smell as the brown shirt with his name. More like a wet paper smell, except none of these boxes looks wet. We are in the biggest room I ever seen. In the middle are these sliding metal belts that move the boxes around. People in brown shirts like Singer's are everywhere: carrying packages, taking boxes off the moving metal, waving to Singer when we walk by. All along the walls are giant metal racks that go all the way up to the ceiling. The racks are full of boxes and packages Singer says get sent all over the world, most of them places I never knew was out there. The racks are so high no one can reach them except with a special machine called a forklift. Singer's job is to drive the forklift.

There's five forklifts driving around right now, lifting the boxes up and down the giant racks. I never knew Singer was so important, reaching up to the top of the rack with his forklift where no one could ever reach without his help. He waves at a woman driving a blue forklift, and she drives towards us. It looks like some kind of monster I seen on the video with two long silver teeth to kill stuff. Singer's work is pretty damn loud, those moving metals and the forklifts and all the people. The forklift lady even got on big ears to block down the sound. Maybe I'll get me some of those to wear when I ZigZag the dishes.

The forklift lady climbs down and shakes Singer's hand and then mine. Then Singer grabs my hand and pulls me over to the forklift. Painted on the side: DINO, and next to that a little skull like on his hat that Jenna took.

"You want to drive it?"

I nod and watch Singer climb up into the seat. He reaches down and pulls me up with him. He sits in the seat, black like my jacket, and I sit off to the side. He starts explaining all the levers and pedals and saying the names and what they do, but I lose track after the first one. ". . . and then this lowers the fork." Then he makes me put on a hat called a hard hat and the big orange ears to block out the sound. He wears a hard hat and the ears, too. When he moves some levers, we start driving forward along the long rack with all the packages. We drive right out the building inside a truck, and he slides those two silver teeth under a big stack of boxes, lifts them up, and we back out of the truck, *beep, beep, beep, beep, beep.* . . . He drives over to the rack and lifts the boxes up to the second level, drives forward, lowers the boxes, and then pulls those silver teeth out real slow, *beep, beep, beep.* . . . All his hands and feet moving so many levers and pedals at once I can't keep track. Singer can drive anything. Mostly I'm thinking about when Singer showed me pictures of the naked women, and my thing gets like the rock again.

Two magazines that show lots of women full naked in all different positions so we can see everything. Pussies all look pretty much the same except a little different. Some are a little bigger, some a little darker or lighter, some more hairy than others. Singer explains everything real good, how when she stands like this with her legs together all you can see is the hair. The hair's all different, too. Some wide, some skinny, a lot of pussies with no hair except the skinny strip that goes straight up. Then he shows how when they spread open they legs you finally see the pussy. I knew they had it hidden down there.

He explains about the soft rounds, the breasts, how they feed the baby after it's been born. I hold the picture up close but can't see where no milk comes out. He says it's a tiny little hole you can't see. Two breasts in case one gets empty, I guess. This makes him laugh, so we laugh together.

Then he pulls out another magazine. This one got naked men instead of women. He explains how men's things, the dicks, is all different sizes and shapes, but they all do the same job. Get inside those pussies and shoot the sperm. This makes Singer laugh again and nod his head like I got it right. None of the men's things in the pictures is like the rock, like when I seen my dad's and Eddie's all shiny. Singer says they can't show them full erect. Don't ask me why, they show everything else.

We already stopped once at a little store. Singer went in alone and came out with a brown sack. All he said was "This should help." Then we drove here, which looked different until I remembered where we were, lots of big buildings except no houses anywhere. No restaurants or stores either. Just gray metal buildings that are big, sideways big instead of up, papers stuck to the melted cold on the street like where Cadillac Tom parks his car. We pulled into the parking lot with the big sign says GLOBAL EXPRESS. Singer parked way over here and pulled out the magazines with the naked people. Singer calls them the visual aids.

"Baby comes out the pussy?"

"Yeah."

"How?"

"The vagina stretches."

It sure don't look big enough for no baby to come out. "Baby comes out alive?"

"Yeah. That's how you were born."

"I killed my mom when I was born. That's what my dad says."

"No, don't listen to him. We don't know what happened with your mom."

I ZigZag down deep into my mind, do a little thinking away from Singer's radar. This all seems strange to me, sperm and eggs so small you can't see them, baby eggs growing inside the pussy, babies coming out that small pussy hole, baby sucking milk out little holes in the soft rounds. Talking to Singer about the pussy makes me sad I ain't never seen my mom. Maybe Singer's right, I didn't kill her when I was born, she's just somewhere else. Maybe she'll come back to see me some day, make her go *oooohhhhhh* when I ZigZag the dishes so fast, make her proud of the only baby come out her pussy. I ZigZag back up to the surface before Singer sees I been away.

We sit for a few minutes, just talking on the inside. The wind's blowing now, whipping some of those papers up into the air. Two big trucks pull out, GLOBAL EXPRESS on the side, and Singer waves and smiles at both the drivers. I pick up the magazine with the naked ladies and look at it some more, flipping the pages back and forth and looking at the different bodies. I ain't never seen something so amazing as a woman's pussy. Maybe soon I'll touch a real one, see how it feels and smells.

"You ever touched a pussy?"

Singer smiles, nodding his head real slow.

"What's it feel like?"

Now he's scratching behind his ear, trying to pull it back. "It's wet. And warm. And slippery."

"Like a greasy plate before I rack it?"

"Something like that."

"I wonder when I'll touch a pussy."

"There'll be plenty of time for that. Stick to the magazines for now."

"When then?"

"When what?"

"When can I touch a real pussy?"

"Uh, not until you're eighteen."

"Why?"

"That's just the age you have to be."

"You have to be one eight to touch a woman's pussy?"

"Yeah . . . yeah you do."

"You said you can make the baby starting when you're one five."

"Well, that's the technical age. For the woman. That's how old the woman has to be. But you . . . see, the man has to be one eight before he can actually touch a woman there. It's complicated."

"I don't understand."

"I know. And you never will because that's just how women are: they're confusing. Just remember one thing, no pussy until you're eighteen."

Inside here everyone waves at Singer and me when we walk by, Singer stopping to stick his head in one of the offices.

"How's it goin, Sarah?"

"Hey, Dino. Good, good. Wow, your little brother is no longer so little."

"Nope. You remember Sarah? She's our comptroller. The lady with all the money."

Both of them looking at me, now she's out of her chair, around the desk and walking towards us. She got a good flower smell.

"I met you when you were this tall," she says, putting her hand out flat. "Still shy, huh?"

"Soon as we get around other people. When we're alone, he talks my ear off. Right?" Singer sneaks his fingers into my side before I can move. It makes me laugh loud and ZigZag out the way.

"So you're off today. What have you guys been doing?"

"Singer taught me all about pussy."

Singer and Sarah both got a surprise look on they faces, looking at each other and then Singer smiling and shaking his head. Now she's nodding her head. "I see, well . . . what are Positive Mentors for? Right?"

"It's not like that." Sarah smiles but she doesn't say anything. "Today was our 'birds and the bees' talk."

"Ahhh, I see. And did we teach ZigZag all the slang terms, or just the choice ones?"

Singer laughs. His whole head is bright red. "So, anyway, moving right along, I came to get my check."

"Right." Then to me, "Singer's our direct deposit holdout."

"I know, I know. It's weird. I like to get an actual check."

I don't know what they're talking about. Sarah walks back to her desk and takes a stack of envelopes out the top drawer. She pulls off the rubber band and flips through them. "Singer, Dean. Guess they didn't fire you after all." She hands him the envelope, smiling.

"Thanks. I'm going to show him around."

"Sex 101 followed by Career Day. Quite the educational big brother you are. What's tonight? Estate planning?"

"Nahhh," Singer says. "We've already done that. Tonight's off-shore tax havens."

Now we're driving back towards the inside of that truck, same thing again, then back toward the rack. I watch him work the levers, backwards and forwards, and push the pedals in and out. Now he's got the teeth lifted up way high, pedal in and out, now forwards towards the giant rack, and then the machine jerks so fast I almost fall off. I grab the bar and look at Singer. Both his hands are on his stomach, eyes slammed shut tight, his face covered with that noise. We're goin fast now, right towards that giant rack, Singer still down in the seat. I ZigZag down close to him, try to help him up, but his hands don't come off his stomach. Then

ZigZag

Singer somehow whispers a plan on the inside of my head. I reach up and turn the little key. When the machine shuts off, it rocks forward and tips up in the air. A box falls off the teeth and almost hits a man in a brown shirt. Then the machine rocks back and sits silent. Now we're surrounded by the people in brown shirts, hands reaching up for Singer. It's like he floats away from me on those invisible hands. Then hands come up to get me, move me down off that machine. They got Singer down on the cement floor, everyone in a circle pulling off orange ears. I leave mine on and just watch mouths move really fast. A lady reaches down and pulls off Singer's hard hat and orange ears, his eyes are still slammed down tight, his hands locked on his stomach. Then someone touches my shoulder, and I feel the ears come off. "Are you OK?" Then my hard hat floats off my head. "ZigZag? You all right?" Things moving in slow motion now, the noise coming up loud at the bottom of my head, right where it hooks into my neck. I turn around. I see the lady who gave Singer his paycheck and then . . .

everything go black

Lunch bastards got lazy and left an extra big stack of bus tubs, big greasy pots, and the oval trays shaped like spaceships. The first thing I got to ZigZag, though, is the heavy black grills that go over the coals. I blast them once with the sprayer, sprinkle on white powder, and start scrubbing before it can turn blue. I see Dale over there splitting heads of lettuce with the black-handled knife. Inside my head I see little cowboy heads lined up on his cutting board and his face all painted up like in the videos. Then when I look again, it's just Dale in the black-and-white checked cook pants and a white shirt with little brown stains down the front. Only part looks Indian is that ponytail. He got the faucet on full blast, the deep metal sink full of cold water, and he sweeps the split heads in there with the side of the blade. When he starts to look up, I drop my head back down and concentrate on the grill, scrubbing so fast smoke comes off the green scrubber.

"You're like a goddamn ostrich, running in and sticking your head in the sand." It's the Toad's voice, close by, so I just ZigZag deeper, grab the next grill, and give it a blast of hot water.

"I know you hear me. You just make yourself available when this detective stops by. Hello? Earth to moron dishwasher?"

The grill slips off the edge of the bus tub and slams down on my fingertip. The noise hurts bad, the finger in my mouth before I got time to remember it's covered with the white scrub powder. I try to spit out the powder, but the taste goes up inside my head and burns my nose. A blast from the sprayer gets rid of the taste, but the hot water burns the inside of my mouth, shaking my head now trying to get the powder taste out.

"Watching you, Louis, is like a round-the-clock advertisement for a vasectomy clinic."

I ZigZag back around and grab the last grill, blast of powder, and then scrub superspeed. The little black balls of burned food fly off the grills, tickling my arms and sticking to my white apron. The Toad walks away yelling at one of the cooks about how she's cutting some meat. I just block it all down and rinse the last grill. Then, one at a time, I carry the grills out front to where one of the cooks already got the coals red as that car lighter. I lift a grill up, the heat coming up in little waves, and drop it in fast before the coals get my arms.

"Careful with that," someone says, except I'm already on my way back for the next one before I can see who said it. Once the grills are all in place, I tear into the dishes superspeed, everyone eyes in the kitchen getting big as I fill the racks and feed them into the machine, my hands blurring together they move so fast. Inside I got a picture of that bottle half full of the noise it sucked out of Singer at the hospital.

When the busgirl comes in to get some clean bus tubs, I ZigZag under the dish station and look to see where she got her thing hidden. I can't see it, but at least now I know where she hides it. I come back up and hand her two clean bus tubs before she can feel my eyes on her.

"Thanks, Louis. You're a sweetheart."

"How old are you?"

"Me?" she asks. "Why?"

"You at least one five?"

"Fifteen? Uh, yeah, I think so. Hello, I'll be eighteen in seven months."

"That's the right age."

"For what?"

I lean over the dish station a little see if she got the flower smell. All I can smell is the wet, silver metal. Her soft rounds are smaller than the ones I saw at the Monkey Club and in the magazines. I can feel the rock coming back again.

"In between one five to four zero. Singer says we don't need a relationship. Just the consenting. But we got to wait until I'm one eight."

"What are you talking about?"

"To do the—"

"Well, well. Figure out where it is yet?" One of the monkey boys is back, that smile on his face again. He's standing next to Tawny on the other side of the dish station. She's taller than him.

"Leave him alone, you jerk."

"Make me."

"You are such an asshole. Ignore him, Louis." She walks out of the kitchen with the bus tubs. Monkey boy's arm comes up, but I ZigZag towards the machine and the handful of pepper sprinkles down to the floor.

"Hah! Almost got you." He leans down and takes three clean bus tubs. "Do it, or I swear to God, you'll get the whole can dumped on your head tonight." Then he turns and walks out the kitchen laughing so loud one of the cooks gives him a look like he's crazy.

When the detective comes in the kitchen, the big clock above the door says eight zero zero. He's right behind the Toad in a dark blue suit and long brown coat. He got a little notepad and a pen in one hand. The Toad got the cigar pointed right at my head as they move this way.

"Louis. My office. Now."

Friday night is always the most dishes. I've been working half speed all night to let the dishes pile up. That way the Toad can't keep me in the office too long, or they'll run out of clean silverware and plates.

"What's with all these dishes? You sandbagging on me, or what?" There's more tubs piled up than what the lunch bastards left.

"Hello, ZigZag." The detective's got a nice voice, and it's good he knows to call me ZigZag.

In the Toad's office it's just me and the detective. He sits in the Toad's chair, where he can look out the little window, still cracked, into the kitchen. Right behind him is the safe. The desk is pushed up against the wall, so I sit on the side near the door in a plastic chair that don't feel too good. The detective has a good smell; not like flowers but something sweet.

"Now ZigZag, your boss said that he already told you about your father and what happened today."

"You sending him to the jail?"

"Well, that's for a jury to decide. He beat her up pretty good. While we had him in custody we asked him about the investigation we're doing here on the stolen money. You remember when we talked about it?"

I nod, trying to sort out fast in my head what I'm suppose to say and not suppose to say. My eyes keep wanting to look at the safe right behind his head, and the more I try not to think about it, the more my eyes want to look over there. Then they do a quick look before I grab them back. He looks at me and then over his shoulder.

"Well, anyway, your dad signed this parental release form today." He unfolds a piece of paper and holds it up. Maybe I could read it with Ms. Tate's help and a few days, but not this fast.

"This gives me permission to question you, on the record, as well as to get your fingerprints. As your legal guardian, he's waived your right to an attorney. Do you understand?"

I nod, but he must see I don't know what he's talking about.

"Let me tell you what we know so far: one, someone went into the safe early Tuesday morning sometime between three-ten, when your boss left with the bar staff, and five past eight, when he returned. Two, whoever opened it had the combination and access to this office because there was no forced entry on the outside doors or the office door. So, in all likelihood our perpetrator is an employee of this restaurant. Three, we lifted a print off the handle that doesn't match your boss's or any of the assistant managers'. So our first step is to check all the employee fingerprints against the one we have. If we find a match, then we've probably got our man, or woman. Do you follow me so far?"

I lean back in the chair, like nothin happened, and nod, slow, slow, slow, try to give my mind some time to think what to say, except it's not sending up any words.

"Now, that's all the background. What I'm really trying to do is figure out who did this. And if whoever did this helps me and works with me, then they won't get in as much trouble than if they try to hide what they did. Do you understand?"

I nod again, slow, trying to sort everything out in my head. "I think I better get back to those dishes. Toad gets mad if they pile up too much."

He grabs my arm gentle and moves me back onto the chair. "We're almost through. Couple more minutes." He pulls a little black machine out his pocket and sets it on the desk. He pushes a button, and the two wheels start turning slow. "This is Detective Jonathan Hawke, interviewing Louis Fletcher, aka ZigZag, regarding case number two three four five seven six dash Adam Charlie. OK, Louis, just relax. The tape recorder is just for accuracy. Now, is there anything you want to tell me about what happened this past Tuesday morning?"

I shake my head, my hands all sticky again and my throat gone completely dry.

"When we brought your father in today, he did not want to cooperate during the questioning. But when I mentioned you, he started to change his tune. We told him if he'd cooperate with us on this investigation, we'd work with the D.A. on the assault charge. Unfortunately for you, Louis, it didn't take him long to roll over. He told us that you took the five thousand dollars."

Every time I wipe the sticky off my hands, it comes back double. My eyes go down to the floor trying to find out what to say. Just outside the door I can hear the waiters and waitresses going in and out the kitchen. The door never stops swinging. My fingers get the tingle thinking about all them dishes piling up, that machine gone cold with a big monkey boy smile.

"ZigZag? Do you have something to say?"

I see my dad bring the Black Beauty over his head, then that little bit of time where everything goes quiet. In that space the voice comes back just like he's standing here whispering into my head:

Ain't no free ride around here. Understand what I'm sayin? You stole this shit from that fat fuck cracker you workin for? You bull-shittin me, boy? How the fuck you get all this? Five thousand dollars here!

Goddamn, Ne—gro. We fuckin stylin now! Clear my ass with Cadillac Tom. . . . where you got five grand, you can get me some more. . . .

Then the flash of black and the noise explodes across the back of my head. I push it all out and grab the side of the desk to keep everything from spinning. The detective is tipped sideways now, his mouth moving but the words coming out all mixed up. He's up out of the chair, out the door.

> alone
> hook up the tube and suck out that noise

hook it up
alone
suck that noise right on out
good
good
noise go away can't never come back

Hospital got a smell makes my head hurt. Like that bleach bottle is under my nose no matter which way I turn my head. A needle stuck in Singer's arm connects to a little tube connects to a bottle hanging over his head. The bottle's half full of clear noise it sucked out of Singer. They got a lot of other tubes and wires hooked into Singer trying to push or pull that noise out, can't tell which. A machine makes a little sound reminds me of Singer's two-teeth monster, *beep beep beep beep beep.*

Lots of people came to see Singer, except only two I know: that lady said I could live with Singer and the lady give Singer his paycheck. The paycheck lady stayed for a while when we first got here, Singer and me riding in the ambulance and everything full speed with the flashing lights and siren. Singer kept saying he was all right, let him up, he don't need an ambulance. All those people he works with in brown shirts said he didn't have no choice. Singer's lucky he got so many nice people at his work. When the noise gets me at the Toad's restaurant, about the only person might help is big Dale. He'd pick me up same as that pan of cut-up chicken and carry me out to the ambulance. If he ain't working, the monkey boys probably just push me under the dish station to keep me out the way, or the Toad, *goddamn moron worthless blob of cunt spunk*. Since Singer give me the sex 101, I can understand the Toad better.

This man and a lady in white pants and blue jackets put Singer into the back of the ambulance on this bed got wheels. He kept shaking his head, saying how ridiculous it was, except I could see the noise on his face. Made me wonder maybe they gonna take off Singer's other ball. I been keeping my radar on these doctors make sure they don't try and slip in there and take his last one while Singer ain't looking.

Everything was crazy when we first got here, Singer getting wheeled around like he's the human dessert cart, about one zero people in brown shirts following behind and me just ZigZag invisible keep an eye on Singer's ball. Without that ball he can't shoot the sperm in a pussy and grow a baby.

Then this doctor lady blacker than me starts yelling that there's too many people in here and only immediate family was allowed to stay. All the people in brown shirts said good-bye to Singer and hugged him and touched his hand. That's when the paycheck lady and the caseworker lady left. Can't remember her name, something like Jam-son or something. Now it's just me and Singer and the doctor lady. She's looking at papers on this metal clipboard and writing something. Then before I got time to ZigZag invisible, she looks right at me.

"Unless there's some African somewhere in Mr. Singer's family tree, you need to leave."

"What?"

"You'd better hurry before they leave."

"Before who leaves?"

"Your group."

"They ain't my group. Singer's my group."

"Well, Mr. Singer needs to rest."

"I'll wait."

"Not in here you won't."

"You said family."

"Right."

"Singer the only family I got."

"How's that?"

"He's my big brother."

She gives me a look up and down, running her radar so hot I can smell it. Then she breathes out and starts writing again. "Five minutes. Then you're leaving."

OK, that's good, cus where else I'm gonna go. . . . Friday, today's Friday, which means I got to ZigZag the Toad's dishes.

"What time's it?"

"Three-thirty."

"Four three zero I ZigZag the Toad's dishes."

She runs that radar over me again, make sure she didn't miss something before. She got eyes so big she probably don't need the radar, plus a face that never changes too much. Now she's looking at the little machine, writing again on the metal clipboard, then checking the wires hooked into Singer.

"What's all them wires for?"

"Different things. Mainly precautionary monitors."

She looks up with one eye while her hand keeps writing. Just behind her there's another bed with a curtain wrapped around it. I can see a bony foot with little white hairs in the space where the curtains don't touch. The foot don't move, just sits there like it's dead all on its own.

"What's he here for?"

She looks up and then over her shoulder. "She. You say Mr. Singer's your big brother?"

149

"Not for real my big brother. But we been together five years."

Now she's folding up her clipboard, slipping the pen in a pocket on her white jacket. "We should let him rest now."

I look at Singer. Somehow he looks smaller in this bed, his whole body sunk way down low, like those machines sucking out everything, bad stuff and good stuff all draining into that bottle together. Looks like he'll sleep fine whether I stay or go.

"You didn't tell me what all them wires are for."

She breathes out and looks at her watch. "Has anyone explained to you that your big brother is very sick?"

"Singer said he got the noise in his ball so they took it off." I flip on my radar extra sensitive and lean in close to her. "You the one took it?"

"No, I didn't." First time she's smiling a little. "One of our best surgeons did the operation."

"Why they take Singer's ball?"

"Dean has what we call 'testicular cancer,' which means there were bad cells in his testicle. By removing the testicle we hoped it would also remove the bad cells."

"Then how come he still sick?"

"The cancer, or the bad cells, had already spread. It spread very rapidly into his abdomen and lungs."

"So he still got the noise inside."

"Yes, unfortunately. The chemo hasn't been as successful as we'd like to see at this stage and today . . ." I ZigZag down low and look at Singer, his eyes still slammed tight. Her mouth is moving in slow speed, words floating away before I hear what they say. I got to watch her close make sure she don't try to grab Singer's other ball. I pick up Singer's hand and hold it like I seen the pay-check lady do. His hand feels small, like he really is shrinking. ". . . the sedative to help him sleep. He should be fine to leave tomorrow; we just want to keep an eye on him for the rest of the night. Do you have any questions?"

I shake my head and squeeze Singer's hand a little tighter to signal him that I'm here. She looks down and breathes out slow again. Now she's looking right at me with those big eyes. "He's very sick. You need to be prepared for the worst."

I nod my head. I flash her the numbers to the Toad's safe just to see if she knows anything. She don't know Singer and me already seen the worst together. What could be worse than the Toad and Jenna coming in the office while we were under the desk?

"Do you have a ride, or do you need to call someone? Your parents?"

Something about this doctor lady don't feel right, so I got to ZigZag out of here quick. "I got a ride. Time to go ZigZag me some dishes."

The doctor lady walks to the door and moves her head for me to follow. I look at Singer again, touch his hand, and just listen to that machine *beep beep beep beep beep*.

Outside the hospital the sun's still full bright, except the wind is blowing now. It feels a lot colder than it looks. I zip up my leather jacket. Down further is a metal fence with all kinds of trash held on it by the wind and beyond that the freeway. Maybe Singer will be done resting when I finish washing the Toad's dishes.

I ZigZag over the fence so fast it gets mad and takes a little bite off my knee, same leg the monkey boys smashed into the dish station. On the other side of the fence I bend down and touch the little tear in my pants. My fingers turn red, except the hurt hasn't got to my brain. Maybe I should go back now, show them my cut leg. They could wheel that white-haired-foot lady out the room and put me next to Singer. Instead I slide down the little hill on my butt and walk to the edge of the freeway.

Cars and trucks go slower when you're inside. Standing here now they're flying by superfast. When the trucks go by, they throw little rocks at me. One of the little rocks hits me in the head. I stick out my thumb like I seen when me and Singer are driving around and try to block out his voice telling me never to do this. I forget what he calls it.

After standing a long time with the thumb out, a green car pulls off the freeway and stops. I run towards the car watching the little red lights glow in the back and the smoke coming out the little pipe, a lot more smoke than comes out most cars. When I get to the side of the car, the man's already leaned over and got the door open. He looks as old as Singer, two nine, except he got a lot more hair and different colored paint all over his clothes and face. His car got a smell like the employee toilet at the restaurant.

"Jump in."

All I can think when I get in is how Singer won't be too happy I used the thumb to get a ride.

"Where you headed?"

"ZigZag some dishes at the Toad's."

"Come again?"

The man moves the lever under the steering wheel, and the car starts forwards. When he cranks back up to full speed, I can hear the little rocks hitting underneath the car. "Where to, partner?"

"You know a restaurant on Riverside, the Grub & Grog?"

"Sounds familiar. What kind of food they got?"

"Same food as everywhere else."

"Ain't that the fuckin truth." The man laughs real crazy like it's the funniest thing he ever heard. Then he takes a little cigarette out the ashtray looks like the Toad's cigar except all white.

"So what's the story at this Grub & Grog? You got some pussy lined up there?" He does that laugh again sounds like a toy machine gun I had when I was little.

"We got lots of pussy now I know where they keep it hidden."

"Fuckin-a, right, brother. Fuckin-a." He pulls the lighter out, and it glows bright red, touches it to the miniature cigarette. He sucks on it a long time and then in a funny voice says, "Wanna hit?"

I just shake my head. Watching the Toad chew his unlit cigar is all the smoking ZigZag will ever need. Then still in that same funny voice, "You don't get high?"

When I don't say nothin, he just looks at me. "That's cool. No problem. One man's chemical is another man's . . . whatever." He laughs again. "What's this place called again?"

"Grub & Grog."

"Grub & Grog . . . so there's a lot of action there, huh?"

"I guess. Toad said I broke his window on Monday."

"I'm with you there. See this?" He turns his head and pulls down his shirt collar. There's a thick scar on his neck runs up past his ear. "I know all about broken windows. Out at the Prairie Dog one night, and this guy gets all tweaked out, said I was hitting on his old lady. I was like, this double-bag bowser here? Fucker threw me through the plate glass window. Crazy coyote damn near cut my head off." He drives with one hand and smokes the little cigarette with the other, most of the time talking in that funny voice. "So anyway, about that action. If there's enough to go around, you think you could hook me up?"

The only kind of hookup in my head is the way they got Singer with all them tubes and wires. "You got the noise?"

"Noise, toys, and evil ploys, I got it all. Payday today. Bought a dime bag to get things cookin, and now I'm ready for some pussy! Tell you what, bro, it's twenty-four seven looking for that little fur triangle."

"Why you got paint all over you?"

He does the crazy laugh again, then starts coughing. He rolls down the window halfway and coughs outside and then coughs some more inside. When he finally stops, he says, "You are too fucking much. So how you know about this place?"

"What place?"

"Grub & Grog?"

"Singer got me the job there ZigZag the dishes."

"You work there? You gonna find me some pussy while you're working?"

"I know right where it is."

He yells like a crazy man, slams the steering wheel, and turns up the radio louder than it's already been. Now he's got to yell for me to hear him. "Fuckin Friday night!" Then he rolls the window down all the way and sticks his head out. "Yeeeeeeeeeeahhhhhh." When he comes back in, he says, "So this woman. She hot?"

"Everyone we got there is hot," I yell over the radio, except he's trying to light that little cigarette again. It's so small now he can barely hold it. When I roll down my window, the air rushes in cold and feels good. Papers start blowing up from the backseat, and I watch one get sucked out his window.

"Tax return. No sweat." Then he laughs crazy again and puts the little cigarette in the ashtray. The freeway is crowded with cars and big trucks, and he has to swerve a couple times to make it over to the sign says RIVERSIDE AVENUE with a big arrow. As we roll off the freeway and slow down on the little hill, the papers start to settle back behind us. Now things look more familiar, the dough-nut store, the video store, then pretty soon the gas station and the Toad's restaurant.

"There it is, right?"

I nod. We have to wait for the traffic to clear before turning left into the parking lot behind the restaurant. The cook who threw the spoon at my head disappears through the kitchen door just as we pull up.

"So how do we play this, partner?"

"Play?"

"This woman. How you gonna get me in the saddle?"

He stops the car by the kitchen door, the engine still running. I roll up my window. Now when I look close, his eyes are red like he needs some sleep. "Don't jack me around, little brother. I gave you your ride. Now it's your turn."

"I got to go ZigZag the Toad's dishes." I start to open the door except his hand grabs my jacket and pulls me back. For a little guy he got a damn strong hand.

"Don't fuckin tweak me out here. You said you were going to hook me up with this babe. Now where is she?"

"Where is she who?"

The punch comes up like a flash of light and snaps my head into the window. No one's hit me since I moved in with Singer, but how it feels comes back real fast. The noise always starts slow, then spreads out from where the hit came like little electricity, then the long, deep hurt that hangs around to remind you where you got punched. Now he's got my jacket again, that fist cocked back, a look in his eyes I seen plenty of times before. "Now you gonna get me laid, or do I have to kick your ass?"

Just like my dad and the Toad, asking questions that ain't got no good answer. I try to ZigZag loose, but his hand has me good. Another punch lands on my shoulder. Now my body goes automatic, tensing up full tight, everything closed waiting for the next blast. I ZigZag down deep inside, away from everything until I get to the quiet spot. Then a loud *WHAM WHAM WHAM* . . . except away from my body . . . *WHAM WHAM* . . . outside the car . . . a hand slamming the car hood. Without opening my eyes, I get a little smile on the inside. This got to be the first time I ever been happy to hear the Toad's voice: "The hell is this?"

I open my eyes, and the Toad's face is in the window, greasy and wet and full of little holes like always, except this time it sure is nice to see.

"None of your business, doughboy."

"Christ, Louis. What now?"

"Just get the hell away from my car."

"Fine. Let's go, Louis. Get your ass in that kitchen before I help this yahoo kick your ass."

I push open the car door, except his little hand still got me. Twisting my body doesn't even break his grip.

"You just back off. Me and him got some business."

Now the Toad's working the little cigar around the corner of his mouth, back and forth, spit a little tobacco flake, now pointing it at the man like it's got magic powers. "You wanna have a little butt party, go find someone else. Louis here has work to do."

"Fuck you, I ain't no faggot."

"I know, sweetie, just let him go and get this car off my property before I cut it up with a meat cleaver."

"Fuck you."

The Toad steps forwards. His hand shoots in the car window, grabs the man's head, and slams it into the steering wheel two times, *WHAM WHAM*. The man's head comes away from the steering wheel with blood dripping from both sides of his nose. He's spitting blood but seems a little confuse about how that hand came in the car so fast. "Fuck you!"

The hand lets go, and I ZigZag out the car. The man looks at me and yells through the window I already closed, "You little punk bastard. We ain't finished." Then he tries to open his door, but the Toad slams it shut.

"Uh-uh, sweetie. You don't want to come out here. You know why?"

"I don't give a shit why, I'm going to—"

"Because I'm ready to start biting, and my bites don't stop until something disconnects from your body. Fingers, ears, nipples, don't matter. I've seen your little gook cocks. No bigger than this." The Toad points his little finger up towards the sky. The man leans away with the same look everyone gets in they eyes when the Toad starts talking.

"Fuckin weirdo . . ."

"C'mon. Whip out your little gook cock for me. I want to disconnect that worthless toothpick from your body. Show me your gook cock."

The tires spin loud, and the car goes full speed ahead and out of sight around the Toad's building. He walks towards me shaking his head.

"How old are you, Louis?"

"One five."

"Fifteen." He just chews his little cigar for a minute and watches the cars go by. The man with the green car and bloody nose speeds by, honking and waving the finger at us. "Fifteen. Now if that isn't a fucking miracle, I don't know what is."

I'm not sure what the Toad means, a miracle I'm one five or if he's still talking about gook cocks, whatever that is, so I just watch him work the white tip on that cigar. He's looking out across the parking lot past the gas station. He points the cigar at the sky. "What the hell is that saying? Red sky tonight . . . red sky . . . red tonight . . . something's all right?" He looks at me and then back at the sky. "I'm asking you? Red sky at night . . . something's all right. . . . Fuck, I don't know."

I'm confuse about the sky, but I like listening to the Toad talk about it. He got a different kind of voice out here than he does in the kitchen, one more like Singer got all the time. We just stand here looking at the sky and listening to the cars drive by. A plane flies over us, and the Toad cranks his head way back to watch it. His body looks even funnier like this, his head bent backwards, then a big round belly, and then skinny legs like a frog. The cold air is sneaking in around us, coming out in little clouds when we breathe. The kitchen door slams open. Now it seems even darker out here when the light from the kitchen pours out. It's one of the monkey boys dragging a garbage can he can barely move.

"Hello, Louis. Seen the pepper can?" He's got that same smile he got when he put the burn in my eye.

"Better ask Dale. He the last one I seen with it."

The smile goes off his face like he don't know what to say. Then he turns and keeps dragging the garbage can towards the dumpster. "We'll see" is all he says.

Toad gives me a funny look and then, "All right, let's go." His voice is changed back now. He's waving the little cigar at me to get in the kitchen.

"Oh, almost forgot. Remember that detective? Small fucking world, but your old man got hauled in, drunk off his ass, for beating the shit out of some crack whore in a pool hall on Nineteenth. Unlucky day for your pop, turns out the crack whore is an under-cover cop. Tricky fuckin cunts, aren't they? Anyway, she was on some investigation with this yahoo Hawke working my case, and when they pulled your dad's rap sheet they made the connection. Said he'll stop by tonight. Wants to talk to you again." The Toad gets in so close with his radar he's got to take out the cigar so it don't poke me in the chest. "Why's he wasting his time chasing you? Your old man roll over on you?"

"Is my dad going to jail again?"

"Beating on a cop? Yeah, I'd say so."

I listen for how this makes me feel. For some strange reason, it don't feel right on the inside, even if all he did was knock the noise into my head. I can see the surprise look my dad got in his eyes when he saw the Toad's money, how for a few minutes I really thought I done something good.

"So he roll over on you or what?"

I ZigZag into the kitchen, punch the time clock, and attack the stack of dishes the lunch bastards left before the Toad can ask any more mixed-up questions, his voice coming back again: "So he roll over on you or what?"

When everything goes bright again, the restaurant sounds extra loud. The detective hands me a glass of water. I suck it down so fast it makes me cough, little bits of the water getting sucked up into my head, then big gulps of air when I can breathe again.

"Slow down, take it easy," he says, a hand rubbing along my shoulder. Always slow down, slow down, slow down. His hand feels the same as when Singer rubs my back after I go black out. When the air comes back normal, I sit up. He closes the door and sits down in the Toad's chair.

"You all right?"

I flash him a quick nod and wipe the wet off my forehead.

"You sure?"

I nod again. Sometimes when I go away like that, somehow I come back with new ideas. That's the special powers Singer taught me. He says you got to look on the inside to find your answers, that all your strength comes from somewhere deep down inside. That's when my radar reminded me how my dad brought out the Black Beauty the time my friend was over at our apartment and broke a window. My friend said right away that he did it so I wouldn't get in trouble. Then my dad turned to me and asked me was that true. When I nodded yes, he told my friend to leave. As soon as the door closed, he started swinging the Black Beauty harder than I ever seen him swing it, *I swear I'll kill you, you ever rat on someone again.* My dad would knock me across the room for sneezing wrong, but he'd never rat on no one. Not even me.

"I know you need to get back to work. Now we've got your dad's statement, and we can get your prints any time. It will make things a lot easier for everyone if you just tell me right now. Did you take the money from the safe early Tuesday morning?"

My mouth wants to yell how there's nothing to worry about, me and Singer are working on a new plan to get that five two four one back in the safe, maybe get that reward money, and move away. Except I got Singer's voice to remind me what to do, *just act like nothin happened.* Me and the detective just look at each other. He breathes out slow and shakes his head. He reaches down and turns off the little black recorder. Maybe now he's done asking questions, which is good because the dishes in the kitchen are giving off that ringing sound.

By the time I ZigZag through the stack of dishes, the clock says one zero one nine. I went and told Dale I was hungry, and he just gave me a smile and told me to wait back by the dish station. A few minutes later he came back with a frying pan covered with a napkin. I thought he was just bringing it for me to wash. I started to scrape it out into the disposal. He grabbed my arm and yelled, then pointed at the full lobster tail all juicy with just a little bit of brown on top. He said eat it quick before the Toad saw. I tasted lobster before out of the tubs, but never hot with no bites missing. Dale even came back again with a little cup of butter so hot it

bubbled. He showed me how to dip the lobster into the cup and
soak up the butter before eating the lobster. The lobster and hot
butter is the best food I ever ate at the restaurant. When I went
back out to ask for another one, he just gave me a look like I was
crazy and said, in a whisper, "That's all I can get tonight."

The monkey boys been back twice, both times with big hand-
fuls of pepper. First time I blasted the pepper right out of the air
with the sprayer. Second time they snuck up quiet where my radar
couldn't see them. I ZigZagged low and missed one handful, but
the other monkey boy threw his from across the dish station and it
landed full in one eye. The burn shot deep in my head worse than
I ever felt while I moved over and grabbed the sprayer. It took a
few long blasts to clean out all the burn. Ever since my eye feels
like that pepper's in so deep the sprayer can't reach it. Tawny's
been back lots of times, dropping off the full tubs. Each time I see
her coming, I ZigZag low and grab the clean tubs for her. She
always smiles nice, my nose working extra hard try to detect the
flower smell. It don't matter how many times those monkey boys
come after me with the pepper. I got to ask Singer how you know
when you got the consenting, but I think me and Tawny have it.
I'd rather see where she got her thing hidden than make her mad
for the stupid monkey boys.

"Louis!"

The Toad's voice always makes me jump, even when I'm pretty
sure I ain't done nothin wrong. I can't see him over behind the ice
machine. "Some lady named Tate called looking for you. You line
up some action we don't know about?"

I still can't see him, but I can hear him laughing with one of the
cooks. "So anyway, this bitch sounded pretty hot. So, naturally, she
immediately took an interest in me and dumped you. Figured
you'd understand."

The clock says one zero three six. I ZigZag into the tub Tawny
just dropped off, rack it, and slide it into the machine. The Toad's
still talking.

". . . she said to tell you she just wanted to make sure you're all right. Ahhh, isn't that sweet?"

Then I remember something that makes my body slow way down until I'm racking at half speed, no hurry, just slow, slow, slow. Most of the night I forgot about the ambulance ride and the hospital and that bottle sucking the noise out Singer's arm. So the longer it takes me to get out of here, the more time I'll have to think up a plan for where to sleep tonight.

When the kitchen door slams shut behind me, I turn and stare at it. After a few seconds the little light around the edges goes black. The last couple hours I let the dishes pile up real good to keep me surrounded by the warm steam. The Toad came back, looked at all the dishes, and told me I was staying until every last spoon was clean and stop milking the clock. Then he walked over and punched my time card and dropped it into the metal rack. That didn't seem right, me cleaning all those dishes for free, so I went back up to full speed and finished in less than two zero minutes. Just before I walked out the kitchen, the clock said one two zero.

Even though I been in there extra time, no good plan came into my head. Singer must be asleep or using all the special powers to get rid of that noise. Normally the plan comes right into my head, in his voice, just like he's whispering in my ear. Only one plan came, in the ZigZag voice, the same plan I always had before I moved in with Singer. Somehow now it don't seem right, though, sleeping in the Toad's attic with everything that happened with the five two four one and that detective and all the questions.

The air feels single digits like it did last night. The little clouds of cold puff out my head each time I breathe and float off my sneakers and the bottom of my jeans. The gate to where the ladder is makes a loud scraping noise when I pull it open, then loud when I close it. Feels strange going up this ladder again, alone, Singer in the hospital instead of right behind me. For some reason, tonight it seems like there's more city lights. They twinkle through the cold in every direction.

When I pull on the door, it doesn't open. I pull harder, and my hand slips off. I fall backwards and land in a patch of crusty snow, then crawl back over to the door until my eyes adjust to the black. Now there's a silver lock that was never there before. Why couldn't the Toad wait until summer to figure out he should lock this door?

I ZigZag back down the ladder and then over the fence instead of through the gate. The lights from a car flash across the building. I just lean into the wall and watch the car pull in, the little red lights in the back going silent. A woman gets out, locks the door, and then starts walking this way. Her heels click loud on the pavement. I almost yell to tell her we closed two hours ago. Instead I sink invisible into the wall and shut off my thoughts so she can't see me. She turns and disappears around the corner by the road she just come off. Now it's like Singer's voice is back in my head telling me to follow her.

I ZigZag behind her, silent, her heels still clicking. She got jeans that fit tight and stop before they get all the way down her leg. The bottoms of her legs must be damn cold. She got a black furry coat to keep the top half warm. A little cloud of cold air puffs out behind her head and floats up into the streetlight. She knocks on the front door of the restaurant and looks at her wrist while she waits. When she looks this way, I ZigZag slow behind a tree and disappear. The door opens, and she goes inside. I rush up quick and catch her smell before it follows her into the building, a smell I know but can't pull back all the way. A plan comes into my head to wait and maybe she'll take me to the hospital where they got Singer. Then I'll ZigZag past that doctor lady and sleep on the floor next to Singer's bed. That will be better than using the thumb. Singer was right on that one: the thumb's not a good way to go places.

It seems like a long time before I hear the heels clicking on the pavement again. I'm sitting in a tight little ball against the wheel of her car with my hands as deep as they'll go in my jacket pockets. I stand up and start towards her. When she sees me she stops, then steps backwards. Her hand comes out her purse holding up something black.

"Back the fuck off," she says.

I don't move. She's still walking backwards.

"My boyfriend will be right out."

"The Toad's your boyfriend?"

She stops, leans towards me like she's trying to get a closer look. "What did you call him?"

"The Toad?"

Now she smiles, then laughs a little. "The Toad. That is the most perfect description I have ever heard. That's exactly what he is, yeah . . . you said it." Then her smile goes away, and she holds up her hand again. "So how do you know him?"

"I work here."

"Sorry to hear that. Well, if you don't mind, I'd like to go home." She waves her hand and starts walking this way again, slow. She goes the long way around me and then back towards her car, her eyes locked on me the whole time with that hand held up. Now she's on the other side of her car, a white one that's smaller than Singer's car and all one color, still looking this way. When I start walking towards her, the hand comes up again.

"Pepper spray. Stay the fuck back less you want this shit in your eyes."

I stop walking. Why does everybody want to put the pepper burn in my eyes? She opens the door and slides in the car real fast, slamming the door and locking it. The engine starts up, now the lights. She's just watching me, running her radar up and down through the glass. Then the window comes, automatic, but not all the way. She turns her head sideways and yells through the little gap, "C'mere."

I ZigZag over, slow, slow, slow, so I don't scare her. I lean down and look at her. Even at full blast her heater's a lot quieter than Singer's. A good flower smell is coming from inside the car.

"How old are you?"

"One five." Maybe she's checking me for the consenting.

"Fifteen? And that creep's got you working this late?" She points at the dark building. "So what do you do?"

"ZigZag the dishes."

She sticks a cigarette in her mouth and pushes in the lighter on the dashboard. She takes out the unlit cigarette and points it at me like the Toad and his white-tipped cigar. People are all pretty much the same.

"You're a dishwasher? You weren't going to bother me."

I shake my head, breathe in the good smell. She's got good radar. She pulls the lighter out, and it glows bright red in the dark. She touches the end of the cigarette, and the red jumps across, now glowing in two places. She plugs the lighter back into the dashboard and blows out a big cloud of smoke.

"Still scared the hell out of me. You shouldn't be hanging around out here this time of night. Your parents coming or something?"

"My dad's in jail."

"Your mom?"

"She died while she was having me. Maybe. Singer says we don't know."

"Jesus . . ." She shakes her head and sucks on the cigarette, then blows the smoke out real slow. "You're gonna freeze your nuts off you stay out here."

"I think they already frozen."

She laughs and shakes her head. Then the window goes all the way down automatic. "Stick your head in here." When she says it, something in my brain clicks, the way she sounded, then *stick my head in his microwave* comes into my head in her same voice, a picture of legs so close I could touch them, the Toad's fat fingers in black underwear. She's running her radar up close on me now, taking long puffs on the cigarette. "What's your name?"

"ZigZag."

"ZigZag?"

"Two big *Z*'s, two little *g*'s. Singer give me the name."

"Who's Singer?"

"My big brother."

She sucks on the cigarette and blows the smoke out slow again, her eyes always on me. "You're a little weird. But you seem pretty harmless. You need a ride somewhere?"

I ZigZag into the car so fast she jumps back a little, holds the can up again just a few inches from my face. I press myself back against the door so she's not scared. She shakes her head, drops her hand, and flicks the lit cigarette out my window. Then my window goes up automatic, the heat already circling around my feet and up my legs.

"You need to learn to slow down. All right?" She presses her hand on my leg and squeezes real soft. "Take it easy. Now where to?"

Now the flower smell is stronger. Last night I only saw her bottom half. Her top half looks real nice. Her hair is straight brown down to the shoulders of the black furry jacket. The jacket has a silver zipper that's pulled halfway down. When I see her soft rounds under a little black top, the rock tingles in my pants.

"Hello? Where to?"

She got a nice smile. All of a sudden the car is real hot, her heater going full speed, so I slip off the black leather jacket. She breathes out, heavy, then rubs around her eyes like Singer does when he's thinking. "You don't have anywhere to go."

When she looks at me, I don't know what to say, wondering whether it's a question I'm supposed to answer and hoping she won't make me leave the warm car. She shakes her head and looks at me again.

"I don't know why in the hell I'm doing this." She moves the gear lever and pulls out of the Toad's parking lot. She turns on the radio, the heater still blasting full speed.

"That creepy boss of yours, the Toad?—god, I love that name— you know he's not really my boyfriend. I was just saying that to scare you. So how long you worked at that dump?"

I try to pull back the number except all I can think of is the numbers to the Toad's safe and the five two four one.

"You don't know how long?"

I shake my head.

"So what's it like, you know, working for the Toad?"

"He yells a lot and runs around with that little cigar he never lights."

"Yeah. What is the deal with that? He is such a pig."

"How old are you?"

"Me," she says, pointing at herself. "Twenty-two. Jenna, by the way. Nice to meet you." Her hand feels soft, and I hold it until she pulls away. Even when her hand's gone, I can smell the flower smell she left on me.

"So where do you stay if your dad's locked up?"

"With Singer."

"Your brother, right?"

"Yeah."

We're on a road I've never seen that's got three lanes both directions and houses everywhere. The street's lit up bright, but the houses all look dark out there like they trying to keep warm in the cold air. I know there's cats hiding under the parked cars to keep warm, but I haven't seen any of the little cat eyes glowing in the dark.

"I could take you there."

"Where?"

"To your brother's."

I think about Singer hooked up to all those machines in that room with that nasty foot that don't move behind the other curtain, those little white hairs. There wasn't another bed in that room, and Singer never gave me my own key to his apartment. I'll have to get that from him tomorrow when he comes home.

"Are we headed the right way for your brother's place?"

"He's in the hospital."

"You're kidding. Well someone sure dealt you a shit sandwich this week. What's wrong with him?"

She touches another cigarette with the red glow and drops her window just a little to suck out the smoke. The cold air whistles outside like it's mad it can't get in here with us, mix up with the warm air.

"They took off one of his balls. Today I had to keep my eye on the other one . . . make sure they didn't take it, too."

"You got a strange way of saying things." She sucks on the cigarette and flicks the ashes out the window while she drives with the other hand. "What's he got, like testicle cancer?"

"Don't know about that. Just sometimes the noise gets him real bad."

"That sucks."

We turn off this road and slip down through the dark onto a freeway. She switches the radio station a lot and then pulls out a little shiny disc, and her radio swallows it up.

"You into hip-hop?"

I really don't know what she's talking about.

"You like metal?" She points at the dashboard.

I nod just to make the questions stop.

The song makes her move her head and smile when she sings. I just lean my head back on the seat and listen to her voice. She sucks on the cigarette in between the words, tapping on the steering wheel with one hand and driving with the other, then blows the smoke out during the singing. A big truck rolls past her window, then a dirty trailer covered with holes. I see some pink noses that look wet sticking out the holes. The trailer has lots of red and yellow lights and black flaps that hang down with silver naked ladies on them.

Jenna turns down the music and flicks the lit cigarette out the window before it closes automatic. "You hungry? I'm hungry. I could go for some strawberry waffles with whipped cream. Doesn't that sound good?"

I don't think I've ever had the waffles, but her voice makes it sound good.

"You're awfully quiet. But I'll take that as a yes. Waffle Shack is just up here." She points this way out into the night. Her fingernails are long and bright red. "My treat."

We pull off the freeway onto a road that leads up to another street that's lit up full bright. There's no houses here, just gas stations and some kind of big white building and rows of different stores up and down the street both directions. She turns right and then right again. The Waffle Shack is a white building with a red sign. She has to drive around the back of the building to find a parking space. We get out and walk toward the building.

"Lots of people eating waffles tonight."

"Yeah, bar crowd and people who got nothing better to do. Basically, the people like us: screw-ups and losers." She puts her arm out, and I hold it.

The light is so bright inside it takes a few minutes for my eyes to come back. There's no tables, so we have to stand inside the doorway with seven other people. There's smoke everywhere, like an indoor cloud that mixes up with the people voices coming from all the booths. One of the screw-ups or losers waiting, I can't tell which, is looking right in my eyes. His hair is almost as short as Singer's, his skin superwhite like the plates at the restaurant, and for some reason he's only wearing a tight yellow T-shirt, no jacket, that says BLOW ME in big red letters. He's got metal rings stuck in his ears, eyebrows, cheeks, lips, nose. I think the girl standing next to him is looking at me, too, but it's hard to tell through her sunglasses. She has purple hair. They don't talk on the outside, just stare at me like they're sleeping standing up. Jenna's talking to a girl, except I can't hear what they're saying.

My fingers get the tingle from the dishes being washed in the kitchen. The sound is coming from over there, but all I can see is the cooks putting the plates of food in the little opening to the kitchen. I could ZigZag back there, rack and stack all the dishes, and float back out here before Jenna lets go of the smoke she just sucked in. Her lips leave sticky red marks on the ends of her cigarettes.

When we finally sit down, Jenna orders us both the strawberry waffles with whipped cream. I tell her I want Dr Pepper, but instead she orders us two cups of coffee, lots of cream, lots of sugar. We're in a booth back in the corner, where all I can see is her head and then behind her the dark parking lot. There's two screw-ups or losers out there sharing one cigarette, the little red glow moving back and forth between them and getting brighter when they pull in the smoke. Jenna's got her black furry coat off now with just the little black top to cover her soft rounds. When the coffee comes, she puts out her cigarette in the ashtray, watching herself squish the end. Then she pulls out another cigarette, sticks it in her mouth, and moves her head towards the flame from the purple lighter.

"So you're probably wondering what I was doing with your boss, right? Well, trust me, I won't be doing this much longer." She sucks on the cigarette and somehow blows the smoke out sideways while she talks straight to me. "It's no big deal, really, the whole escort thing, but it's not like something I want to do forever. Once I finish school . . . I don't know, I mean, where else can I make a thousand dollars in three hours?"

She takes a sip of coffee, then a quick puff, and keeps talking, so I don't tell her about the five two four one I made in less than five minutes. ". . . OK, granted, sometimes it's a real drag. Guys can be such total sleazeballs, but you just turn off. It's all such an act. You don't know how many high-powered guys in this city have me on their payroll, wives, kids, two dogs and a cat at home, the whole thing, and they're out fucking around . . . it's just disgusting when you think about it. But hey, is that my fault? This whole business wouldn't exist if the demand wasn't there. Then again, some of the girls say what we're doing is just as bad, you know, putting out for money. So . . ." She sucks on the cigarette. "I don't know."

When she says this, she blows out a long smoke, then takes another drink of coffee. "So your boss, the Toad. He's the perfect example. Met him, I don't know, couple weeks ago. Wife at home, I don't know if he has kids. God bless those mutants if he does. But he calls me all the time. 'Jenna, can you come by tonight after we close? Jenna, can you meet me at the Lift?' My friend Jordan, she's the one got me started in this, her motto is 'The uglier the mash, the sweeter the cash.' Isn't that great? She says it's like an ugly tax. So someone like your boss? He pays double what I charge my other clients. Don't tell anyone this."

She pulls a roll of money out her jacket pocket, covering it with one hand and spreading it out with her other hand so no one can see it except me. Then she leans closer and says, "Took him for two grand tonight. S-u-c-k-e-r." She leans back, rolls the money up and puts it back in her jacket pocket, then takes another drink of coffee. "So what was I saying?"

I drink my coffee for the first time, which don't taste as good as Dr Pepper. I add more of the cream and the sugar, see if that makes it taste better.

"Oh yeah, about finishing school. So even if I want to do something else, where am I going to make this much? I don't know, some of the girls have met rich husbands, and then they're out. My friend Tia finished her degree, she's a teacher now. If they only knew, she's probably clamped nipple rings on half her students' dads. But she still only started at like twenty-five a year. Twenty-five? I can make double or triple that easy. So . . . I don't know. I'm twenty-two. I'd like to be doing something else by the time I'm twenty-five. But what? Who knows . . . your boss offered me a job last night. You believe that? I could come work with you."

Just as she says it, the waitress brings the waffles. Jenna puts out her cigarette, takes a big bite, and smiles at me while we chew. The strawberry waffles with whipped cream are so good I ZigZag through the whole plate before Jenna finishes her first waffle.

"Didn't like it, huh?"

She got me confuse, so I shake my head.

"It's a joke. Here." She takes my empty plate and slides hers in front of me. "I'm not that hungry." Before she can finish her cigarette, I eat all her strawberry waffles. The Waffle Shack isn't as loud now, no more people waiting to sit down by the door and some of the tables empty in the dark reflection behind Jenna's head. The smoke cloud don't smell good and makes my eyes burn. The clock above the kitchen door says three zero two.

"You've got nice skin color," she says, blowing the smoke out sideways, then pointing the cigarette at me. "You could be a model, I bet. You're fifteen . . . high school, right? You have a girlfriend?"

"I go to the Fellowes School with Ms. Tate."

"Fellowes School. Never heard of that one. Where is that?"

"It's pretty close to the Toad's restaurant."

"Hmmm. Girlfriend?"

"No. Singer just told me about the consenting, so I'm still looking for one. You could be my girlfriend."

"Ahhh," she says, touching my arm with her soft hand again. "You're sweet."

"You're the right age."

"The right age? For what?"

Landon J. Napoleon

"One five to four zero. To make the love."

She smiles, then laughs. "Well we're not shy anymore, are we? No, actually . . . I think I'm a bit old for you."

"Did you make the love with Toad?"

She swallows the coffee and shakes her head, then sucks on the cigarette and blows out the smoke while she says, "No, sweetheart, I'm afraid not. What I do with him is about as far from love as you can get."

"I don't understand."

She sucks on the cigarette and smiles, blowing the smoke as she talks. "That's private stuff. Besides, you're not old enough yet."

"One eight. I know."

"So what's going to happen with your dad?"

"The detective said he'll go to jail again."

"Again? What he do?"

"Beat up a crack whore was really a cop."

"Ouch." She lifts her cup and points at it when the waitress walks by. The waitress stops and fills it. I watch the steam come off the cup and disappear. "So what happens to you now?"

"I live with Singer now."

"How old is he?"

"He's two nine."

"Twenty-nine? And you're fifteen? That's quite an age difference."

"Difference for what?"

"*Difference* meaning he's a lot older than you."

"He's not my brother for real. We only been brothers for the last five years."

"He's like a volunteer?"

"Yeah."

She sips the coffee, makes a face, tears open two more packets of sugar, and dumps them in her cup. "I thought about doing that once. Be a big sister, a role model. You do stuff like this, right? Go out to eat." She waves her hand back and forth between us. Then she doesn't talk for a while, just sips her coffee and stares up at the ceiling. "Don't know why I never did it."

The waitress leaves the check on a little black tray. Jenna pulls a two zero bill from her pocket and sets it on the tray. "So what's your favorite thing you and your big brother have done?"

"I dunno." I never really thought about a favorite thing.

"Come on, there has to be something. Has he ever taken you somewhere like . . . I don't know. Disneyland, some shit like that?"

I shake my head. "We never went nowhere like that. Singer ain't got much money. Said his wife took him to the cleaners in the divorce."

"Well . . . maybe he'll take you when he gets better."

The waitress takes the check and money and then comes back with the change. Jenna slips on her furry black coat. "Not going to tell me your favorite thing?"

"Now I know."

"OK, what?"

"One time me and Singer stole the Black Beauty from my dad."

Jenna leans forward, waving her hand at me. "And? You gotta give me more than that. Tell me what happened." She takes a drink of coffee and smiles real nice. She's easy to talk to like Singer.

"So . . . c'mon. What's the Black Beauty?"

"It's this bat he'd always hit me with when he got mad. We drove way far outside the city to the country to some place with this bridge. Singer let me throw the Black Beauty off the bridge, and then we watched it float on down the river. That was already a pretty damn good day, except that wasn't all, we didn't go home right away, we drove a little farther and built us a big fire ring with these rocks. Singer showed me how to carve the stick, and we cooked hot dogs on a real fire."

Jenna puts her cigarette out in the ashtray, nodding her head. When she looks up she's smiling, then she reaches out and squeezes my arm. "That does sound like one hell of a good day. Better than Disneyland."

● ● ●

Outside the air feels even colder. Jenna smiles when I offer to scrape the cold off the windows while she waits inside the car. Her scraper's not as good as Singer's; it's too small, and it doesn't have the brush on one end to sweep off the cold, so it takes me longer than usual. When I finally get inside the car, I'm frozen up pretty good.

"So is he at Samaritan General?"

"Who?"

"Your big brother."

She's already pulling out onto the road, which only has a few other cars on it now. "I think so, but we don't have to go there."

"Well, I've got to take you somewhere." She turns on the radio; a quiet song plays with no words for her to sing.

"Maybe I could just stay with you."

She shakes her head. "That's not a good idea."

"Why not?"

"Just isn't. It's way late, and I don't want to piss someone off. Like your parents. Or your brother."

"I told you my dad's in jail, my mom—"

"Look, I know. I'm sorry. But that's just the way things are. OK? Buying you breakfast is one thing. What, I'm going to take a fifteen-year-old kid home? No way. I'm sorry. I can't."

I nod, wishing still that I could stay at her apartment. She's got a nice smile and smells good, probably has a real soft bed. Anyway, I didn't like the smell at that hospital, that bony foot with the little white hairs, no good places for me to sleep. I'll sure be glad when Singer comes home tomorrow.

She finds the hospital no problem, the sign lit up SAMARITAN GENERAL just like she said. The place looks a lot bigger coming in this way, lots of little buildings stuck together and going up different levels. Up high on the building in the middle is the red lights. Most of the windows are dark except quite a few with the lights still on. I try to guess which window is Singer's and whether it's lit up or dark, but there's so many I can't tell. Jenna pulls in along the curb where the lights are full bright. There's two ambulances painted orange, white, and blue parked just ahead of us, just like the one Singer and me rode in. A woman in blue pants and a blue jacket closes the back ambulance door and walks in front of the car carrying a big black box that's got tools to fix people like Singer.

"So you never told me your real name."

"ZigZag. Two big Z's and two little g's."

"OK, ZigZag. Well, it's been nice. You're a good breakfast partner. Hope your brother feels better."

"He'll be coming home tomorrow. Singer got the special powers."

"And don't say anything to your boss about our breakfast. Creep's freaky enough as it is. Our secret, OK?"

I just nod. She reaches into her coat pocket and pulls out the roll of money. She takes a one zero zero bill and hands it to me. "Surprise your big brother. Take him to do something nice."

I take the money and put it in my jacket pocket. Then Jenna leans over and gives me a hug, that good flower smell filling my whole head when she's this close. I move my arms up and hold her tight, her furry black coat tickling my chin. Then she pats me a couple times and kisses my cheek as she pulls back into her seat. I ZigZag out the car. She's saying something, but I can't hear what, the car door slamming, now floating inside the hospital with the radar on to make sure that doctor lady doesn't find me, Singer's room number mixing up with Jenna's good flower smell in my head.

Today the doctor lady hooked something called a morphine pump onto Singer's side. It's a special black bag so when the noise gets too bad, all Singer has to do is press a button and the morphine goes automatic into his body. Singer said morphine is a drug that makes the noise go away. One time at the Fellowes School, we learned about the drugs with police talking to us, and pictures of what the drugs look like, and videos of what happens when you take them. They talked about crack and heroin and marijuana and PCP and brought in the real drugs so we could see what they look like. The police said drugs fry out your brain, that you'll go to the jail if you take them. They never talked about the morphine pump. I'm a little bit confuse how some drugs are good drugs and some drugs are bad. You must only go to the jail if you take the bad ones, but who decides which is which?

The great thing about the morphine pump is that it means Singer can come home today. Whenever that noise gets him, he just pushes the button and the morphine blasts away the pain. That way, he don't have to waste time coming here and seeing the doctor every time the noise comes. I'm glad Singer got the morphine pump.

Earlier this morning, a nurse woke me up before I found Singer. She started yelling what was I doing here, get the hell out or she'd call the police, and this ain't no damn hotel. It took me a minute to wake up, and then things started to come back into my head: how Jenna dropped me off, and I looked all over this hospital for Singer's room, that room number over and over in my head, except when I found the number Singer wasn't in there. Neither was that bony foot with the little white hairs. By then the sleep was rushing in on me fast. I looked around the room, and since it was empty I went down on the bed just to rest for a minute. My eyes slammed shut before my head hit the pillow.

After giving me some strange looks, the nurse looked up DEAN SINGER on her computer and said, *Follow me*. I don't know how I got so far away from Singer's room, but it was a long walk from where we started. Singer was up when we got there, sitting on the bed with his legs hanging over the edge reading a magazine about cars. He smiled big when he saw me and then hugged me good for a long time. He kept saying how sorry he was that he wasn't there to pick me up from work, that he called me at work three times and was going to send a taxi when I was done, and did the Toad give me the messages (Singer got mad when I told him the Toad didn't say nothin), that he even called Ms. Tate to see if she could come pick me up, but he couldn't get her so he just left a message. Singer was happy when I told him the Toad said Ms. Tate called me at work. I didn't tell him I forgot to call her back.

Then Singer got real interested when I told him about Jenna coming to see the Toad again and how she took me to the Waffle Shack for the strawberry waffles with the whipped cream and coffee, lots of cream, lots of sugar. That made Singer laugh. He said, *Only you, ZigZag, could be hiding from her under a desk one night*

and getting her to buy you breakfast the next. I didn't really understand what he meant, but we laughed good about it. I told Singer
how Jenna took two zero zero zero off the Toad without even making the love, and how I asked her to be my girlfriend cus she is so
pretty and has the best flower smell I ever seen. We did a lot of
talking on the outside, more than we usually do, right here on his
bed. The nurse even sneaked in an extra tray of the scrambled
eggs and toast and sausage for me.

It's better today cus the bony foot is gone, no little white hairs
watching us from behind those curtains, which are opened all the
way up, the bed stripped down with no sheets or blankets. Damn,
I'm glad that foot is gone.

"Where's the lady was over there, Singer?"

Singer takes another bite of scrambled eggs. He finishes chewing, wipes his mouth with the napkin. Then he looks out the window without saying anything for a long time. Finally, all he says is
"Died this morning."

We take a taxi from the hospital back to Singer's work to get his
car. It looks funny, his car alone way on the other side of the parking lot, probably wondering why we left it here since yesterday.
When the doctor lady was explaining the morphine pump, she
told Singer, "From now on, under no condition are you to drive.
You might feel perfectly fine one minute and then have a severe
onset of pain at seventy miles an hour. The pump will alleviate the
pain, but unfortunately morphine and automobiles don't mix."

"How am I supposed to get around? Take him to school? Get
to work?"

The doctor lady stopped adjusting the pump and stared at
Singer, then at me, and back to Singer. "Mr. Singer, this cancer is
in an advanced stage. Your courage is admirable, but pretending
will not help you or those you care about. Have you prepared this
young man for all the potential outcomes?"

Then Singer did something I ain't never seen him do: he just started crying, so I hugged him. Every time it seemed like he was going to stop, he'd start up again even harder. The doctor lady left us alone. It felt a little weird, me holding Singer while he cried like that. He held me a lot of times when I cried, so I guess maybe what Singer said about the reversal is true now, how it's my turn to take care of him.

Singer gives the taxi driver some money, and we watch him drive off. The sky looks like the water at the bottom of the bus tubs where all the cigarette butts and grease float off the dishes and ashtrays. I lift my arm and squeeze like the sprayer's attached instead of a hand, blast everything away so the sun can shine down on us and chase the cold out. Some birds fly over us so high you can't see their wings, higher than the airplanes, just a giant V-shape floating in the sky. I watch for a long time until they disappear.

"Where those birds going, Singer?"

He drops his head back, scratches the corner of his mouth. Out here in the light I notice little hairs poking through his head. "Geese. Headed south."

"Why south?"

"Warmer in the south."

"Why don't we fly south, Singer? I hate scraping the cold off everything."

Singer looks at me, scratches the side of his head. Then a big smile comes on his face, the biggest one I seen since that noise put him in the hospital. "Yeah, why don't we?"

"Why don't we what?"

"You just said it. Why not?"

"I just said what?" I'm not sure what Singer's talking about, but this is the happiest I seen him since that noise grabbed him yesterday. Now the smile is off his face.

"Yeah, right." He rubs his face and breathes out slow. A dog starts barking over somewhere behind Singer's car. "With what? Unless . . . let's do it."

"Do what, Singer?"

Singer don't answer, he just slips away when I'm not looking and starts walking towards his work building, then turns and waves with his hand. He starts laughing, louder and louder, until he sounds like maybe that morphine already fried his brain.

Inside we walk down the same long hallway with all the glass offices. There's not many people here today like there was yesterday, everything quiet on Saturday at Singer's work. We stop at the paycheck lady's office. She's in her chair behind the desk and jumps a little when Singer knocks on the glass.

"Jesus, you scared me."

"Sorry, Sarah."

Then she's around the desk and hugging Singer before she says, "God, how are you? We were worried sick last night. What are you doing out of bed already?"

Singer pulls back, holding both her hands and smiling. "Slow down. I'm fine."

"Hey there," she says, sneaking a tickle into my side. Then back to Singer, "Are you sure? The doctor said it was OK to leave the hospital?"

"Yeah. There's not much they can do at this point. I told you I didn't need the ambulance. Besides, I've got this now." Singer lifts up his shirt and leans over so she can see.

"What is it?"

"Called a morphine pump. Pain gets too bad, I just push this button and voilà, no more pain."

She don't say nothin, just wipes her nose and hugs Singer again. "I'm sorry." Now she's the one crying, Singer hugging her tight and rubbing her back like I did for him at the hospital.

"It's OK, Sarah. I'll be fine."

"I know, I know you will. I'm sorry. I just hate . . . I'm sorry."

She cries for a long time, but Singer don't seem to mind. He rubs her back slow and pulls me into the hug circle. Hugs got a way of making you feel better no matter what kind of noise got you. When she pulls back, she gets a tissue from her desk and blows her nose a few times. "Well . . . I promised myself I wasn't going to do that. So . . . what the hell are you two doing in here on a Saturday?" She's got a big smile now like she had yesterday. My radar gives me a good feeling when we're with the paycheck lady.

"I need to ask a big favor, Sarah."

"Dino, you know I'll do anything for you."

Singer looks back, then walks over and closes the door. "Can we sit down?" Sarah walks behind her desk, and me and Singer sit on this side in two chairs that don't match. Singer picks up a paper clip and starts bending it different ways.

"Couple of things have come up lately, financially, so I wanted to ask you about taking a loan from my retirement plan. You're the one that does that, right?"

"The one and only. How much do you need?"

"Well, as much as I can get, I guess."

"Let's check it out."

Sarah puts on a pair of brown glasses and starts typing on the computer, which beeps when she hits some keys. After a few minutes she says, "OK, as of the last pay period you have a total of $2,756, and you're fully vested so that's all yours."

"That's it?"

"Yeah, let's see . . . you're contributing fifty dollars a month . . . three years plus company contribution . . ." She punches some numbers on a calculator. "Sounds about right."

"So can I borrow all of that?"

"No, limit is fifty percent. So that would be . . ." She punches some more keys. "The absolute maximum would be $1,378. And it has be repaid, or you'll get hit with an IRS penalty."

Singer scratches his head for a few seconds. "They pretty strict on that, the maximum?"

"Unfortunately. This all falls under the IRS Code and Department of Labor. Lots of red tape and rules."

"Shit. So that's the most I can get?"

"Technically. Hold on." She spins in her chair, pulls open a file drawer, and then comes back around with some papers in her hand. She starts reading, "Internal Revenue Code of 1986, blah, blah, blah, regulations thereunder, blah, blah, blah, here we go: 'loans will be made for any reason. If the participant is married,' you're not married . . . OK, 'Any loan will be subject to the following conditions: (a) the loan will be in the form of cash, not a distribution of securities; (b) the amount of all loans by a participant may not exceed fifty percent of the participant's vested account; (c) the loan must be repaid within three years.' That's it, then. So, yeah, you could get the full $1,378."

"Shit. There goes the trip south."

We just stare at Singer since we don't know what he's talking about. Then finally he says, "Well, give us what you can."

"Sure."

She takes out another piece of paper and starts writing on it. "OK, I'll need you to sign in the three places I've marked with an X. I'll have to get this signed off on Monday, then process it, let's see . . . " She opens a little book on her desk and looks at some different pages. "Next pay cycle is . . . can probably have a check for you by . . . two weeks from Monday?"

She hands the paper to Singer. I can smell her good flower smell. Singer takes the paper and breathes out slow, then leans in close and puts his arm on Sarah's desk. The paper clip is a square now. "You know I wouldn't be asking you this if it wasn't important. I really need this money, like, right away."

"OK, well . . . for you, Dino, and only you, I will use up all my favors. How soon are we talking?"

Singer looks down at the floor and scrapes his shoes around like maybe the answer is down there somewhere. "Well, first thing, I'm going to use my last five days of vacation time. We've got some business things to take care of. Can you let Bob know I'll be out all next week?"

"Sure. No problem. Which means you need the money by?"

"I've seen you work miracles before," Singer says, unbending the paper clip into a *U*. He breathes out slow and looks up at Sarah. "Is there any way I can get it today?"

The hardest part about driving is that you have to keep so many different things in your head, and it all gets mixed up with the talking you're already doing on the inside. I try to block everything down except the driving stuff, push out all the different numbers I repeat, and Jenna's good flower smell, and the feel of that safe lever when it clicked open; just breathe like Singer's telling me, breathe, let the clutch out slow, and press the gas slow at the same time, everything slow when you're driving. Then something jumps in my head I can't push out: the numbers to the lock that's got my bike chained by the trash cans at the restaurant. Next thing I know, when I get them numbers pushed out, the engine's dead, stalled the car again. We keep doing the same thing, over and over and over, Singer repeating the steps in order, slow, slow, slow, his hand on top of mine on the gear lever, his voice saying, *Clutch out, slow, good, little more gas, now slowly let the clutch all the way out. . . .* Stalled again. I keep telling Singer maybe he should drive instead, but he just shakes his head and says try it again.

After we left the office, Singer unlocked the car door and slid in the passenger seat. He slammed the door and rolled down the window, which is broken so it only went halfway. "Well, today's your big day."

"But you're on my side, Singer."

He banged the side of the door with his hand. "You heard the doctor, I can't drive. So we're going to accelerate your driving lessons." Then he smiles. "No pun intended."

"I don't get it, Singer."

"Get in."

I went into the driver's seat and slammed the door, my hands a little sticky already even though we ain't started the engine yet.

"You need to learn how to drive so you can take us out tonight."

"Where we going?"

"Well, my first plan was to fly south like you said. Some place warm. Florida. Maybe the Caribbean. Always wanted to go to Jamaica." Singer has come up with some good plans, but this has to be the best ever.

"But, unfortunately, we probably couldn't get out of the state on what we've got. So we'll just have to celebrate here tonight. Live it up a little."

"How we going to live it up?"

"I don't know. Any ideas?"

"Ideas?"

"Yeah. What would you like to do? Something we've never done."

First thing sneaks into my head is Jenna's good smell, the way her shirt only covered half of her soft rounds. "How about we go on a date with Jenna?"

Singer smiles big, then laughs a little. "I don't know, she's a lot of woman for your first girl."

"Yeah. That's what I like."

Singer laughs again. "So, what, like the three of us go out and do something?"

I nod. When I think about me, Singer, and Jenna together, the noise goes far away. Then Singer snaps his fingers at me and smiles. "You are a pure genius. This is perfect."

"What?"

"Perfect. We find Jenna, tell her you want to see her again."

"I do want to see her again."

"Right. And then I tag along as chaperone."

"What's *chaperone*?"

ZigZag

"I can check her out, see if maybe she has an angle on the Toad. She's that close to the guy, she's gotta know what to do."

My mind's still locked on *chaperone*, see if maybe I can pull back what it means if I concentrate harder. When nothing comes up, I drift on back to Singer. He's talking on the inside now, real hard, trying to pull out the plan for how Jenna can help us get that money back in the safe. We just sit for a while, silent, the wheels in Singer's mind turning so fast I can smell them.

We keep trying the driving for a long time, but every time the car goes dead. First few times my body tenses up automatic, thinking maybe he'll blast me for messing up again. I know in my head Singer's never hit me, but I guess my body still ain't convinced. I jump when he starts yelling, "That's it. That's it. You got it!"

Then I look around and see he's right: the chain-link fence next to the car is moving. No, we're moving! ZigZag is driving the car! Except now I freeze up cus I ain't never driven the car for real. The building is straight ahead of us, Singer saying something, but I can't hear the words cus everything's blocked down except that building, closer, closer, closer, everything moving faster when you on this side of the car, wishing I was back in my own seat like always, Singer's words coming full blast into my head, his hands on the steering wheel, pulling, pulling, pulling, except my hands won't let go, now the building huge, right in front, got to ZigZag low, got to ZigZag low

> float on down to rack and stack
> rack and stack
> rack and stack
> rack and stack
> stack and rack
> take those monkey boys and burn them down

strawberry Jenna smells so fine
so good
tickles my face when she leans so close
kiss me again strawberry Jenna
strawberry waffles with Jenna every night

my girlfriend be Jenna
lots of cream, lots of sugar
strawberry waffles with Jenna every night
strawberry waffles with Jenna every night

When the sound comes, the sun is coming in full bright and warm on my face. Then something blocks down the sun, Singer's head covered with those little baby hairs. Somehow I did the ZigZag down into a hole here in the car, Singer here to pull me out.

"It's OK," he says. "Come on."

His hand's reaching out for me. Then the sun goes away, and the smell of Singer's car comes back, me climbing out from under the steering wheel. The building's gone. Then I look in the mirror and see it small behind us.

"You ready to try again?"

I look at Singer, then at the building in the mirror again, then back to Singer. "How we didn't hit that building?"

"Lucky, I guess. It's OK. No one's going to notice a few more dents in this car." Singer laughs and squeezes my leg with his hand, then lets out a long *ahhhhhh*. Now he's just smiling.

I ZigZag out the door and stand on my side of the car before he can finish what he was about to say. I'm done with the driving for today. Back in the car, Singer's still working the new plan.

"This could just work. Only one question: why would she want to get involved with this mess? Chances are she won't. But unless we come up with something better, we've got to find her and fast."

"How we gonna do that?"

"What was her friend's name?"

"Whose friend's name?"

"Jenna's, the one she said got her into the escort business . . ." I got no idea who Singer's talking about. ". . . when we were under the desk? Shit. What's her name?" After a few seconds the name jumps into Singer's head: "Jordan. We find Jordan, and she tells us where to find Jenna."

"How we gonna find Jordan?"

Singer looks at me and starts the engine. "We go back to the Monkey Club."

Singer doesn't have any problem driving and never has to press the button on the morphine pump. While he drives, I tell Singer about the detective and all the questions, how he said my dad told him I was the one went in the safe. This makes Singer scratch his head, slow, but he don't say nothin. After a few minutes he tells me to keep going, what else, don't leave anything out. I empty out my head, everything I can remember about my dad going to the jail for beating up that crack whore who's really a cop, how the fingerprint on the safe don't match the Toad or any of the assistant managers, case number two three four five seven six dash something something, the pepper the monkey boys threw and how I blasted it out the air with the sprayer, how I acted just like nothin happened early Tuesday morning.

"Are you sure? You didn't say anything?"

"Nothin, Singer. Just like you said."

Singer's biting his fingers now, steering with the other hand. We're cruising on the freeway, cars and trucks all around us.

"I can't believe they picked up your dad." He's shaking his head. "Not good."

"Don't worry, Singer, he didn't say nothin."

Singer looks over at me and then back to the road. "No? What makes you think that?"

"My dad brought out the Black Beauty when I ratted out my friend for breaking the window. My dad hates it when people rat."

Singer doesn't say anything, just looks in the mirror and slides over into the next lane. A tow truck is next to us hauling a little white car that looks just like Jenna's. I flip on my radar to see if maybe she's in the truck, but it's just the driver who stares back at me, a man so big he got to bend his head sideways to drive.

"Who knows? Maybe he said something, maybe he didn't. But if he didn't, why is that detective so interested in you all of a sudden?"

Most of the time I don't have answers for Singer's questions, so he just keeps talking and he usually comes up with his own answers. "Could be just trying to scare you." Singer turns on the signal, drives the car slow off the freeway behind a yellow car. The sky looks even darker now, like that bus tub water is extra dirty.

"What will we do?"

Singer shakes his head and pulls to a stop behind the yellow car. Singer's car doesn't sound too good when we stop, like it might shake itself apart. "Let's just hope the Jenna factor pays dividends. Gives us some leverage."

"What's *leverage*?"

Singer's shaking his head. "Trying to get clean by doing something dirty. I just don't know. . . . Any chance he'll drop the case if we can put the money back?"

Now I can see the Monkey Club, that long black car silent in the same place it always is. Singer parks on this side of the street, across from the black car, and turns off the engine. He reaches in the glove box, pulls out the envelope, and counts out one three seven eight. Then he puts the money back in the envelope and slides it in his jacket pocket.

"OK. First we find Jordan. Then I got another idea. You don't suppose Mr. Community here will reduce the vig for early payment?"

Good thing Singer's got the ideas, cus I got no clue what he's talking about.

ZigZag

● ● ●

Singer tries to open the front door of the Monkey Club and then pounds loud when no one comes. We wait a few minutes and then walk around to the back, the door open this time. I flip on my radar extra sensitive to listen for that little man with the black-handled knife. Singer knocks and then sticks his head inside. "Hello?" he says, stepping inside. I follow him.

The Monkey Club is real quiet now, no loud music that shakes the walls back here. There's boxes piled up along the walls all the way down the hallway and these big silver metal cans with dents. Singer says, "Hello? Anyone here?"

We walk past the room where I saw all the naked and half-naked women. We stop, and Singer pushes open the door. The room is silent now, black, and Singer slides in until the black swallows him up. I follow slow until my eyes come back and then ZigZag slow behind him. There's no one here but a pretty big mess everywhere: clothes all over the chairs, all kinds of tall hair spray cans and little bottles on the long row of white tables with mirrors. Singer leans back and whispers real quiet, "See if we can find a phone number somewhere."

Singer flips a switch, and the row of white bulbs around the first mirror goes bright. He opens the drawer at the table and moves a bunch of papers around, looking at them one at a time. We spend a long time doing this, opening drawers and digging through all kinds of papers, fingernail polish, little brushes that leave black on your fingers, little curved metal tools I never seen before, bottles with white pills, razor blades, little mirrors with dust, packs of gum with all the pieces already gone, half a candy bar that's too hard to bite, and then a bunch of these strings with soft white bullets.

"What are these, Singer?"

His head comes out a tall locker. "Those are women things."

"What kind of women things?"

Singer's head is back in the locker. "Never mind. I'll explain later. Look for Jordan's phone number. Or better yet, Jenna's."

I keep going through the drawers, and Singer works on the tall lockers. When I find a little book's got all kind of numbers in it, Singer smiles and gives me the wink. We turn off the light and walk to the office where Cadillac Tom gave Singer the five zero zero zero the other night. When Singer knocks, the door opens a little bit. "Hello?" He pushes the door open all the way. The light's on, but the office is empty.

"Place is deserted." Singer closes the office door and keeps walking down the hallway towards where the music was coming from that night. We walk up a long black ramp and through these heavy black curtains. Now we're standing in a big room with lots of empty tables and chairs and mirrors on every wall. A man is sitting on a stool over by the bar with his back to us. A woman with black hair is moving around in front of him, facing us, in jeans and shoes but no shirt. She's doing some kind of silent dancing, no music. We walk across the room, and when her eyes lock on us, the man turns around. It's Cadillac Tom.

"Hey, the dynamic duo. Freakman and Baldy. Wasn't expecting you boys so soon." Cadillac Tom is holding a tall skinny glass with the same kind of yellow drink makes my dad's face go crazy.

"What the hell is this?" the girl says, covering her small soft rounds with her hands.

"Can we talk?" Singer says.

Cadillac Tom looks at the girl and back at Singer. "We talkin right now, brother."

"In private."

"I'm doing an audition here." He takes a big drink from the glass, except his face don't change. "So you got something to say, say it here."

Singer runs his tongue around his lips, then pulls the money from his jacket pocket. "I don't think we should do this, you know, in front of her."

"I don't give a goddamn what you think. Now you . . ." He points at the girl with his glass. "Dance."

"I don't believe this," she says.

"What? You getting shy on me in front of these two butt jumpers? How you gonna dance when the room's full of two hundred drunks with hard-ons?"

"You've seen what you need to see," she says, letting go of her soft rounds and pulling a shirt off the bar. Her body looks nice. She puts on the shirt and starts to button it.

"I didn't see shit. You need to get down to your panties. That's what you'll be dancing in, sweetheart."

She finishes with her buttons and stares at Cadillac Tom.

"Come on," he says. "Just go in the back, get down to your panties, and then come back out. I'll put on some music. I can't hire you until I see a few bend overs, see if you got what it takes."

She's shaking her head slow. "Fuck you." She picks up a purse and puts it over her shoulder. She steps closer to Cadillac Tom and says it again, twice as slow, "Fuck. You." Then fast again, "Fuck you!" We all watch her walk away and disappear between those black curtains. Cadillac Tom finishes his drink, then stares at us.

"Stupid assholes." I see the flash of light leave his hand and ZigZag low. I hear the glass go by my head, *whooo*, and smash back there somewhere. I still got my radar on for that little man.

"Stupid fucking assholes. You see how hot she was? They don't just walk in off the street like that every day, and you fuckin nut sacks . . . why am I talking to you?"

Singer walks over and hands Cadillac Tom the envelope. Cadillac Tom counts the money with one eye while the other eye stays on Singer. "This your first payment?"

"C'mon, it's barely been two days," Singer says. "If I can get you the other $3,600 before Thursday, will you drop the vig?"

Cadillac Tom laughs, tosses the envelope back at Singer. "Fuckin amateurs, Ziggy told me. Should of listened to that little prick."

Cadillac Tom goes low and then comes back up on the other side of the bar. He's pouring from the bottle.

"Anything else, ladies?"

Singer reaches down and picks up the envelope, gives Cadillac Tom a long look.

"Hey, sweetie, vig kicked in the minute you left here. Kinda like buying a car."

"What?" Singer asks.

"Depreciation, you know? Soon as you drive that baby off the lot, fucking value drops twenty, thirty percent. Besides, should charge you another grand for fucking up my audition."

Singer shakes his head and starts back this way. He points at me with his eyes. Then Cadillac Tom's voice coming from behind us, "Nice seeing you girls again. Don't forget first payment's due Thursday. Five days."

Singer guides me through the curtains with his arm. He stops halfway through and turns back towards Cadillac Tom. "Hey, one small favor. You gotta girl named Jordan works here?"

"I got four girls named Jordan work here."

"Four?"

"Popular stage name. And all four of them are royal pains in my ass. Tits out to here and attitude to match."

"How about Jenna?"

"Hey, Kojak, I look like a goddamn Rolodex? Get the fuck out of here."

Singer shakes his head, gives Cadillac a long look, then says, "That girl that was just in here had it right."

"Yeah? About what?"

"Fuck you."

When we get to Singer's apartment, the noise grabs him bad right before we reach his door. He goes down on one knee, that strange sound coming out again, *AIIEEEEEE*, holding his stomach and lifting his shirt with his other hand. He pushes that button, and then his face, slow, slow, slow, goes relax, the morphine pump killing that noise fast. I help him stand up, and he breathes out a few times before he walks to the door and unlocks it. I close the door and help Singer sit on the couch. He's looking at his watch.

"Almost eleven. Your lady friend should be up by now."

Singer sits on the couch and starts looking through the little book I found.

"Lady friend?"

"The one and only Miss Jenna." Singer's smile makes me smile back. "Here we go." He punches in seven numbers and then hangs up. "Shit. Number's been disconnected." He flips through the book some more. "Nothing under Jordan, either . . . here's one. Amber."

He punches seven more numbers. After a long time, "Hello, Amber? Hi, I'm a friend of Jenna's. She used to dance with you? Jenna . . . Jenna with a *J* . . . yeah . . . I don't know her last name. . . . You just started last week. . . . Right, well, I really need to get in touch with her, sort of an emergency. Do you know Jordan? You know two. . . . Great . . . oh, right . . . really? . . . the music guy? . . . OK . . . great." Singer grabs a pen and writes something while he holds the phone with his head tipped sideways. "OK, thanks a lot."

Singer hangs up and shakes his head. "She just started. Doesn't know Jenna and met two of the Jordans last night but doesn't know their numbers. But she gave me this address. You ever heard of Timothy Drake?"

I shake my head.

"Drake Records? Well, he's this big-shot record producer who's supposedly having a major blowout tonight. Amber said most of the dancers are going after work tonight, two, three in the morning. She said all the Jordans will definitely be there. Which means we can go out before."

I'm a little bit confuse about how one minute the noise has Singer down on his knees, and now we getting ready to go out.

Then I remember how he has that morphine pump to blast away the noise whenever he wants. Singer don't need no doctors anymore; the morphine pump is like having his own doctor no matter where he wants to go. Now he's dancing around like a crazy man. "Yah mon, we be jammin."

I don't know what Singer's saying, but he ain't never been wrong since I known him. Watching him dance around and talking crazy makes me laugh. Good thing he got that morphine pump so we can do whatever we want.

All day long Singer just stays in the bed to get rested up for our big night out. I just watch the TV and sleep a little. Finally, Singer wakes up and says how we'll go for a fancy dinner first, two hundred dollars, just me and him. I don't have too many clothes, so he helps me iron a black T-shirt and the black Guess jeans he keeps in a special drawer for when I gotta look nice. I only got one pair of shoes, the black sneakers I use to ZigZag the dishes, so they got a funny restaurant smell stays in them no matter what. Now that he's got some money, Singer says he's going to buy me a brand-new pair of whatever kind of sneakers I want, probably those black-and-white Air Jordans I seen on the TV.

We both take a shower, Singer first and then me, Singer shaving while I disappear in the hot steam. When I come out, Singer got everything shaved smooth again, face, head, the only hair now those two thin eyebrows. While we're getting dressed, he even lets me drink some of his Coors, except it tastes worse than the coffee with lots of cream, lots of sugar. I get a Dr Pepper instead. Singer blasts me with the spray gives us the good smell, so I blast him back. We blast each other like that a few times until we really got the good smell.

"We forgetting anything?" He sits back on the couch, slow, holding his side.

"When do I ZigZag the dishes next?"

"Monday."

"I ain't never missed a day at work."

"I know. Let's hope we can keep it that way. I figure we have to have that money back in the safe before you work next. Otherwise it will be too risky for you to go in. That detective could show up again and really put the heat on you."

"I felt his heat pretty good already."

"And then Mr. Cadillac will be sending his boys around on Thursday. We've got to figure out how we're going to come up with a grand."

I'm confuse about all the numbers, five two four one back in the safe and then more back to Cadillac Tom, but Singer got that look on his face like he always does when he knows what he's talking about. Singer breathes out slow and scans the apartment with his radar make sure we're ready. There's a lot of dishes piled in the sink sending out the ringing sound. Singer got all kinds of papers piled everywhere, too, on the table and kitchen counters and on top of the TV. Now he stands up and looks at me with a big smile.

"Well, tonight's our night. Ready, Sir ZigZag?"

I give him the nod. When we walk out the door, all I can think is how my dad said I'd never be anything, how I wish he could see how I am being somebody, all dressed up in my black jeans and shirt with no wrinkles, me and my big brother headed out for the dinner costs two zero zero.

If Jenna asked me the question again, I'd tell her the ride to the restaurant is my favorite time with Singer. He puts in a tape, and when the music starts he acts like the crazy man again, singing louder than I ever seen. I'm not too good with the words, but I ZigZag low and move to the music while Singer yells out. The music makes Singer happier than I seen him in a long time, so I hope this song just goes on forever. Singer's tapping my leg and driving fast, in one lane, out one lane, over to another lane, that music blasting the whole time.

I watch Singer move in the seat, his body somehow smaller now, like the noise been eating it away from the inside. His face looks like he needs to be doing a lot of sleeping during his week off. After we drive on the freeways for a long time, I see an airplane come down low across the road, right above the car as we shoot underneath. I spin in the seat and watch that big silver bird float down, down, down, back wheels spitting smoke when they touch the ground, then the front wheels down quick but no smoke. Singer turns off the freeway and drives us on a road that leads away from the airport. Along the wall on my side they got the sleeping planes with just they big tails all different colors sticking up above the wall. Singer makes some more turns, and we float silent under three walkways filled with people and then up a ramp into a dark garage. Singer pulls a ticket out the little machine, and the black-and-white arm goes up for us. I can't wait to ZigZag into the restaurant and eat the lobster hot off a plate instead of cold out the bus tub water.

Inside the restaurant we get in a line. Lots of people must have the same plan about eating the hot food. Couple times while we were walking Singer had to stop, go down low, and lean into the wall until the noise stopped. He didn't press the button on the morphine pump, he just bent down and used all the special powers to blast away at that stuff inside him. Then after a few minutes he stood up slow, breathed a few times, and started walking again. While we wait, Singer starts singing the song again, except now his face is wet like the Toad's. Singer keeps wiping it with his hand.

"You OK, Singer?"

He nods and wipes the wet away again. "Yeah. I'm fine. I'm ready for some prime rib and crab legs. A little surf and turf, baby." Singer got on a black jacket looks real fancy. He pulls out the envelope with the five zero zero he told me to count out. He blinks one eye at me, like he always does to make me smile. Finally a tall, skinny white man with the white hair looks up at us from behind a wood stand.

"Reservation for Singer. Nonsmoking."

He looks at Singer, then at me, and scans us hard with his radar without saying a word. Then he looks at Singer. "Does the young man have a jacket?" Then he looks over at me like we done something to make him mad.

"Actually, no," Singer says. "Is that a problem?"

The man breathes out slow and points to a little sign. Singer scans it fast. "Well, looks like you're going to have to make an exception."

"No exceptions."

"Really?"

He's looking at Singer: "Really."

Singer looks at me, smiling and nodding his head, then back to him, "You know the great thing about cancer?"

"I'm certain I don't follow you."

Singer looks at the man like he didn't understand what he just said, then at me. He's got that same look like when I told him about the money I took from the Toad. Singer leans across the wood stand. "Follow this, gramps. Either we're seated in the next sixty seconds, or I'll ruin your whole night."

"Are you threatening me?"

"Not you, no. Your little business here. I'll bet I can destroy five-grand worth of shit before you can say nine one one."

The man gives me a long look, his radar smoking, then Singer again. "Eloise." He snaps his fingers. A woman comes out from a little room with a black jacket. My coat floats off me, and the black jacket goes on. I ain't never been to a restaurant where they give you free clothes.

"Seat them at twenty-one. Next to the kitchen." The man hands two thick menus to the lady without looking at us again. Then the lady gives us the same long look with her radar. Singer leans in when we walk by and says, "Thanks, gramps. Knew you'd see it our way."

At the table, Singer orders us a bunch of stuff I've heard about at the Toad's: oysters rocket fellers, two shrimp cocktails, and two baskets of garlic bread. There's all kinds of clean plates and forks and knives and spoons and different glasses just for me and Singer. I never sat at a table with all the dishes and the tablecloth clean.

Then four waiters come all at once and start moving the silverware around and filling our water glasses and taking some glasses and leaving bread and butter and asking Singer a bunch of questions. Singer said the doctor lady told him to drink lots of water, so I guess that means I'll be drinking lots of water, too.

"We need to have a little talk," Singer says, chewing on a fat shrimp dipped red.

"More of the sex 101 talk?"

"No," Singer says, smiling, "I think you've got that down pretty good. You've already been on one date."

"Date?"

"With Jenna." Her flower smell comes back into my head, the way her hair tickled my face when she kissed me in the car. Now I wished I was eating the strawberry waffles with the whipped cream instead of the shrimp cocktail, except the shrimp cocktail is pretty damn good.

"No . . . we just need to talk about me and, you know . . . my condition."

"What condition?"

"Well, you remember what the doctor said this morning, right?"

I try to pull it back, all the stuff I heard the doctor lady say, except Jenna's flower smell is crowding everything else out my head.

"You know . . ." He's pushing a shrimp around in the red cocktail sauce. It bends and then disappears in the little pile of red. ". . . about preparing you for what might happen?"

"I don't understand." I'm trying to listen to what Singer is saying, but mostly I'm thinking about how good Jenna smells up close, my date with her later if we can find Jordan at the big-shot record producer's party.

". . . well, I told you before how they did the surgery and the chemotherapy, that's what made my hair fall out, how it didn't stop the cancer. You remember?"

A little, but I nod like I remember full.

"Now what the doctor's saying is that . . . well, there's nothing else they can do to help me."

"But you got the morphine pump, Singer. That helps you."

He looks down at his side and eats another shrimp, a little cocktail sauce on the corner of his mouth. "The morphine pump helps the pain, but it doesn't make the cancer go away."

"I don't understand."

"I don't either," Singer says, his eyes getting full of the tears. We eat our shrimp cocktails and the rocket fellers without talking on the outside. I watch the waiters with big trays in each hand floating through the dining room. A man is playing a giant black piano, biggest one I ever seen, up on a little platform with a jar full of money. He looks funny, like his head is too small for his body.

"OK, here. It's like at work, when you're doing the dishes. Suppose you wanted to get rid of all the dirty dishes so you never had to wash another one." Who knows why, but OK, I keep listening. "So you wash as fast as you can, fast, fast, fast, but no matter how fast you wash, you never get rid of the dirty dishes. To stop the dirty dishes, you'd have to close the front door so no more customers ordered food. The source of the dirty dishes is the customer, so washing faster won't make the dishes go away. Does that make sense?"

"A little. But why would I do that?"

"Well, you wouldn't, but if you did . . ." We're sitting by the kitchen, so the door keeps swinging open and closed, back and forth, the smells and sounds coming out the kitchen so familiar I know the Toad is hiding back there. ". . . happen. Do you understand?"

He breathes out slow and finishes a piece of bread. Now he reaches across the table and holds me by both shoulders. "I need you to understand this. I'm very sick. Very sick. And sometimes when people get very sick they die. That's what could happen to me."

I think on this for a minute. "You won't die, Singer. You got the special powers you taught me. That noise can't get you."

"We all die. I might die sooner. That's all. OK?"

I nod, except I'm watching the kitchen door swing back and forth out the corner of one eye.

"Now I need you to promise me you'll do two things if . . . when something happens to me."

"What?"

"First, promise me that you'll keep going to the Fellowes School and get your G.E.D."

"What's the G.E.D.?"

"Remember we talked about this? It's the same as if you graduated from a regular high school, Graduation Equivalency Diploma, something like that. Do you promise?"

"That's easy. I promise, Singer. What else?"

"Second, that once you finish school and have your G.E.D., that you become a big brother for someone else. This might not be for a long time, maybe ten years from now. I just want you to promise that some day you'll help someone the way I've tried to help you."

"Like give the sex 101 talk and kill the Black Beauty?"

"Yeah," he says, chewing some more bread. "And all the other things we've done together."

I got to think on this one for a minute cus it's a lot harder than the G.E.D. Singer's always been the big brother, ZigZag the little one. I ZigZag low and see a little guy who's afraid of the Black Beauty, someone who needs a name give him the special powers and to think up good plans. When I come back up, I'm still a little scared about being the big brother. "I don't know, Singer. That sounds too hard."

"It is hard, but it's also rewarding. And I'm not saying right away. I didn't become your big brother until I was twenty-four. That's nine years away for you."

Nine years. That seems like forever. When he says it like that, it seems easier.

"So do you promise?"

"I promise, Singer. I'll finish the G.E.D. and become the big brother."

Singer starts talking about our plan to find Jenna and where we should go on our date with her. I got it blocked down, though, my mind already thinking up names to give the little brother the special powers.

When we're done with our prime rib and crab legs and filet mignon and lobster tail, the noise attacks Singer worse than I ever seen. When he stands up to go to the bathroom, that noise sneaks in low and grabs Singer in the legs. He drops down on one knee, fast, then all the way down and curls up. His head hits the chair, and the envelope full of money goes all over the floor. A tight little noise is coming out of Singer, *aaarrrrrhhhhhh*, people crowding around while I scoop up the five zero zero. Voices are coming down all around us, man voices and woman voices are closing in tight around us and getting all mixed up.

"*Is he all right?*"

"*Somebody call a doctor.*"

"*What happened?*"

When I get the money picked up and back in the envelope, Singer's still curled up. He's got his hands on his stomach, his eyes slammed down tight. I ZigZag over and put my hand on his head, which is covered with the wet and feels cold. My other hand slips down to his side, the fingers on they own looking for the button to that morphine pump, anything to make those sounds stop coming out of Singer, *eeeeeeeiiiiiiiii*. I get his shirt pulled up, the little black bag there now, except he never showed me what to do. Instead I take his hand, which gets a mind all its own and don't want to leave his stomach. I got to pull hard to move his hand on top of the pump. Then when his fingers see where they are, they go automatic and press the button to release the noise killer. It takes a few minutes, and then I feel Singer's hand go relax in mine, slow, then he uncurls a little, and finally his whole body goes relax. I help him go flat and hold his head in my hands, which feels like one of the Toad's wet cantaloupe at the restaurant.

Now his eyes open back up, slow, people still crowded in looking down at us. I block out all the voices and just protect Singer's head from all the eyes. He's looking up at me now, his head shaking like he can't believe how bad that noise got him. I guess we're doing the reversal again, Singer on the ground instead of me, his head in my hands instead of the other way around. A hand touches my shoulder.

"He gonna be all right?"

It's a man I never seen before, bent down low right next to us. The man's moving his head different ways and looking down at Singer. Then his hand starts to touch Singer's shirt, so I grab it up.

"It's OK," he says, not trying to pull his arm away. "I'm a doctor." I flip on my radar and scan him good. He sure don't look like the doctors we saw at the hospital. He ain't got the long white coat or the thing around his neck to listen to Singer's insides. He looks like a regular person in a black suit with a shiny purple tie.

"Can I have my arm back?" He looks down at his arm and smiles. My hand lets go and he looks at Singer again. "If you let me take a look, I might be able to help your friend."

I ZigZag out the way so the man can lean over Singer. He still don't look like a doctor to me. He picks up Singer's shirt a little and nods his head when he sees the black morphine pump. "How long has he had this?"

"Just got it today."

Singer gets up on his elbows shaking his head like he just woke up.

"How you feeling?"

"Not so good," Singer says. His face is covered with the wet again. The man takes a little white cloth out his back pocket and rubs it on Singer's forehead.

"Cancer?" the man asks.

Singer nods, his eyes opening and closing slow.

"I know I'm not your doctor, but you should try to get as much rest as possible. That pump is only to make you more comfortable." Then he looks up at me. "You need to get him home and in bed. He needs to rest." The man touches Singer's arm. "You need to take care of yourself. Lots and lots of rest. OK?"

Singer nods slow. The man stands up and gives us both a smile before walking back to his table. The people start to move away, talking real low where my radar can't pick up what they saying. It takes me a minute to help Singer get on his feet. First he has to stop halfway and rest on his knees, then finally give me the nod to pull him all the way up. He's holding on tight to my arm. "I'm fine. I'm fine. Right here, hold on. Need to rest a minute."

"You gonna be OK, Singer?"

He's nodding, everything now in slow motion, still wiping that wet from his head. I got him back in his chair now. Singer starts to say something, but the noise cuts it off. He closes his eyes and holds his stomach with one hand.

"I'm fine. See." Singer pushes himself up, but the chair grabs him right back. Now two of the waiters are back.

"Would you like us to call someone to help you?" Singer shakes his head and starts to push himself up again.

"No. We got it covered. Dessert first."

Singer just drinks water for the dessert, but I get strawberry cheesecake. Then Singer sees how much I like it, and he orders me another piece. When the check comes, he lets me count out the money, which is two zero zero with the tip. Then Singer takes my arm, gripping it harder than he ever has, and stands all the way up. The waiter just smiles, nods, says, "You take care of yourself," and walks away with the check and the money. I look back at Singer, his face superwhite and still covered with the wet, his eyes real tired.

"Don't worry," he says, giving me a little smile. "We're going out tonight if it kills me." Then he looks at me and laughs. "You know what I mean."

It takes us a while to get back to the car, slow, slow, slow, that noise freezing up Singer's legs good. We don't talk too much on the outside, me holding his arm to keep him from falling. I say something about the reversal again, but Singer don't say anything, maybe cus he's tired; but I keep reminding him how I always got to take care of him now. We go through the covered walkway so the cold doesn't blast us until we step into the garage. There's a wind now, strong, with a smell like the drains in the kitchen. The cold makes me think about the geese and how they're all warm down south.

When we get to the car, Singer gives me the keys so I can unlock the doors. I help him slide in, close the door, and ZigZag over to my normal side. Singer puts the key in the ignition but doesn't start the car. He looks like maybe he'll be going to sleep any minute.

"You OK, Singer?"

He shakes his head and rubs both sides with his hands.

"Yeah. One hell of dinner, huh? Two bills. Feel like I'm going to explode."

We wait for a long time, but Singer's too tired to drive. So I ZigZag back over, help him out, lock the doors, and we walk down the stairs to where a bunch of different colored cabs are lined up on the street, some white, some blue, some yellow. Singer raises his arm, and a white one moves towards us. I help Singer in, and the cab drives away, the cells in my head still buzzing about the best dinner we ever ate.

The noise got Singer so good that all he does for seven hours is sleep. His radar knows it's coming, though, because when we get back from the restaurant he walks straight into his room.

"Where you going, Singer?"

"Sleep."

It seemed funny the way he said it, like he was going away for a vacation and we wouldn't see each other for a long time, which is pretty much what happened. Then a minute later he calls my name. When I walk in, just his head is sticking out, his big black comforter tucked up all around his neck.

"C'mere." I float over by his bed and lean down. He still looks more tired than I ever seen Singer look, fat dark patches under both eyes, his head white as flour and covered with the wet.

"Decide where you . . . later . . ."

His eyes close slow, then open again, slow, that noise stealing Singer's words before they make it outside. Then his eyes close again. I watch him for a long time, wondering if maybe those eyes will open up and he'll finish what he was saying. Every time I'm about to walk into the other room, he breathes loud like maybe he could sense me leaving. So I sit back down on the edge of the bed and wait and wait and wait. When Singer starts breathing real deep, I know he won't be finishing that sentence. I float off the bed, silent, and put the TV sound real low so Singer can concentrate on getting rid of the noise. I even chew quiet when I eat some pretzels later. All the time I keep one ear on the TV and one around the corner in case Singer needs some water, except he never makes a sound all night. The only light in the apartment is the flash of the TV, and my head starts to hurt because I'm crooked on the couch.

I peek in Singer's room from the doorway, and it looks like he still hasn't moved, his body frozen solid by the noise. Then as soon as I take one step toward his bed, his radar goes off and he breathes real hard, coughs, opens his eyes. He stares at me for a few seconds like his brain hasn't caught up with his eyes. I wonder if maybe he's about to finish that sentence. Then his eyes slide shut, and he's gone again. I walk to the bed and look at him, touch his shoulder, and shake him real light.

"Singer? When we going on our date?"

I try a few times, each time shaking him a little harder until his head is going crazy all over the place, but the sleep has him good. I get hungry so I call for a large pepperoni the way Singer taught me.

"It's one o'clock in the morning," the voice says at the pizza place.

"So?"

"So I'm just the cleaning guy. Thought you was my wife."

"So?"

"So call back tomorrow, you moron."

Then he hangs up. I try the Chinese number, but no one answers there. I watch TV and think about Jenna's flower smell, careful now to keep my head in a good position on the pillow. Then I go peek in Singer's doorway just to make sure he didn't wake up and go on the date while I wasn't looking.

I'm in the Toad's office, except instead of hiding under the desk with Singer or opening the safe I'm with Jenna. She kisses me on the cheek again, that flower smell in my head, her hair tickling my face. Then there's water running somewhere, and Jenna jumps. She says if we don't turn off the water the Toad will find us. So I try, but the water just keeps pouring out faster and faster, the Toad in the little window now coming across the kitchen—

". . . sleepy head."

That voice familiar, close but not too close.

ZigZag

"Hello. Party time."

Then I pull apart the two worlds, the inside and the outside, Singer's voice coming from the outside. I ZigZag awake so fast he jumps back. He makes a noise like maybe I'm hugging him too hard. It doesn't matter, though, cus at least he's finally awake. Singer stands up like he ain't in no hurry at all.

"How long you been asleep, Singer?"

"Shit, it's two thirty in the morning. We've got to get to that party."

My head feels like it's stuck between the two worlds, inside and outside, half of me wanting to float down to the sleep again, half wanting to go find Jenna. Singer got his face up close to the mirror looking at his teeth from all different angles. "We've got to call your teacher tomorrow."

"Ms. Tate?"

"She'll be worried that you were out on Friday." Singer is breathing slow, holding his stomach with his hand. He's still got the noise on his face, except Ms. Tate ain't got nothin to worry about when I'm with Singer.

It takes a long time to find the big-shot record producer's party. He lives in a house way up in some hills Singer says I seen a lot of times just never up this close. We keep driving down the wrong roads, little streets that don't go anywhere except to more houses, Singer driving with one hand and reading the little paper with the other. When we finally get to the house, we step into the cold and look at each other, both our minds thinking about how all the lights look from way up here, flickering on and off, but we don't say nothin on the outside. Singer's face looks better like the seven hours of sleep shrunk up those black patches under his eyes.

I want to ask Singer about the geese. How they all know where to go and how big is the south? Do all the geese fly to the same place and just sit there until their geese bodies get warmed all the way back up? What I really want to know is why the geese don't just stay down there where it's warm. Why the geese always fly back where it's cold? Maybe that's what Singer's thinking, that once we get the money back in the safe we'll be a new kind of smarter geese that just flies south once and never comes back. No more Toad. No more noise.

I don't say nothin now just in case the Toad or that detective got secret agents hiding up in the trees blowing back and forth in the wind. Singer turns, looks at me, and nods. We float toward the big shot's house, a real tall place with a wall all around it and big black gates that are already open. There's cars parked every-where. We ZigZag through all the cars and people out in front sharing the cigarettes. When we finally get to the doors, Singer grabs my hand before he leads us inside. "Stay close" is all I hear before the music blasts his words away.

When we step inside the house, the party blasts us full bright with the heat. My body goes automatic and starts soaking up the hot light and sounds and smells, everything going deep and melting away the cold been frozen up since the last time I washed the dishes. The party is like standing at my dish station, hot and sticky all around me, my radar scanning just to make sure the Toad isn't hiding up in one of those high corners in the ceiling. Singer takes off his leather jacket. The heat's already under mine and warming the jacket up good. The party got a smell reminds me of Jenna, sweet and warm like when she got up close and tickled my face with her hair.

"So I wonder if the Jordan we met that night is the one we're looking for," Singer says. Then Singer makes a face and grabs his side, a little blast reminding him he can sleep seven straight hours but that noise is still waiting for him wherever we go. My body tenses up, wondering if maybe now we'll have to leave without finding Jenna. All this way up into the hills . . . after a few minutes Singer's face goes relax, the smile back, and he nods at me that he's beat the noise again.

"Ready to party?"

Singer's fingers sneak in and tickle my side before I can ZigZag out the way. I don't know about Singer, but my body's already soaking up a lot of the party, my hand coming away wet when I wipe my forehead.

The party is the best place in the world, air so hot and wet it sticks to your body and keeps the cold from ever coming in. It's like I'm at work except Singer's with me at the dish station. We're going through all different rooms, rooms bigger than I ever seen. Singer looks at me and shakes his head, raises up his shoulders a little. The party is blowing fast in our faces, hot and loud in every room, different music, smoke, voices, and so many bodies jammed in we have to ZigZag sideways through them.

A little man in a purple suit with gold earrings runs up to me and scans me hard, his drink spilling out onto my arm. "Welcome to Little Cuba," he says in a funny voice, smiling at us. His face is all wet like the Toad's, his fingers scratching at a skinny beard. "Friends of the bride or groom?"

Singer looks confuse. "Didn't know it's a wedding."

"Not in the traditional sense. It's a marriage, though," the man says, tapping me in my chest and spilling more of his drink on me, "a marriage of decadence and bliss." Singer moves between me and the sweaty little man.

"Nice to meet you. Dean Singer." Singer puts out his hand, but the little man just looks at us and disappears into the crowd of people.

"C'mon," Singer yells, pulling me through the bodies. We go back into the corner by a long couch where we can scan the room better. Singer leans back, and we watch out the windows onto a patio filled with more people, puffs of cold coming out their heads while they talk and drink and smoke. I flip on my radar extra sensitive see if I can pick up Jenna's smell through all the smoke and talking and music.

"Shit . . ." Singer's looking around the room, his face trying to come up with a good plan. He's scratching his head. "We need to find her before Mr. Big figures out we crashed the party." Singer watches the people some more.

I'm confuse about two things: who's Mr. Big and how do you crash a party? Singer points at the morphine pump and leans in close to me. He has to yell for me to hear him: "Least we brought our own drugs."

I ZigZag my mind up to full speed to help Singer, scanning hard, trying hard to pull a good idea out my head. Then behind us two men start yelling at each other. When we turn, one of the men hits the smaller man in the stomach, and he drops down on one knee like Singer does when the noise gets him. Singer grabs my arm and pushes me back the other way. Another punch lands on the man's back, then another and another until he's down on the shiny wood floor, not moving except for his back breathing up and down.

"I think it's time we changed venues. Quietly."

My heart's going extra crazy now, the sting from my dad's punches somehow rising up each time he lands one on the little man. Singer's got to grab my hand keep it from shaking off my body.

"It's OK. I got you." I nod but still got to swallow hard to knock back the noise coming up my throat. Everyone in the little group is still circled around the little man, who's on his hands and knees now spitting blood, the taste rising up warm in my own mouth like when my dad starts swinging the Black Beauty.

We ZigZag, quiet, away from the little group with the music and hot air and smoke all mixing up around us. Then the yelling gets louder, and more people are fighting, glass breaking now, the people jamming up around us. My heart goes extra crazy, Singer stopped now and looking back. All I can see in my mind is my dad running this way, the shiny Black Beauty in his hands ready to blast us with the noise.

"C'mon."

Singer's hand pulls me along, floating against the people, between furniture and a big white elephant that gives me a little wink. The elephant is cold when I press my hand against its head. Then Singer opens a door, and we're in a room so dark my eyes don't work. It's even hotter inside this room, little sweat balls rolling down both sides my face. A weird sound comes out of Singer: *eeeii*. My eyes come back slow . . . slow . . . until I see Singer with his back against the wall, sliding down, both hands on his stomach. I ZigZag down fast and grab him before he hits the floor, then lower him down easy so he don't get hurt.

"You OK?"

He's nodding, his hands pulling up his shirt and then a finger on the button to the morphine pump. Good thing we brought our own drugs. His face goes relax . . . slow . . . and all the noise drains out like it's looking for some place to hide.

Back in the party we spend a long time walking through long hallways and rooms looking for Jordan. Singer talks to lots of different women except none that work at the Monkey Club. Most of them are real pretty, but not as pretty as Jenna. Now we're talking to one called Alex who does work at the Monkey Club.

"So we're looking for Jordan. She here?"

"Which one? You know her real name? We got three of them." Alex has real black eyes and straight black hair.

"Actually four."

"No shit, four? Who's the other one?"

"This one's a friend of Jenna's."

"Don't know any Jenna. I know a Jenny and a J.J. And Jandy. You sure it's Jenna?"

Singer gives me a look, and I nod.

"You a cop or what?"

"Not hardly. I drive a forklift."

ZigZag

"What's with the shaved head?"

"Long story. Look—"

"Why doesn't he talk? Hello?" Then she yells at me, "You speak English?"

"Forget it. Let's go." Singer grabs my hand, and we move away from Alex. Then she yells back at us, "Hey, don't get like all uptight and shit. There's one of them right there."

Jordan is shorter than Jenna but has the same color brown hair. She's in a short red dress, tight everywhere, with two skinny straps to hold in her soft rounds. Big gold hoops, one on each ear. She's at full speed, words and smoke blowing out her head so fast I got to ZigZag superspeed and grab the words before they mix up with the music. A black man with no hair like Singer gives Jordan a brown glass jar with a spoon way smaller than any we got at the Toad's. I feed a spoon that small into the machine, and we'd never see it again.

Jordan takes the spoon and sucks a tiny pile of white stuff up her nose. Singer's showed me a lot of stuff before, but never anyone suck food up they nose. A voice yells above the music, "Shit will fuck you up, Jordan."

Then Jordan yelling back, "Like to see you dance in stiletto heels for six hours without a little boost."

Singer has to touch Jordan's shoulder three times before she turns around, her smoke coming straight at me now and tickling my noise before I can ZigZag out the way. She scans Singer hard with her radar, leaning in through the smoke to get a closer look, then back away and over to me. Must be something about us cus it's got her words blocked down.

"Oh my fucking . . . Jesus . . . I am fucking tripping out here. Wayne, this is him, the fucking kid I was telling you about. Backstage. No way . . ."

Wayne is blacker than me and got eyes look single digits. He and Jordan stare at me like maybe I'm from a different planet, which most of the time is how I feel. They're shaking their heads,

217

sucking on the cigarettes, laughing. Jordan looks real nice, her eyes a different shape and her skin a soft color in between Jenna and me. They're talking now, they mouths flying double speed, laughing, the smoke cloud rolling up and mixing with the big cloud that goes all the way to the ceilings higher than I ever seen. Jordan's back up to full speed, words and smoke and another little pile of the food up her nose. "This is, like, way too bizarre. I mean what, you looking to attack me again?" She pulls down the top of her dress, and one of her soft rounds pops out. Then before I got time to really see it, she's got it tucked back in. That makes Wayne laugh and yell. Then Jordan up close: "So hello? Do you speak? You tripping again?" She got a different kind of look in her eyes, like maybe they got some noise in them. Jordan's eyes roll up, and she shakes her head. "You believe this fucking kid?"

Singer steps between me and Jordan, makes her back off: "We're looking for Jenna."

"Yeah, and who the fuck are you?" Jordan blows her smoke straight into Singer's face, not out sideways like Jenna when we're having the strawberry waffles.

"I'm with him, and he's with me. We need to find Jenna."

"Your little pal here attacks me, and I'm going to turn you nut jobs loose on one of my friends? I don't think so."

"No one attacked you, he's totally harmless. He got into some trouble. He's already been out with Jenna—"

"He's been out. You mean you guys are tricks, and she cut you off because you're psychopaths. Get lost." She turns back to Wayne and sucks some more of the white powder. Singer breathes deep, touches her shoulder again.

"Thought I told you to get lost."

"Please, just a phone number. What can that hurt?"

She scans Singer hard, blowing the smoke, then me again see if we're the psychopaths. "What do you think, Wayne? These geeks look hard up or what?"

Wayne pinches his nose shut to keep his food from falling out, then sucks it back hard into his head. Then he just stares at us and starts laughing. "I think you should throw them both a little action, Jordan."

"Shut up, Wayne."

Wayne leans real close to me. His eyes got the little red lines, the same smell rolling out his head my dad gets when he drinks from the bottle. "You ain't lived, little brother, until you've tasted her magical charms—"

"Just shut up, Wayne." Jordan's pulling Wayne away from me, then Wayne looking down at me real hard, nodding his head slow. "I shit you not, little brother. She will rock your world."

Jordan pushes Wayne backwards. "You're wasted, and we're leaving." Then she follows him into the crowd. Singer grabs my hand and pulls me. "C'mon. We can't lose her."

We got to ZigZag slow through the party, people jammed in, laughing, talking, yelling, the music rising up louder and louder when we move towards the black speakers floating up in the corners. When we get through the people, we're in a big hallway, but no Jordan or Wayne.

"Shit." Singer looking both ways now, his mind searching for the good plan. "Out front." We run down long hallways, loud tile under our feet, big paintings on the walls, people everywhere we turn we got to ZigZag around, over, and between. We find the huge front door and blast into the night with our radars still locked on Wayne and Jordan. A car is backing away slow, headlights coming straight at us. "There! C'mon."

We run down onto the grass, slippery and crunchy in the cold, and jump little statues. We reach the car, and Singer pounds on the hood, then knocks the window. The car stops. It takes my eyes a few seconds to come around in the dark, then Wayne's face on the side where I always sit. The window comes down automatic, Singer's head leaning in but the engine blocking down his words. Jordan starts yelling, and now Singer yelling back. The door opens on the other side, Wayne coming up now. Wayne looks confuse, his body moving sideways, then forwards, backwards.

"Back the fuck off . . . the car . . . before I . . ."

Jordan jumps out the car and walks towards Wayne. "Jesus Christ, Wayne. Get back in the car. Wayne, right now. Get in."

"This the little brother attacked . . . my baby?"

"No he didn't. Just shut up, Wayne."

Wayne's still moving towards Singer, across little patches of snow that crunch and trip up his feet, his arms swinging down and then back up. Jordan's following behind him slow.

"Wayne, my goddamn feet are fucking freezing. Now get in the fucking car."

Wayne stops walking and swings again at Singer, who moves to the side before Wayne can connect. "This the one tried to rape . . ."

"Oh, Christ. You are fucking pathetic." Jordan turns back into the headlights and starts walking this way towards the sound of the running engine. "You boys want to freeze your nuts off out here? Fine."

Wayne says, "We're not leaving . . . until someone explains exactly . . . not until I have a little talk . . . no one touches my baby. I'm gonna tear the motherfucker's head off."

My eyes aren't working too good in the dark, but they don't need to see anything to know everyone's eyes looking this way now, that the motherfucker's head about to come off is the one attached to my body.

When you got the noise, it sucks all the power out your body. With the morphine pump Singer can't fight regular, so he's just backing away, Wayne coming in fast and swinging with his fists. Jordan's screaming at them to stop, shaking her head, then flashing her eyes over here let me know what she thinks of me. Singer's moving in circles, which works good cus Wayne can't walk too good.

Every time he swings, Wayne's body moves sideways, and he has to stop and wait for everything to get balanced up again, then another swing, and Singer moving back the way he just come. So it doesn't really register when somehow Wayne's fist hits Singer across the face and sends him down onto the grass right in front of the headlights. Everything goes silent . . . the sting of the punches rising up inside me now, the smell of the breath when they just keep coming ain't nothin you can do except block it all down and wait for the noise to go away. Then another punch deep into Singer's stomach, right where he keeps the morphine pump.

My body goes automatic, everything locked in, silent, my fists squeezed together ready to blast. I ZigZag over, cutting through the headlights, and take Wayne off Singer without even feeling it, his head snapping back and hitting a patch of black ice along the edge of the pavement. I float down on top of him and sit on his chest, grabbing up his jacket and shaking his head up and down onto the ice. Screams are coming up behind me, voices, then someone's hands pulling at me from behind. Then I float off Wayne without even trying, big hands now pulling me up and away, Jordan going down low, her hand coming away wet from the back of Wayne's head.

"We gotta get outta here," Singer says. "C'mon."

Wayne's head is moving side to side real slow, low moans coming out his body.

"I didn't mean to hurt him none," I say before Singer pulls me away. We start back towards the house where we parked Singer's car. I got to hold him up so he can walk. Jordan's voice is back there screaming at us, her words blurring together and eaten up by the night.

Singer slides in his side, and I ZigZag over to mine, the car iced down good out here. The heater starts up loud and blows cold. "Well, no Jenna . . ." Singer's shaking his head and holding his stomach. Then he turns and gives me a smile. ". . . but that was one hell of a sweet tackle."

Worst thing about cancer is being stuck in Singer's apartment. When we first came in from the big-shot record producer's party, the sun was already full bright, the first time I ever stayed up so late it was the next day. Singer was hurting bad, so I did the reversal again and got him all tucked in the bed. He was talking crazy, something about he was sorry and how when he wakes up we'll go find Jenna. I don't know if Singer can make it out his bed, so how's he going to find Jenna? He left money out in case I get hungry for the pizza. His head was covered with the wet, so I got a cold washcloth and pressed it on his head to cool down his body. After a few seconds his eyes slammed down.

The other bad thing about cancer is Singer ain't cleaned his apartment for a while, so it's got a smell like the long hair snake I pulled out the drain in the employee toilet. The Toad started yelling at me cus there was water all over the floor and coming into the kitchen. I unscrewed the drain cover and started pulling on this big piece of hair jammed in there. The hair didn't stop coming until I was holding a three-foot hair snake smelled worse than it looked.

There's a lot of cats hanging around the apartment, too, three or four or five every time I open the door, all different colors, dirty, real skinny ones with little patches of hair missing. Sometimes I ZigZag down low and pet the cats. We do our talking on the inside, my radar scanning the smooth patches where the noise blasted away the hair like on Singer.

Mostly I watch TV. One time the movie with the cowboys and the loud guns wakes up Singer. It's full black in the room now except for the light from the TV on his face. He stands there with his eyes open but doesn't say anything for a long time, that same look as when he never finished his sentence. I watch the TV with one eye and keep the other eye on Singer. Any time the TV woke my dad up, it didn't take long until I'd feel a shoe or a rolled-up magazine across the back of my head. Even sitting here in Singer's apartment, my body is tensed up just in case.

"What time is it?" Singer is rubbing his eyes.

There's only two places I know what time is it: the Fellowes School and the restaurant, both with big clocks. Everywhere else it don't matter. Singer must remember this cus now he's reaching for his watch. "No way." He looks up at me. "It's one-fifteen in the morning."

I don't know if this is good or bad, Singer's face not telling me either way. He breathes out deep and puts his head on the wall, his eyes still open. A siren sound gets louder and louder, coming in from the front window, and then shuts off real close. He yawns loud like a lion on the nature shows and sinks down low onto the couch. "Stuck in this dump all night. I'm really sorry, I just . . . god, I don't have any energy. Don't worry, we'll find her."

I'm glad we're going to find my girlfriend. When I look over to tell him I'm excited about seeing Jenna, he's already disappeared back into the bedroom . . . silent. I float in, his eyes already closed down, his mouth open to suck in the sleep. I do the reversal again and tuck the blanket up around his neck.

After a while days and nights blur together with Singer in his bed the whole time. I try to find Jenna, but no matter how far I walk in every direction I can't smell the flowers or see the white car. I even try to find the restaurant where I ZigZag the dishes, but who knows where it is. Everything's real boring when all Singer does is stay in his room sleeping except when I help him to the bathroom.

I float down the street with my radar on extra sensitive, scanning the eyeballs looking at me from the dark doorways. Then something grabs my leg from down low. I ZigZag away fast and look back, a man with wild white hair on the sidewalk saying something that don't make sense. I sneak back over, slow, and ZigZag low to listen. The smell coming off him makes my head roll back. He's still talking crazy, not the Spanish but not the English either, probably some kind of other special language. He's holding his stomach, like Singer does with the noise, and pointing at his mouth.

I pull the food money Singer gave me out my pocket, two zero, and the crazy man tries to grab it. I ZigZag back, more crazy words coming out his mouth. I'm about to give him a five-dollar bill when I hear Singer's voice come into my head.

One time when me and Singer were walking, a lady with a little baby was asking people for money. She was real dirty and had a little cup on the sidewalk with a sign that said PLEASE HELP BABY. The baby was wrapped up in a dirty blanket, silent. Singer talked to the lady a few minutes and told her we'd be back. We went to a store and got a bunch of baby stuff: food and diapers and a soft little blanket. We also stopped at a phone booth and wrote down the name of a place that gives the homeless people food and a place to sleep. That's when Singer said, "Always give more than you take. The best gift is to help someone help themselves."

When I walk away, the crazy man starts yelling, but who knows what cus it's in a language no one could understand. He don't know I'll be back with some stuff to help him help himself. My mind floats back to Singer, how he finally woke up. He said he couldn't believe he slept four days straight, that today's Thursday, that I missed school all week and two days at work, Monday and Wednesday, first time I ever missed. Then he said today's the day the first vig is due to Cadillac Tom, one zero zero zero. Singer gave me two zero and told me once he eats something he'll be ready to go find Jenna. I sure hope so; I want to smell the strawberry up close.

I walk past a brown building with a good smell coming out the door. The sign says PACO'S TACOS, which is right cus tacos is all they got. It's hot in here, wet dripping off the faces on the three guys behind the counter. I buy one five tacos and three large Cokes with lots of ice. On the way back, I give five of the tacos and a Coke to the man with the bad smell. He smiles big, nodding his head while he eats, reaching up and shaking my hand, and trying to pull me down to the sidewalk.

"Sorry I ain't got no phone number to give you." Instead he gets the one zero zero Jenna give me so he can buy some shoes keep his feet from freezing off.

He's already on the second one, eating the taco and talking so fast it all gets mixed up in his mouth. I watch him take a bite of the yellow paper along with the taco and swallow it all down with a big drink of Coke. Next to him is a shopping cart filled up with his stuff, lot of different junk tied to it with string. I give him a little wave and ZigZag away. All the way down the block I can hear him back there, yelling that crazy language no one understands. Then I ZigZag up to full speed, around the corner, past the blue refrigerator been out in front of a house since I can remember. I climb the steps and ZigZag into Singer's apartment. What I see makes me drop the tacos and Cokes, the big cups popping open when they hit the floor and splashing everywhere.

Singer is curled up tight in a little ball, naked except for that black morphine pump strapped to his side, his body superwhite and covered with the wet. I seen the noise curl him up like this before, except I ain't never seen this look on his face. I ZigZag down low, reversal, and take hold of him. He's shivering like he's cold and wet like he's hot, the cancer mixing up everything. I grab some towels from the bathroom and dry him off, then wrap him up tight like a little baby. He's got his eyes slammed down, his face locked in on breathing slow and easy. Then he opens his eyes and smiles, looks at me like I never seen.

"I'm not afraid anymore."

"Of what?"

"Of anything." Then he squeezes my arm and says, "Weird, isn't it?"

Singer must be having the wet dream: so real on the inside makes your body go automatic on the outside. Maybe now's a good time to tell Singer about the plan I come up with, make him feel better. "Singer, how about if when we get that reward money, you and me and Jenna fly south like the geese?"

Singer nods and smiles. "Sounds pretty good, huh?"

"Sure do."

He thinks about it for a minute, nodding his head. He smiles and squeezes my arm. I give him a smile back. I like how we're talking about going to the warm, his voice sounding better like maybe he's finally got all that noise out his body. He moves up a bit, and I help lift him up onto the bed. He points outside. "Can you get the door?" I step on one of the tacos and then in the pool of Coke on the carpet. I close the door and ZigZag back to the bed.

"You hungry?"

He looks down at the floor, the tacos squished in a pile and covered with Coke. "I was."

I grab up one of the tacos, shake off the Coke, and unwrap it. The warm smell that comes out wakes up my stomach. Singer takes a bite and chews slow, then swallows. He looks at the taco and takes another bite. "Not bad," he says with his mouth full. "Any of that drink left?"

I check, but both cups are spilled. Instead I fill the cup with water from the bathroom faucet. He takes a long drink and burps. We both laugh. He hands me the taco back.

"Want the rest?"

My answer is to swallow it whole and then grab another taco off the floor. Seeing Singer look better knocked the hungry back into my stomach. He goes relax on the couch while I eat up the tacos. I wish the Coke wasn't spilled. Singer stands up, takes off the blanket, and pulls on his underwear. His body is small and white, smaller than I ever seen. The little belly he used to have is gone. He pulls on a pair of shorts and a white T-shirt says GLOBAL EXPRESS—ON TIME BIG TIME and rubs his hands on his fuzzy head. He sits back on the couch, slow, careful now that he don't stir up the noise.

"How do I look?"

"Like a skinny dude in shorts."

He laughs, then starts coughing so hard I'm afraid he might knock something loose and spit up his insides. I rub his back a little until he stops. He takes the cup and drinks some water.

"Shit . . ."

Singer's looking about the worse I ever seen since he started taking the medicine made all his hair fall out. The patches under his eyes are real dark again, his face sort of sunk in on itself like he's growing backwards. He didn't even eat one taco, and, except for the fancy dinner, all he's done since he came home from the hospital is sleep. I'm getting a little worried if we'll ever get that money back in the safe. Singer starts to talk, but every time he tries the coughing starts again. Finally he says it real quick before the coughing can sneak in there: "We'll head out as soon as I get dressed." He looks down at the black bag. "I'll just get loaded on morphine. And away we'll go."

We leave Singer's and walk to the front of the apartments by the busy road. The sun is out, but the cold still bites us good. Singer says the taxi is too expensive, so from now on we take buses and walk so our money don't run out. When we walk to the bus stop, some of the cats I been talking to follow us for a while, running between our legs and tripping Singer a couple times. He yells at them to get away, and when they look at me I block down my thoughts so Singer don't know they my friends. It works pretty good cus those cats finally stop following, Singer checking me once with his radar just in case. Just before the top of the hill, my radar smells the bus before I can see it, a warm sweet smell that sticks in my throat.

"So what'd you think about our dinner? Lobster. Filet mignon."

I got to think on this for a minute, pulling back how the food tasted hot off clean plates. "I think it's more amazing than the woman's pussy."

Singer laughs, grabbing his side, and then starts coughing again. I got to remember not to say funny things so I don't make Singer cough, my hand going up automatic to rub his back. He shakes his head when he stops coughing, just smiling now and nodding towards the bus coming up the street.

"That's ours."

I like the rhythm the city makes all on its own, riding the bus, sounds and smells and different people all crashing down together, so loud they go invisible, silent, just floating around like ghosts. When Singer stops coughing, he taps on my shoulder. "Look at that." When I turn and follow his arm across the bus, I see the most amazing thing he ever showed me coming up from behind the tall buildings, all different colors, a giant rainbow curving right up into the clouds. Singer got the look same as me. "Don't see that too often."

I look at Singer and we both smile, and then back at the rainbow. It's the first rainbow I ever seen not on TV, so close you can reach out and taste the colors. I move my hand up and then back and forth through the different colors, close one eye to bring the colors closer. Then the clouds move, and the rainbow fades away. I watch the sky for a few minutes hoping the rainbow will come back. Instead the sun comes out brighter. The rainbow stays gone.

Then Singer says something he doesn't say much on the outside: "Love you." I can't see his eyes behind the sunglasses. He reaches up and squeezes my arm, then keeps hold of me while he puts his forehead flat against the bus window. Singer's hand slips off my arm. I reach down and put my hand on his. I like to just sit here, the bus rolling along, and soak up the sounds and smells of the city. One eye stays on Singer, while the other watches the sky to see if the rainbow comes back.

When the noise grabs Singer now, it don't mess around. I see him fine one minute, talking, laughing, walking away from the bus stop, then he's on the sidewalk, pushing that pump, waiting and waiting and waiting for the morphine to blast the noise so he can breathe normal again. I help him onto a bench, and he goes away for a long time. Then I help him up, and we keep moving, always doing the reversal, Singer barely able to walk when that noise gets in deep.

I float in and out when we walk so slow, ZigZag back to the blue refrigerator see how the old cats are doing. We walk past a trash can, and the flies buzz around our heads when we get too close. We float further down the street, through the cold air slows down your movements and makes us lean into doorways where the wind can't blast us. All the windows got black bars on them, music blasting out the buildings and the cars flying by both directions. The city's turned up real loud today.

"How bout a date, sweet thing?" She's a tall, skinny lady with pink everything: hair, makeup, coat, pants, and shoes.

"You're all pink."

She smiles and steps out from the wall, rubs my shoulders. "Ain't the only thing pink, sweetheart." She's licking her lips. My radar's picking up some kind of bad smell I don't think was there before she got so close. Singer shakes his head, tells her no thanks. We ZigZag half speed, slow, slow, slow, float away silent around a corner, her voice out there somewhere but Singer's laughing blocking it down.

After a long walk up and down different streets, we're standing in front of a door says two five. My radar's trying to pick up the strawberry Jenna smell behind the door. Singer knocks, and we wait. When we couldn't get Jenna's phone number from Cadillac Tom or Jordan or Wayne, we got a new plan: come here to where Jenna works, place called Angel Escorts except no sign anywhere.

When the lock turns, the flower smell rises up in my head. First an eye just stares at us from a crack in the door, then the door swinging open and the smell rushing out fast.

"Oh my god! Hey, how are you?" She's out into the cold hugging me now. I grab her up and squeeze tight to get a good smell.

"What are you doing here? I mean, how'd you find me?" She pulls the door closed and steps outside.

"Singer found you."

"Singer?"

Singer gives her a little wave and reaches out his hand. "Hello. Dean Singer."

She shakes his hand. "Ahhh . . . the big brother who's not really the big brother?"

"That's me." Singer's got hold of his stomach, blocking down the noise, his eyes real tired from all the morphine. He does most of his talking on the inside, like me, when he's on the morphine pump. "ZigZag's talked about you so much I feel like we've already met."

I flash Singer the smile let him know I remember what he said about we shouldn't tell Jenna we saw the Toad sticking his fingers in her underwear.

"Is that right? About our big night at the Waffle Shack?"

They both look at me like I'm supposed to talk. Jenna starts again before I got a chance: "So you like my new wheels?" When I see Jenna pointing to a purple car, it confuses a little. I flip on my radar extra sensitive and float out to where I can touch the car.

"Just got it. Mustang. It's next year's model."

The Mustang is real shiny except where the black snow is already hooked on behind the wheels. The license plate says J-NA so she can remember which one is hers.

"V8?" is all Singer says, whatever that means.

"I guess. You believe someone already had JENNA? I came up with that." She points at the front of the car. "It's not stupid, is it? I don't know . . . I like it."

I shake my head. Nothing I ever seen about Jenna or her car is stupid. She's silent a minute, rubbing her arms to keep off the cold, and then, "Well . . . so, I've got an appointment in a few minutes."

Singer flashes me a quick look and then back at Jenna. The cold's getting her good cus she's got the bumps all over her arms. "Right, well . . ." Singer's looking for the words. "It's OK . . . what you do. That's why we're here."

Jenna flashes me a long look, then down at the ground. She's shaking her head and kicking at the little pebbles on the step. "All right. So c'mon on in, I guess. I'll give you the spiel." She starts to open the door.

"No, no, no, no," Singer says, shaking his head and waving his hand. "No, we're not here for that."

"You're not?"

"No, god, no. Nothing like that. We're here because, well, we were hoping you could help us with something."

She closes the door again. "Yeah? Like what?"

"Well . . . a little problem we're having."

"Can't be any worse than what I thought was just happening. Jesus, I was like . . ." She smiles and slaps my shoulder, then pinches my ear and twists it. "You goof. I thought you were . . . what a relief."

"I understand if you don't want to help, but we don't know where else to turn."

"So what's up? I mean, I barely know the kid. How can I help?"

"Well, you know who he's in trouble with."

She looks at me and nods her head real slow. "Let me guess. Would this man be one of my—"

"Yes, he is."

"Oh my god. No . . . his slimeball boss?" Singer gives her the nod. "I knew that fucker . . . sorry. Knew he was trouble."

"What do you think? Can you help us?"

She looks back at the door and then down at me. "Look, I don't know . . . I've got, you know? In a few minutes." She's looking at her watch.

"Right. No problem. Could the three of us meet later?"

"I don't know. You know? I'm trying to get out of this business. Did you tell him that too? That I'm trying to get out." She looks at me but starts talking again before I got time to answer. "So I don't know if I want to know too much, you know?"

We just look at her, Singer nodding and me not knowing what to say like always. It's hard to think of words to say when her smell's this close.

"I'm sorry. I can't. But it was nice to see you. I hope you understand. Maybe we'll run into each other again at the Waffle Shack, huh?" She steps back inside. Singer and I step away and start back down the street. We only take a few steps before Singer is down low, his face cold and white like the butter ramekins, his eyes black and sunk way back in his head. He reaches up, and I grab his hand. "Don't worry, I'll . . ." The noise grabs the words out Singer's mouth. He's flat on the ground holding his stomach, my hands holding his head so he don't hit the sidewalk. Then I feel the flower smell rising up again, and Jenna's on the other side helping me pull Singer back up. Her face don't look too happy. We move Singer over to some steps, and Jenna keeps shaking her head back and forth. "I just know I'm going to regret this."

One good thing about cancer is you get to ride in the purple J-NA. The noise slammed Singer down so bad Jenna said we had to bring him back here to see the doctor lady. Now they got Singer hooked up to all kinds of machines again, tubes and wires all plugged into his body trying to suck out the noise. The doctor lady and two nurses hooked all those machines into Singer before I had time to ZigZag down make sure they don't take his other ball. Then the doctor lady scanned me hard with her radar before she and the nurses finally left us alone in here with Jenna.

"Wow . . . I don't know," she says. "I don't know if that's such a good idea."

The noise has Singer's eyes, up and down, up and down, up and down real slow trying to fight back the sleep. "Just a day or two . . . until I get out."

Jenna got skin real white and smooth, no little wrinkles or black patches under her eyes like Singer, no little holes fill up with sweat like the Toad. Except now she's chewing on her finger, and little wrinkles somehow jumped around her eyes.

"I'd really like to help. I would." She's looking at her watch. "This is awkward. Please don't think I'm like a total bitch, but I have to work tonight. I already missed one appointment to bring you here, and I've got another one."

Singer's eyes are slammed down all the way now. "He's no trouble. Promise. Just . . . pizza, let him watch TV."

"Shit . . . I'm already late. Hold on."

Jenna pulls a little phone out her purse, flips it open, and punches a number. She floats over to the corner of the room, talks real soft for a few minutes, now coming back this way. "I'm sorry. I can't reschedule this. . . . how about if I drop him off at your place? Get him set up there?"

Singer nods his head so small I got to use my radar to see it. Then Singer pulls me in and whispers, "In the freezer . . . the money." I come away from Singer repeating five two four one in my head, but not too loud cus of all the machines in here. Jenna squeezes Singer's hand and kisses him on the forehead before we float past all the doctors and nurses, down the elevator, and back into the cold night to find the purple J-NA.

At Singer's apartment I go straight to the freezer and take out the ice cream carton. Instead of chocolate chocolate chip inside is the five two four one inside a plastic bag, which I tuck in my pants like Singer showed me. Jenna's looking around at Singer's stuff, not saying anything. Then she turns and looks back at the door, her face looking a bit confuse, now pointing at the door.

"Did you guys lock that when you left?" I got to think on this for a minute, my mind trying to pull things back in the right order about when we were here and when we left to get on the bus to visit Jenna at Angel Escorts. My mind goes superspeed when I see Cadillac Tom come out Singer's bedroom back behind Jenna, then my body automatic pulling Jenna the other way, screaming, out the door, her heels clicking loud down the steps, shouting and yelling back there, but my mind locked down, everything blurred, J-NA, purple J-NA, no bike cus we got the purple J-NA. She runs to her side and jumps in, the engine firing up loud and two beams of light blasting the cold. I ZigZag to my side, but before I close the door something's got me, a strong hand on my neck, Jenna still screaming, another man on her side pounding on the window, now the Mustang moving forward, choking . . . choking . . . the hand choking off the air, pounding on the car, door still open, lights blurring fast now, choking, Mustang swerving back and forth and then the hand is gone, floating off my body with the black leather jacket Singer gave me. I slam the door before the cold can jump in, and Jenna makes the Mustang engine scream loud down a different street.

"Goddammit, that was Cadillac Tom. What in the fuck was Cadillac Tom doing at your friend's apartment? What are you getting me into? I don't need this shit. He said this was about your boss, so what the hell's going on?"

I ain't never seen Jenna mad, my body tensed up in case she wants to bring the noise.

"No, goddammit, you will not pull this silent shit on me. Cadillac and one of his goons pounding on my new car because of you." Jenna slams the brakes, and the car slides, the tires screaming loud. Now we're sideways in the road, no other cars on the street. "You tell me what the fuck that was all about, or you're walking."

Seems like no matter what, everyone always wants to throw the noise at me, even Jenna with the good flower smell.

"Talk, goddammit!"

Except no noise comes. . . . I ZigZag back up and take a look around. . . . Just two big eyes waiting for me to talk. "Singer owes Cadillac Tom six zero zero zero."

"What?"

"I stole from the Toad, and now somehow Singer owes six zero zero zero to Cadillac Tom."

"Hold on. You stole . . . the Toad from the restaurant?"

I nod.

"How much?"

"Five two four one."

"Five grand?" She thinks on this for a minute. "And you blew the money, so Singer went to Cadillac. To cover your ass?"

I don't know she's talking about me blowing money, but I nod anyway to keep the noise away.

"Jesus Christ. You know what a . . . oh boy. I got a friend still dances at his club, and this guy is like—That's why I got out. He's not someone you fuck around with. It won't be long until he finds Singer at the hospital. So this is your little problem?"

I give her the nod. She pulls the cigarettes out her purse and pushes in the lighter. We wait, silent, until the lighter pops out. She moves the red glow up and touches the end of the cigarette. The window goes down automatic, the smoke blowing out sideways into the cold while she puts the car in gear, still shaking her head. "Well, fuck . . . looks like I'm in it now."

Jenna lives in a place she calls a townhouse with a special garage for the purple J-NA. The garage door goes automatic when she hits a button inside the car. While we're watching the door roll up slow, she sees two men standing by the front door.

"Shit." She puts her window down automatic, little clouds floating out her mouth when she yells into the cold. "Sorry, guys. Be right there." She pulls into the garage, and the door closes automatic behind us.

"OK, we need to talk." She turns in her seat and takes my hand. "Remember when we met, when we had breakfast?"

I nod. "Strawberry waffles with whipped cream, coffee with lots of cream, lots of sugar."

"Right," she says, laughing a little. "Remember how we talked about what I do?"

Not really, but yeah, I nod anyway.

"OK, well these two guys here, both married, are into ménage à trois big time, OK? Regulars. So this is like one of my best money gigs. So I need you to go into the back bedroom and stay in there until I come to get you. OK?"

I nod. No problem.

"OK, no matter what now, you go in there and keep the door closed. Promise?"

I promise. We jump out the car and run in the house, dark, Jenna pulling me through so fast I ain't got time to see where she lives. Then a light goes on, and I'm in a little room with nothing except a desk and some boxes.

"I'm sorry. Two hours tops, and then pizza's on me. And you're going to tell me everything. I guess teaching that pig boss of yours a lesson wouldn't be so bad."

I nod. Pretty much everything she says sounds damn good. She gives me a little kiss on the cheek and shuts the door. Two hours in a little room with nothing to do. I go flat on the carpet, close my eyes, and pull Jenna's good flower smell into my head keep me warm.

There's so many screw-ups and losers at the Waffle Shack we have to sit way in the back. We pile our stuff on my side of the red booth, both jackets hers since Cadillac got my black leather. She orders us the strawberry waffles and the coffee, lots of cream, lots of sugar. The window behind her head is all steamed up from the talking and smoking, and beyond that some of the worst damn cold you ever seen. I sure wish me and Singer and Jenna could have flown south like the geese.

Jenna puts out a cigarette that's only half gone and pulls out a new one. As soon as she touches the tip to her mouth, the red jumps off her lips onto the white. She lights the cigarette and stares at the flame from the purple lighter. "Tell you what . . . I've about fucking had it with you men. Excuse my French." I sneak down low, but I don't see what she means about the French. Jenna talks fast. So by the time I ZigZag back she's already somewhere else. ". . . hands me this and I'm like, 'Don't even give me this shit.'"

She stops talking and puts her forehead on the back of her hand, the smoke floating up through her hair. I wait to see if maybe the sleep got her, too tired from all her dates. Then she looks up, pushes her thumb into the side of her head with the cigarette burning in the same hand, and breathes out real slow. "Don't you hate it when a headache goes back behind your eye? See him yet?" She looks at her wrist and then scans the screw-ups and losers. I look around, too, but he's not here yet.

"Anyway . . . what was I saying? Oh god, fucking Loose-Change Charlie. Guy probably makes two hundred grand a year, and he starts giving me all these baggies filled with coins and like all these rolls of pennies." She leans in close. "Always get the money first. Full payment, cash up front. Period. No exceptions. I don't care if it's Donald Trump and he gives you his platinum Visa; the dude better have cash, or he's going home with blue balls. So, OK, it takes me forever to count all this shit. I even made him put the change into little stacks, quarters, dimes, nickels." She blows out a long cloud of smoke and shakes her head, laughs a little. "Fucking forty-five-minute drive, and I'm counting nickels and dimes . . . know what he said? He collects loose change in this big jar and once a year calls an escort. Says that way it's not like cheating. What kind of fucked-up logic is that?" She pulls out another cigarette, lights it, one still burning in the ashtray, and rolls the purple lighter between her fingers while she's talking. "God, I'm tired. Where was I?" I barely got time to give her a look before she starts up again.

"Oh yeah . . . so, OK, I guess technically a bunch of fucking rolled-up pennies is cash, but I'm like—" She points back towards the door. "That him?"

Jenna waves her hand to clear the smoke for me to see. There's so many people I can't tell at first. Then a little group moves to the side, and I see the long black ponytail, then Dale turning this way and moving towards us like he still got that pan of cut-up chicken. He got a black leather coat goes down below his knees, jeans with a hole in one knee, and black boots that make him look even bigger than in the kitchen. I turn and give Jenna the nod. She got a surprise look on her face. "Hello . . . looks like that Indian guy, what's his name? The actor? Except bigger."

After Jenna got done with the ménage à trois at her townhouse, we started working on the new plan. She said if we're going to get the money back in the safe, we need someone on the inside, someone who can back us up, someone I trust. My mind went to work on all of that for a while. I could only come up with three people: Singer, Ms. Tate, and Dale. Singer's out, she said, cus he needs to rest. So I told Jenna all about Ms. Tate, how she taught us about the self-esteem, except no, Jenna said, Ms. Tate wasn't on the inside. And maybe she'd want to go to the police. Then I told her how Dale got me the lobster, hot with the melted butter, and how he's the only one really talks to me at the restaurant except the monkey boys. I sure don't trust no damn monkey boys try to blast me with pepper all the time. She asked could we trust him. I pulled back how many times me and Dale done our talking on the inside, no outside words, both of us coming away with a smile.

So we drove by the restaurant, and I sneaked in the kitchen, silent, radar scanning for the Toad, to see if Dale would meet us here at the Waffle Shack after work. I found him back by the walk-in with a white bucket full of green goddess salad dressing. He said, yeah, if I needed help count him in, except he was going out with a buddy. Dale said he'd meet us afterwards, two in the morning, and did I know a good place.

Jenna tells Dale the whole story again, Dale on her side of the booth now and the jacket pile over with me. He's eating the eggs and sausage and drinking the coffee except no cream or sugar. He laughs for a long time when Jenna tells him I took five two four one off the pig slimeball Toad, slaps me the high five, and says I'm the king, whatever that means. Jenna tells him about how Cadillac

Tom's looking to take his overdue vig out someone's ass, mainly mine and Singer's, and my interview with Detective Hawke, and how Singer and me already tried once to put the money back. The only part she leaves out is that me and Singer saw her with the Toad when we were under the desk, but I don't think about that too long cus of what Singer said. The story takes Dale through his sausage and eggs, him not talking much on the outside like usual, now just sipping his coffee slow and nodding, then finally a question, "So you need to get the money back in the safe and pay off this Cadillac Tom. That all?"

Jenna taps the cigarette in the ashtray. "That and teach this pig a lesson."

"I'm still a bit fuzzy on that one. How you know him?"

"Let's just say . . ." She taps the cigarette again, moves it to her lips, and blows out the smoke. ". . . that he's a business associate of mine."

Dale nods. "What sort of business?"

"Does it matter?"

Dale nods again, slow. "What sort of business?"

Jenna taps out the cigarette and lights another one. She's rolling her eyes up and shaking her head. "He's a client of mine. OK? Or you need a color diagram?"

Dale just keeps nodding his big head. "No offense. I just need to know everyone's motivation before I get involved in something." Dale takes a drink of the coffee and raises the empty cup at the waiter. "So that's all you're looking for here, a little revenge?"

"Yeah, so? What's wrong with that?" Dale doesn't say anything on the outside, just lets Jenna start up again. "OK, yeah. The guy creeps me out. But you know, maybe what really creeps me out is that every time I take his money, I just . . . fuck, I don't know, I just want out. This creep is like—I need to do something else with my life."

Dale smiles and blows on his coffee, takes a little drink. "See? It's all about motivation. Now we're getting somewhere."

"Yeah? You think so?" She gives Dale a smile, who smiles back. Then they both drink coffee and look at me. I got no idea what to say, so I just float away, block it down, let Dale and Jenna start talking again, come up with the new plan. Jenna starts talking on the outside when the waiter brings the check.

"So you got any ideas?"

Dale's nodding again, looking my way. "No way you can get in that safe again?"

I pull it back, the night I smelled the Jenna flowers for the first time, the Toad's fat fingers in her black underwear, how those numbers didn't work no matter how many times we tried. I shake my head, no, no way I can get in that safe again.

"You got the money on you?"

I pull out the plastic bag and slide it over to Dale. He takes it down low, below the edge of the table, and counts it out even though I already know it's five two four one. He slides it back in the bag. "First thing, we need to keep this in a safe place until we pull this off." Then his eyes down at me. "How about if I hold it for you?"

"Whoa, whoa, whoa. Wait a minute. Why you? How about if I hold it? How we know we can trust you?"

"We? *You* don't. But I'm the biggest one here, and I'm already holding the bag. Looks like you don't have any choice." Dale flashes me a quick look, lets me know the money will be safe without saying a word on the outside.

"OK, fine. You hold the money. So what's our plan?"

Dale looks at me. "When you work next?"

"ZigZag the dishes Monday, Wednesday, Thursday, Friday."

"OK. Friday it is. That's tonight. I'm off, but I'll switch so I'm at the restaurant. By the end of your shift, my friend, everything will be taken care of."

"Oh yeah? Just like that?" Dale gives her a slow nod. Jenna's still got another question: "And what about you, Mr. Motivation, whatta you want out of this?"

ZigZag

"Me?" Dale says, pointing to his chest and throwing some cash on top of the check, shaking his head. "Nothing."

"Oh yeah. Right. C'mon, you don't want anything for yourself? Little revenge? What? C'mon."

"You might know the Toad, but I've seen him in action. Worked there four years now. So . . ." Dale puts his big paw on my shoulder and gives me the wink. "This guy here's my motivation."

"Touching." Jenna reaches in her purse and pulls out a big roll of cash. "Let me get this."

Dale holds up his hand. "My treat. And I never let a lady pay."

Jenna blows out some smoke and tucks the money back in her purse. "Chivalry . . . you know. Don't know whether I should thank you or be insulted."

Dale smiles. "Neither, really. I'm a hopeless romantic."

They must be using the supercode cus I really got no idea what they talking about. Jenna's smiling at me, lighting another cigarette. "Good looking, unselfish, and a hopeless romantic. Where'd you find this one, ZigZag?"

"I told you he's a cook at the restaurant." They're smiling and laughing again.

"So . . . anyway . . ." Jenna says, leaning sideways towards Dale. "You going to let us in on this plan of yours or what?" I lean forward to hear the plan, too, Jenna's hair tickling my nose.

"Like I said, we do it tonight. ZigZag and I will work our shift like normal. I'll have the money on me. Then just before closing we're going to need a diversion." Dale gives Jenna the big smile.

"That would be me."

"Exactly."

"What, just . . ." Everyone goes silent when the waiter comes to take the money, Jenna leaning closer to Dale. "Just show up?"

"Yeah."

"And do what?"

"Think you can get the Toad into the office, get him to open the safe?"

Jenna thinks on this for a minute. "Maybe. Last time I saw him he went in there to get money to . . . you know."

"Perfect."

"What's perfect? I show up, no appointment. He always has me come late. Twelve. One. He might flip out I show up earlier, unannounced. And then I've got to get him to open the safe? And oh, by the way, Mr. Toad, could we please have six grand to pay off a loan shark?"

"One step at a time." Dale's got a way of talking that slows Jenna down, makes me feel good just to listen to his voice. Jenna breathes out and then pulls some smoke off the cigarette, listening close now to Dale's words. "I've got an idea, but I need to check something out first. Leave that part to me. We've got all day to figure this out."

"Uh, pardon my pessimism, here, but this all sounds really weak. Figure what out? Do you even have a plan? And I don't know, maybe you and I should each hold half the money."

"Trust me," Dale says, reaching across the table now and putting his big paw on top of Jenna's hand. "You just turn up an hour before closing. Wear what you're wearing now, same perfume, something low-cut like that. Do that, and our fat little friend will be a goner."

Jenna blows the smoke out sideways, taps the cigarette into the ashtray. "Think so, huh?"

Dale nods real slow, then gives me the wink and a smile, then looking back at Jenna: "Oh yeah. Guaranteed."

Now they got tubes in Singer's nose that the doctor lady said go all the way down into his body to breathe for him. The worst part, though, is now when we come to see him he can't talk with those tubes blocking down all his words. His eyes are floating open and then closed, the sleep trying to grab him back. Jenna's on the other side of the bed, and when I see her take up Singer's hand I do the same on this side. There's a tube sticking in the top of Singer's hand with a piece of white tape covering it, probably another one of the tubes sucks out the noise. Singer's got his own room now, some place called the Intensive Care Unit, whatever that means. Right through the window there's plenty of nurses and doctors when Singer needs the morphine. One bad thing about this room is that there's no window for Singer to look out and see whether it's day or night. I ZigZag down supersmall and climb in the machine that keeps making the beep sounds, float through the tube inside the back of Singer's hand, chase that noise out, and come back before his eyes open back up.

"Hey, Singer," Jenna says. He gives me a good smile and nods his head a little. His eyes look different, smoke clouds in them like at the Waffle Shack. "So tell him what we're doing. He'll be proud of you." When Jenna talks, Singer's head starts to roll her way a little but then comes back like it's too much work. I'm not sure what Jenna means *what we're doing.* "About the plan," she says.

I nod. I'm a little bit confuse about the plan, but I remember what Jenna said. "We got a plan, Singer, to teach the Toad a lesson." Singer smiles again. There's no sound on the outside, but I can hear his big laugh on the inside.

"Keep going."

"What do you mean?"

"The money . . . the Toad and Cadillac, how he doesn't have to worry." I'm confuse, so I just shake my head. Jenna starts talking fast again, except she's over on this side now so Singer don't have to move his head all over the place. ". . . better. Best part is he's off the hook. Sound good?"

Singer smiles, gives a little nod. Then he lifts up his hand and gives me the thumbs up, like we really got us a good plan. Then his hand drops back down real quick. His eyelids are going up and down real slow. Jenna and me both got hold of the same hand. She turns to me. "We should let him rest. Let's go do our thing, and we'll come see him later with the good news."

I nod. That sounds like a good plan. I'm a little bit confuse about leaving Singer or going with Jenna. No one's ever been the big brother like Singer, but I sure do like going places with Jenna and her good flower smell.

"We're going to get out of here," she says while she leans down and gives Singer a little hug. "Take care of some business, you know. We'll be back." Then to me, "See you out here."

When Jenna leaves, the room gets real quiet except for the *beep beep beep* . . . Singer's eyes are slammed down tight now, his head real still. I give him a little hug, too, and squeeze his hand and move away real slow so I don't wake him up. Singer sure do have the best radar I ever seen cus even asleep he gives me a little smile let me know our plan is real good. I watch him a little longer from the doorway, see if maybe he'll just jump on up, use all the special powers he taught me, some kind of new name for himself like ZigZag except even better, just rip all them wires and tubes out and start laughing and come with us to get me off the hook. Then I remember about the reversal, how it's time for me to get things fixed right with the Toad. Just ZigZag on in there and do it myself, automatic, everything back the way it was before I took that damn money. It's easy to think about now, far away from the Toad and the warm stink in that office and the sound of his voice when he yells my name. Even with Dale and Jenna helping, my hands get the warm sticky when I call up the plan and try to sort out everything I got to do. I ain't never done something this important without Singer. Can ZigZag go automatic all alone, or will the noise swallow me up? I wait, slow, slow, slow, see if maybe Singer hears me and jumps on out this bed to help me. Except Singer don't move, and his eyes stay blocked down. I listen to the machines beep for a long time before I float away silent.

One day maybe Jenna will let me drive her purple Mustang with the license plate says J-NA. The car is damn fast, floating in and out of traffic with no bumps or noises or heater so loud you can't talk. The Mustang heater blows so hot and quiet you forget it's on except your toes are so damn warm it reminds you. Jenna's got the radio on, and when I see her pull out a cigarette she lets me work the lighter, pushing it in, waiting, waiting, then the pop sound and moving the red onto her cigarette. Everything goes automatic in Jenna's car: heater, locks, windows. Maybe when Singer gets out the hospital, the three of us can go back out into the country and dump his ugly car in the river with the Black Beauty and then ride around in J-NA all one color.

"You ready for this?" The window goes down automatic just a little to suck out the smoke, which she blows sideways out her mouth towards the gap. The air out there is the single digits again. All day just sleeping and watching TV at Jenna's townhouse, Jenna on the phone with Dale so many times I stopped counting, then back to the hospital, where Singer didn't even wake up he's so tired. Now already four zero zero Friday and time to do the plan. Only seven hours until one hour before closing. My hands get the warm sticky.

"I'm a little nervous," she says. "I mean, the guy is a pig, no question, but I just . . . I don't know, I still feel a little guilty. Is that weird, or what?" I'm not sure *or what*, but I know Jenna real good now: her mixed-up questions don't matter cus she'll start talking again whether you answer or not. ". . . money if he does. But he should have to pay for the way he treats you. Right?"

I nod.

"OK . . . here we go."

She turns off the freeway and then onto another busy street. She slows down and turns into the restaurant. She drives around back and parks by the trash cans. Jenna's already talking. "I think you're going to pull this off," she says, "I really do." I nod, and she gives me a nice hug.

When I punch my time card, my heart is going extra crazy, especially when I hear the Toad's voice for the first time. Before he comes around the corner, I can see that little cigar he never lights and his face all shiny with the wet. But then my heart does a ZigZag back to normal speed, slow, slow, slow, cus Dale walks by and puts his hand on his stomach where he's got the Toad's money hidden. But then everything gets all mixed up—the plan, Dale's got the money but when do I get it from him?—everything sliding sideways and crashing together, the roar starting up deep in the back of my head.

"Your ass is in deep shit, moron." The Toad rolls up right behind Dale, so close I can smell him. "Where the hell you been?

ZigZag

Lucky I didn't fire your retard ass. That detective's been looking for you. Don't you punch out tonight until I get him back over here. Got it?"

I float into position, my hands so wet now I can't rack right. Dale never said nothin about the detective coming back. Only thing keeps my head blocked down is the giant stack of dishes the lunch bastards left. I blast through the stack so fast everyone walking by rolls back and then forwards all together, my hand moving the sprayer so fast they can't help but watch. I float into two places at once, stacking and racking, stacking and racking, my arms and legs blurred together but everything real quiet on the inside. The machine got the biggest damn smile I ever seen cus it thinks maybe it can beat ZigZag, bright silver, laughing that I missed some days, dish hole so big might swallow my arm I'm not careful. A little fear jumps in my head, the detective, all the questions he asked the last time, but I block down the thought before the machine's big shiny radar can pick it up. I push down deeper, deeper, deeper. . . . Before I go all the way down, I see Singer out the corner of my eye, smiling bigger than he has for a long time, watching me from his bed at the hospital, that noise gone away for now. . . . Then I go automatic, everything silent except the sound of my radar.

> rack and stack
> rack and stack
>
> choke it down
> smoke it down and choke it down
> choke it smoke it choke it smoke it
> smoke it down good don't never come back

Something pushes me from behind . . . a body, a little skinny cook back there trying to get some pans, his body in slow motion next to me. I ZigZag back up to full speed, feeding the racks so fast now the machine got a little surprise look, the cook backing away slow, shaking his head cus he never seen no one ZigZag the dishes. . . . Some waiters and waitresses are yelling and laughing and clapping, my body flying so fast I back off a little just to make sure it don't go out of control, the machine choking down now cus it knows ZigZag got it beat. I empty another tub and blast the sprayer to rinse, a cloud of steam rolling up and sticking to my face. I can see Singer out there at the hospital, clapping, happy, the noise blocked down.

Two hours before closing, the Toad is in the bar getting loopy on tall Jack Daniels and Coke and hitting on two saleswomen from Toledo. That's what Dale said, whatever that means, when I told him the detective was coming back tonight to ask me more questions. We talked out front where Dale and all the other cooks work, flames jumping up through those grills and making the steaks and fish smoke and cry. Behind the cooks is the salad bar and out beyond that all the people at the tables. Friday night's always the busiest at the Toad's, people jammed in the lobby, every table full, and a long line at the salad bar. One of the cooks yells, "SBA!" Dale explains the code to me. *SBA* is what the cooks yell when a pretty girl is at the end of the salad bar cus that's where she's got to lean across towards the cooks to get salad dressing: salad bar alert. Dale said a lot more, but mostly my mind was locked down on the filet mignon and prime rib Singer and me ate.

One hour before closing, Jenna walks into the crowded lobby in a knockout black leather dress with stiletto black boots and a long coat. And right behind her is a guy says his name is Detective Hawke. That's what Dale told me just now, when he blasted back into the kitchen with a confuse look on his face, a wide spatula in his hand still smoking from the grill. I ZigZag low see if I can see the bump where he got the five two four one, but he's got it hidden good.

"C'mon." Dale waving that smoking spatula at me. "We gotta hide you. We can't let him talk to you now."

"What about the dishes?"

"Forget the dishes! C'mon."

As we ZigZag away, the door on the other side of the kitchen, over by the Toad's office, slams open. "Louis, goddammit. Get your skinny coon ass in my office right now."

We're behind the ice machine, stuck out in the middle of the kitchen. Ain't no way we can make the other door without the Toad seeing us. "Louis, goddammit . . . now." I know what Dale means now about the tall Jack Daniels and Coke making the Toad loopy, his words coming out slow and all stuck together just like my dad when he drinks from the bottle. "Your detective friend's here to see you."

"Hello, ZigZag." The detective's voice closer now like they walking this way.

Dale holds up his big paw, then lifts up the door on the ice machine and points at me to get in, my mind not having time to think how damn cold a bunch of ice cubes can be, everything going black when the door goes closed behind me, the Toad's voice so close now it makes me shake.

"Dale, seen the moron?"

"Just saw him out collecting bus tubs."

"Holy mother of Jesus, how many times I told that idiot to stay outta the . . . let the busboys bring back the dishes." I can hear the Toad taking a drink of the tall Jack Daniels and Coke, ice cubes against the glass. "C'mon. See what I mean, place is like a fucking turd factory."

I hear the kitchen door swing back and forth, and the light rushes inside the ice machine. "C'mon," Dale says, pulling me out and brushing off the ice stuck to my clothes. "I know right where to hide you. Last place he'll think to look."

"Where's that?"

"The office."

Instead of using the door over by the dish station, we go out the same door the Toad and Detective Hawke took, away from the office, Dale saying we'll circle in behind them and slip me under the desk. There are waiters and waitresses jammed in the bus station when we float through, everyone grabbing trays and punching in numbers on the computer. Dale points up ahead, where the Toad is cutting through the crowded tables, the detective right behind him with that little notepad already in his hand.

"Shit. Why did he have to show up?" We ZigZag back through the cook line, towards Jenna, people jammed around her. We're at the end of the salad bar, the Toad talking to Jenna now and pointing back towards the kitchen. "C'mon. Let's get you into place."

Dale tucks me in on his left side, grabs a pan of dried-out baked potatoes to hide me, and walks us back. We pass so close I can smell Jenna and hear the Toad saying something about the moron dishwasher. Dale slips a key into the lock and pushes open the office door.

"How you got a key?"

"Assistant assistant manager. Sometimes I lock up for him."

I ZigZag low, under the desk like me and Singer did, and go flat against the wall so fast Dale gives a little laugh. Then his head comes down low in the opening. "Little sooner than we planned, but everything else . . . just like we talked about."

I give him the good nod, the plastic bag with the five two four one coming this way. I take the money from him and hold on tight, my hands already going wet on the plastic. The room goes black . . . the door closes . . . and then swings back open again, glasses with ice and drinks being poured. I can see Jenna's black boots and the Toad's fat little legs. Maybe I could just ZigZag out of here real quiet, breathe in some cold air outside, and then be back before they got time to see me, the heat starting to close down on me, things blurring, the Toad's laugh that makes my body go automatic every time I hear it.

". . . what's with the fucking surprise visit? I told you thousand times I don't like . . . no surprises." Toad lets out a burp I can smell down here: tall Jack Daniels and Coke.

"Can't a girl drop in on her favorite guy without making an appointment?"

Even though I can't see they faces, I got my eyes closed anyway, make the radar go supersensitive, everything tensed up in case he blasts her with the noise when she teaches the pig a lesson, my hands slippery on the plastic bag full of money.

"No. Yes. I got this goddamn detective nosing around, can't find that moron. I know that little bastard's got something. I'm your favorite?"

"Course you are."

All I can see is down low, the Toad's belly hanging over the wide brown belt, pants got a couple stains, brown shoes coated with slime they been in the restaurant so long. They legs are pressed together now, Jenna giving the Toad a hug and a kiss right on the lips. It's got to be the only time in my life I wished I was the Toad.

"Look," the Toad says, pushing Jenna away and taking a big drink, "I can't do this shit right now. Come back later and we'll . . ." The Toad takes a long drink from the tall Jack Daniels and Coke.

Jenna moves in close again. "Come on, baby. Half price. Five hundred, and you can do whatever you want." This makes the Toad go silent, his radar scanning Jenna hard.

"What are you up to?"

"Nothing."

"I'm drunk . . . but I'm not . . . stupid."

"What are you talking about, baby?"

The Toad pushes Jenna away again, his voice rising up now. "Show up on a Friday night, unannounced, offer to do me for half what you normally charge? Something stinks . . . here. You knocked up or some shit?"

My eyes are locked on the safe. I got to get the money back in there, except it don't look like Jenna is going to get him to dial the combination. My whole body got the warm sticky now, the air choking me off under here. I wasn't suppose to bring in the money until Jenna got the safe open and got the Toad out of here. A loud knock on the door pulls me back, the door opening, then a voice, the voice making my body go automatic with fear: Detective Hawke.

"Am I interrupting?"

"No. She was just leaving. And thank you. I'll keep your application on file."

I can't see Jenna's face, but she stays silent and walks out the office with the safe still closed and me stuck a few feet from the Toad and Detective Hawke.

"You find him?"

"No, goddammit. You see him?"

"I was waiting for you."

"Look, you circle back around that way, and I'll go through the kitchen. Moron's gotta be back there by now. Go."

Except Detective Hawke don't move. "You're really starting to irritate me here. What's going on?"

"I don't know, he's a slippery little bastard."

"No, what's going on? She wasn't applying for a job."

"Good for you, Dick Tracy. None of your business what she was doing here."

"Unless of course I'm here to investigate. How about we take a new slant on this whole thing."

"What?"

"Like maybe you're dealing."

"Dealing, fuck. You think I'd put up with all these idiots I was dealing? She's a whore, all right? A high-priced whore who makes this shit-hole barely tolerable. And yes, I'm married, so cut me some fucking slack." The Toad finishes his tall Jack Daniels and Coke.

"Maybe you'd better slow down on those."

"Fuck you!"

Detective Hawke slams the Toad in the chest with both hands and sends the Toad backwards onto his chair, which rolls back and smashes into the wall. The shelf breaks, and a bunch of big phone books and papers fall on the Toad's head.

"You will not disrespect me, you little slug. Now . . . I'm going to make one more pass through this dump, and if the kid doesn't turn up I'm outta here."

The Toad grabs at his throat and starts coughing. "You can't fucking . . . I'm a goddamn taxpayer."

The door slams, and I go automatic, the noise rising up so hot inside the Toad now I can smell it. "Goddamn worthless government . . . civil servant piece of . . ." The Toad throws a heavy book against the office door, then another and another until he starts laughing. The Jack Daniels and Coke must still got him loopy cus the Toad keeps falling into the desk and knocking papers and pencils onto the floor when he gets up from the chair.

Then he does something so amazing I got to rub my eyes make sure it's real: he leans down and starts spinning the combination dial, around and around, still laughing. I use all the special powers Singer taught me to push out all the old numbers floating in my head but somehow remember them at the same time just in case. He slides a new cigar between his teeth and chews the white tip while he works the dial, around and around, my mind locking in on each number he stops at, then the handle going down with a loud *CLICK* sound and the Toad's arm going in the safe hole. I start repeating the numbers in my head, over and over and over, at first in the same order then backwards and forwards just to make sure I got them all lined up right.

When the Toad's hand comes out, he's holding a small metal bottle. He kicks the safe door shut and spins the dial, now unscrewing the metal bottle and drinking so fast it's spilling down his neck. Then the Toad shoves everything off his desk, pushes it all on the floor.

"Fucking ass—" The Toad just sits in his chair, rocking back and forth, taking drinks from the metal bottle, and working the cigar with his tongue. "That goddamn moron." He pushes himself out the chair, takes another drink from the bottle, and blasts out the door.

My body freezes up when the door slams, all alone in here in the dark, my heart going so crazy feels like it's going to jump out my chest. Now's when you really got to use the special powers, just like Singer taught me, slide on over there, ZigZag, and put the money back. Except what if he comes back in? How long I got? What if those numbers don't work right? The wet's pouring off my face now, the heat choking me down in here, the noise starting up low in the back of my head. Singer ain't here to whisper no plan into my head. I gotta go now, do it before the Toad comes back and blasts me with his drinking noise.

I ZigZag automatic, slow, slow, slow, out from under the desk now, sliding along the floor so silent no one could see me if they were standing right here. The kitchen glow's coming in through the little window still cracked, same as the night I went into the safe the first time. I pull back the new numbers and start spinning the little black dial around and around like a clock. Everything the same as the first time, plenty of spins to get it warmed up, first number, back around to the second, just like before. When I'm spinning the third number, I hear the Toad's voice, screaming, right on the other side of the kitchen wall, yelling something about how he's not going to hurt me, he's just going to give my moron ass what it deserves. It makes my body freeze up, the sound of all them pans being thrown around, the noise so close I can smell it, but I got to keep spinning numbers.

The Toad messed me up, so I got to start over, around and around, get the dial warmed up again, then start to empty the numbers out my head. I give the silver handle a little squeeze to warm it up and then freeze up when I hear the loud *CLICK* sound. The safe door swings open easy, now sliding the plastic bag inside the dark safe hole, the words Jenna typed on the little paper we put with the money rising up in my head:

> I'm returning the entire amount borrowed from you, $5,241, with the full faith that you will forgive my mistake and cancel the investigation. Justice, it seems, has already been served.

The sound of the Toad's voice coming back towards the office sends the fear rising up in my head so fast it chokes down my breathing. I jump up and slide to the corner by the tall filing cabinets just as the Toad comes in, a new bottle in one hand, and slams the door closed. I block everything down, numbers, smells, breathing, to keep him from looking back here, just like nothin happened, my body tensed up just in case I got to blast him with some of my own noise. He's digging around in the desk now, drinking, the office still dark.

Then I see I left the safe door wide open. Only thing must be keeping him from looking at it is the booze, which got his radar all clogged up. I try to block it down, Singer's voice rising up in my head, *just like nothin happened, just like nothin happened, just like nothin happened.* But it don't matter when the Toad's got his secret frog agents tell him everything that happens around here.

"What the fuck?"

He sets the bottle down on the desk and goes down low to the safe. He runs his hand over the door like he can't remember did he leave it open? Now from where I'm standing I can see Detective Hawke through the little cracked window, walking back this way through the kitchen, stopping now at my dish station, so close I can smell his confuse. What happened to the plan? Jenna gone and where's Dale? The wet's got my hands good now, the hot air choking down my throat. Then the detective is gone from the little window, probably headed back this way.

I ZigZag my mind back to the Toad, who's bent over and sliding his hand in the safe. That's when something clicks automatic in my body, detective coming back and the Toad about to find the bag of money with me standing right here. So my mouth makes a little whisper noise, all on its own, get the Toad's attention.

"Who's there?" He spins this way and starts to stand, except I'm already moving towards him with the fat phone book squeezed tight in both hands, everything silent, automatic, the Toad about to feel what it's like to get a little ZigZag noise. The first blast comes from down low, the phone book swinging up and snapping his jaw shut before he got time to say anything else. The ZigZag blast pushes him back into the wall, his hands going up so the next blast comes from the side, my foot kicking the safe door shut and spinning the dial all in one motion, then the last blast coming down on top of the Toad's head and sending him flat onto the floor. Everything happens so fast I got to replay it slow motion in my head a few times make sure it was real, me giving out the noise instead of the Toad. I reach down and check to make sure the safe's locked tight, then wipe the safe handle clean with my apron just like Dale said. I stand up tall and look down at the Toad rolling around slow and moaning something about what the hell just happened.

Doing the reversal on the Toad gives me a new feeling, like everything's different now with the money back in the safe. I laugh on the inside when I see the Toad's broken cigar on the floor, knocked clean out his mouth by ZigZag.

"Ahhh, yes, of course. He's right here in the office." The detective moves up behind me so fast I ain't got time to ZigZag his radar. "You know I've been looking for you for the last twenty minutes?"

I turn towards him, squeezing the phone book tight again, my body slow but my mind superspeed, everything silent, ready for the next blast. . . . The detective steps forwards and looks down at the Toad.

"Pathetic. Drunk fucking loser." The Toad has gone silent, still confuse in his sleep about what kind of noise could hit him right here in his own office. Detective Hawke's so close I can see the little black hairs pointing out his chin. My fingers get the tingle, thinking maybe I got to blast him, too, just run out of here and don't never come back.

"Sit down, ZigZag." His eyes look like maybe he's ready to bring some noise. "We need to talk."

I start to bring the phone book up, blast him like I did the Toad, but somehow he pulls it out my hand like I'm moving slow motion.

"Sit. Now."

I sit and do a quick look at the money inside the safe with the ZigZag vision. Detective Hawke leans on the corner of the Toad's desk and pulls out his little notebook and pen.

"Now, we need to get this story straight, you know, for my report. OK?"

I give him the nod, my mind locked in on what it's going to be like in the juvenile.

"So first of all," he says, "our proprietor here got all tanked up on Jack Daniels, and the dumb bastard goes and knocks himself out cold." Detective gives me a long look and nods his head so I nod mine.

"Right," he says, still nodding, "Now our perpetrator, well, he or she must have got a guilty conscience because at some point during the evening the money was returned. Isn't that what you heard from the cooks and waiters?"

My mind goes confuse about what he's talking about, so I just nod see what else he got to say.

"So with the money returned and no harm done, other than the Toad's self-inflicted accident here, there's only one other question we need to resolve." I try not to think about it, but Detective Hawke pulls the thought right out my head before I can pull it back. "But I checked it out; the print we lifted doesn't match any of the employees. Not even the dishwasher." Detective Hawke writes some more in his notebook, then closes it up and slides it in his jacket pocket with the pen.

"Thanks for all your help," he says. "And strictly off the record . . ." Now he leans towards me and whispers real quiet in my ear. ". . . looks like a mirror from the kitchen, but just get real close to it, and you can look in here any time you want."

Then he pulls back and knocks on the little window still got a crack from that skinny cook. I just stare at Detective Hawke, my body froze up by the confuse in my mind.

"You're free to go." He gives me a big smile and then pushes on my arm real soft. "Go ahead. It's over."

So I slip out the office and float back to my dish station, all the things the Toad done going right through me now and drifting away with the steam.

Somehow Singer died the same night we taught the Toad a lesson. Don't ask me how; I was keeping my radar on him the whole time make sure they never took his other ball. Not even the supertuned cells in my head could save him. Jenna was waiting in the parking lot after I finished the dishes and drove me to the hospital. We told Singer about how good the plan worked and how Dale went to the Monkey Club and cut a deal with Cadillac Tom: instead of cash from Singer, the Monkey Club got six zero zero zero worth of booze delivered no charge. Dale called in the order from a pay phone and said the Toad wouldn't even notice the charge to his account since his bookkeeping was so sloppy. The best part was telling Singer how I remembered the new safe numbers and put back the five two four one all on my own, gave the Toad a little ZigZag noise. That made Singer really happy. Finally, I told Singer how I got to kiss Jenna right on the lips even though I'm only one five.

ZigZag

That was the worst day of my life and the best day of my life all wrapped up into one. I'm still trying to sort that out, getting the Toad and then that noise taking Singer away for good. Not even all those machines could suck the noise out of Singer.

Ms. Tate says it's been one year now since that day and how the first year after someone dies is always the hardest. Ms. Tate is right about that. The real bad hurt melts away . . . slow . . . slow . . . slow . . . until your mind can't pull back how bad you hurt when it first happened. Now all of a sudden it's a year later, and more of the good things about Singer stay in my head.

I went so crazy when he died my body froze up solid like the single digits. Not too long after Singer died I wrote a paper for the Fellowes School about me and Singer:

the pramis
by ZigZag

my best frend was siner. his real name is dean siner but I always jsut called him siner. we were bruthers for five years. Mostely just hanging out and doing fun stuff.

siner got a thing called the cancer in his balls. it got so bad the doctors took off one of his balls. he took speshul medcine made all his hair fall out. siner taught me importunt stuff. one. all about the woman and where they got the pussy hidden and how when you make the love with a woman a baby starts to grow inside. don't ask me how. two, always give more than you take.

three. don't be afrade. ain't no one suppose to hit you so insted kill the black buty. jest throw it in a river and watch it flot away.

siner got the morfene pump and got better.

the most fun we had was when we ate the primrib and lobstur we also ate tacos. one time we saw a rainbow when we were on the buss. the only one I ever seen outside.

siners hair was jest staring to grow back. except don't ask me how but he still died

i wish i would of give him a name with the special powers like he did for me. ZigZag. two big Z's, and two little g's. ain't nothin can catch you when you ZigZag.

I made a pramis to siner before he dyed.
Two things.
one. get the ged.
two becum the bigg bruther.

I sure miss him alot. he was my best frend. ever.

ZigZag

Ms. Tate liked the paper so much she gave me an A for it. I don't get too many of them. Then she showed my paper to all these people work at the government. I had to go to a bunch of meetings at the state capitol with Ms. Tate, something about this group called the State Commission on Volunteerism. Ms. Tate coached me on how to read the paper into a microphone in front of the group. We practiced at the Fellowes School with just me and Ms. Tate in the room reading into a microphone.

The people at the state capitol liked the paper so much me and Ms. Tate took a trip to Washington, D.C., to another group called the National Commission on Volunteerism. Ms. Tate took me shopping for that trip and, with her own money, bought me a black suit with a nice shirt and shoes and belt and a purple tie cus that was the color of J-NA the purple Mustang. When you go to Washington, I guess you got to wear a suit cus everywhere we went the men and women were wearing the suits.

Then I read my paper a bunch more times, and the last time was in a place called the Senate, where everyone had a dark suit and mostly white dudes. It was hot in there. A bunch of those senators shook my hand. Ms. Tate said they make the laws for the country. I asked why they don't make a law about no more cancer that takes away your best friend ever. She hugged me when I said that but never answered my question.

While we were in Washington, we visited a bunch of places. My favorite was a place called the Washington Memorial. It's a tall, skinny white building with a point on top and a long pool of water out front. I like the way you can see the building real and in the water both at the same time. Reminded me of the day me and Singer saw the rainbow, how the rainbow was real but you couldn't touch it. When you put your hand in the water at the Washington Memorial, the building gets blurry and then goes away like the rainbow did.

Ms. Tate also took me to a place called the Smithsonian Institution where they got all kinds of airplanes and rocket ships. I seen lots of the airplanes and rocket ships on TV but never up close. We spent a whole day looking at all the different stuff. We learned the same stuff Ms. Tate taught us about the planets, but it's better when you see it up close at the museum. Who needs a rocket ship to go places when you can ZigZag? The trip to Washington, D.C., was fun, but I still wish it was Singer instead of Ms. Tate.

After the trip, I didn't have anywhere to live. I told the caseworker lady, Jasmine, that I could still live at Singer's apartment even if he wasn't there. I told her about the time I took care of Singer when he had the noise for four days and how the pizza man brought the large pepperonis. She said you can't live alone until you're one eight. I know, same age as when I get to see the pussy for real. She gave me a look like I gone ZigZag right out her universe. She also said I couldn't go back with my dad since he's still in jail for beating up the crack whore who's really a cop.

I asked if I could live with Jenna, but Jasmine gave me another look like she couldn't believe I had a girlfriend. I told her all about Jenna, that she's two three now, how we went on the date to the Waffle Shack and had strawberry waffles with whipped cream and coffee, lots of cream, lots of sugar, how she took me to the hospital to see Singer and kissed me on the lips. I told Jasmine that Jenna used to be an escort but was going to get out the business someday. Jasmine gave me another long look and said I have something called the *vivid imagination*, which I don't know is good or bad.

Jasmine finally tried Jenna's number at Angel Escorts, but all we got was a recording that said the number was disconnected. It made me sad I couldn't see her again to go out for the waffles. Maybe sneak another kiss on the lips. Sometimes I'll still focus the special powers and pull back Jenna's flower smell when I want to see her. Only two more years I'll get to see her pussy for real.

Jasmine signed me up for a new big brother a long time ago, but so far no one. She said most of the new big brothers want the little kids like five or six and none older than one zero like when I met Singer. No one wants a little brother taller than they are. Anyway, who knows if I want the new brother cus it wouldn't be the same as Singer.

So until my dad gets out of jail I have to stay at a place called Miller Foster Home for Boys. I share a room with four other boys, all one six like me. None of us has any parents anymore, our dads either dead, in jail, or disappeared like money around that patch of hair the Toad calls the Bermuda Triangle. No moms, either; all moved away, dead, or in jail.

One day when I was playing the checkers with a kid named Ben, I got a call from the paycheck lady at Singer's work. She wanted me to come visit where Singer used to work, so I asked

Ms. Tate to go with me. When we got there and walked down that hallway with all the glass offices, it reminded me of the day Singer took me there and crashed the forklift. Singer's smell was everywhere, that wet cardboard box smell that was always in his brown work shirts. As soon as the paycheck lady, Sarah, saw me, she was around her desk and hugging me just like she did that day with Singer. She cried just a little but wiped the tears away quick and gave me a big smile. Then she gave me all of Singer's work stuff: hat, orange ears, and brown shirts except they say DEAN so I don't wear them.

One good thing about living at the Miller Foster Home for Boys is that I can ride my bike to the Fellowes School and the Toad's restaurant. The Toad came up to me that first day back at work after Singer died and got up real close, that unlit cigar back and forth in his mouth. I missed a whole week of work, Monday, Wednesday, Thursday, Friday, so that's why he was in my face.

"That lame fuck detective cleared your name, Lee Harvey." He points the cigar so close I can smell the wet on the plastic white tip. "Don't worry; I'll find the motherfucker takes me the rest of my life."

As usual, who knows what the Toad's talking about? Once Singer died, I pretty much pushed all of that out my head, so now the Toad staring at me waiting for an answer is making the sticky build up on my hands. Then a plan comes into my head that's so good I look around just to make sure Singer's not whispering right into my head, the first good plan I've come up with all on my own. "I'm not afraid anymore," I say, wiping my hands on my jeans. Maybe I'm afraid a little, but he'll never know.

"Not afraid of what?"

"Of anything." I get the bumps on my arm each time I say Singer's words, like he's right behind the Toad with a big smile on his face.

"The hell does that mean?"

I look around the kitchen make sure no one else is too close. The two cooks by the sinks can't hear us. "Seen Jenna lately?"

The Toad stops as soon as I say it, turns real slow, then comes back up in my face with that cigar. I can smell his equipment overheating trying to figure out how I know.

"You fucking little smart aleck. The fuck you know about that?" He's so overheated the little sweat pools all over his face are bubbling.

"Nothing much. Just a name I heard." I never talked to anyone like this, ever, not my dad or the monkey boys or the Toad: ZigZag is the one in charge now. Almost want to tell the Toad to get over there and wash those damn dishes been piling up. I can smell the confuse still burning up inside the Toad's head. He smiles and shakes his head.

"You sneaky little bastard." He touches my chest with the cigar. "Sometimes I think this moron gig is all an act. Is it?" He breathes out a few times, his fat belly rising and falling each time. He steps closer and scans me hard with his radar. "I'm watching you."

And that's the last time me and the Toad ever talked about case number two three four five seven six dash something something. For a long time I got the wet dream that I could float into the police station, silent, and check whether they still had my fingerprint. Then that wet dream stopped coming into my head. At work, though, I still keep my radar on extra sensitive, but the Toad ain't never said a word about the stolen money again.

I punch the time clock and float into position at my dish station, bus tubs stacked to the ceiling from the lunch bastards. I tear into the tubs so fast the whole stack vibrates from the speed, blasting the plates and racking them all at the same time. The silver metal on the sprayer touches my arm and leaves a little heat mark. I start feeding the racks into the machine at full speed.

> stroke it and choke it
> stroke it and choke it
> choke that machine down
> choke it down good

When I pull the racks from the machine, the steam rolls up around me and sticks to my face like the air at the big-shot record producer's party. The full winter cold is outside now, so the only warm air until spring is here at my dish station. Today's the first day in a long time the sun is shining, except the air still feels single digits like when I ride my bike here from the Fellowes School. Even with the sun it feels like that night me and Singer tried to go back into the safe, those little cat eyes glowing at me from under the car.

Most of the time when I'm at the Fellowes School or the Miller Foster Home for Boys, I don't think about Singer too much cus my head's already full. But at the dish station my body goes automatic, relax, and everything drains out my head. This is when I think about all the stuff me and Singer used to do, the good plans he helped me think up, and the time we cooked those hot dogs on sticks.

I can hear Dale's black-handled knife on the cutting board, *foop foop foop*, chopping the lettuce. Dale's cut a lot of damn lettuce since I known him. I ZigZag behind the ice machine and watch him for a few minutes. His black ponytail goes halfway down his back. Nothing moves on Dale when he's cutting lettuce except his arm, *foop foop foop*. I ZigZag next to him, but he don't surprise none; his radar's too good. "Hey, Dale."

"ZigZag."

"Chopping lettuce again." He nods and smiles. "Ever get tired of chopping all that lettuce?"

foop foop foop foop foop

"You ever get tired of washing the same dishes over and over?" He points towards the dish station with his knife.

"Guess not."

"I chop a lot of lettuce, but each time it's new lettuce. This lettuce here," he holds up a full head, "will only get cut once while it's on this planet. And I'm the one who gets to cut it."

I never thought about it like that, how I'm always washing the same dishes over and over and over and Dale gets to chop new lettuce each time. "Can I try?"

foop foop foop foop

"I don't know. You ever handled one of these?" He holds up the knife, and the sun flashes off the blade. Up close it looks a lot bigger. I shake my head. "Well . . . better not. You might get hurt."

foop foop foop foop

"I won't get hurt."

He stops chopping and looks around. "I don't know . . . the Toad wouldn't like it, you over here cutting lettuce."

"Please . . ."

He looks around again, dries his hands on his apron, and then dries the black handle. He moves to the side and puts the knife in my hand. Now he's behind me, his big bear hand over mine on the knife. "You hold it like this, and then cut like this."

foop

foop

The knife is heavy and slices through the lettuce no problem. He takes his hand away so I can cut some alone.

foop

foop

"You and Singer ever read a book called *The Adventures of Tom Sawyer*?" he asks.

I shake my head. "I don't read too good."

foop foop foop

My lettuce cutting is starting to sound faster but not like Dale's. "You'd like it. It's about a kid and his friend Huckleberry Finn."

"That's a funny name."

"So's ZigZag."

"So's Dale for a Indian."

He laughs. "Part Indian. Part European. Part Asian."

foop foop foop

"Read the book sometime," he says, "and you'll see the irony."

Why's Dale talking about ironing? And what's chopping the lettuce got to do with some book? Dale must not be too bright, just about as smart as he looks. Chopping all this lettuce must get you a little confuse. He takes the knife and points it across the kitchen. "You'd better get back."

I ZigZag back to the dish station just before the Toad comes around the ice machine, his voice saying something now to Dale except I can't hear what. The Toad slows down when he walks past me, still moving but his head turned this way, that little cigar tucked in one corner of his mouth. He don't say nothin, just stares, all our talking on the inside. I can hear the wheels smoking in his head, how he wants to say get my ass in his office, that Detective Hawke is here with a fingerprint they got off the safe handle. . . . I just flash him back one word I keep hidden away except for times like this, *Jenna*, the flower smell rising up in my mind when I say it. The Toad nods a little to let me know he heard and walks out the kitchen looking at the end of a cigar that's never touched fire.

The sun's coming in full bright now through the window high up on the wall on the other side of the kitchen. This is my favorite time of day, when the dishes are stacked high and the little square block of light shines on the wall in front of me, my body cutting through the sun side to side when I slide from racking to stacking. I start racking, blast and rack, blast and rack, feeding the machine the full racks. My body goes automatic, relax, everything quiet on the inside but my hands flying so fast they blur together, my mind outside my body somewhere just watching the ZigZag show. Singer comes back like he always do when I'm at the dish station, that day on the bus when we saw the rainbow, the city sounds and smells rising up in my head right now. My hands scoop up a big black pan filled with slippery white grease, my mind still on the bus. I blast the black pan with the hot water, steam and grease and hot spray flying everywhere, sticking to my face and dripping off my arms. I watch the spray float down through the sunlight and make a little grease rainbow that comes right up out the garbage disposal, the first rainbow I seen since the day Singer died. It looks the same as the one that came out from behind the buildings that day, except a lot smaller, the tiny drops of water and grease floating down slow. Somehow I wish I could keep the rainbow there the whole night while I rack and stack, my fingers already itching from all the dishes piled up.

Then I squeeze the sprayer, and the rainbow is gone, my hands back up to full speed racking the dishes. I ZigZag deep inside to the place where the noise can't find me, everything blocked down, silent, the only sound my mind repeating the rainbow colors so I can pull them back later.